Stone Maiden

By
Tina Gerow

Published by Triskelion Publishing www.triskelionpublishing.com
15508 W. Bell Rd. #101, PMB #502, Surprise, AZ 85374 U.S.A.

First e-published by Triskelion Publishing
First e-publishing: October 2005
First printing by Triskelion Publishing
First printing October 2005

ISBN 1-933471-46-8
Copyright © Tina Gerow 2004
All rights reserved.

Cover art by Triskelion Publishing

PUBLISHER'S NOTE: This is a work of fiction. Names, characters places, and incidents are the product of the author's imagination. Any resemblance to persons living or dead, business establishments, events or locales is entirely coincidental.

Dedications

To my two favorite men, my husband Jon and my son Darian who have given me my own personal happily-ever-after.

Special thanks to my critique group Judi Thoman, Beverly Petrone, Alexis Alexander and Paula Eldridge. I wouldn't be here without you. Thanks for always believing in me and pushing me to keep plugging.

CHAPTER ONE

"Take your hand off me or I'll remove *it* and several other of your favorite appendages."

Ariel Knight stood toe to toe with the goliath blocking her way and stared him down. She'd faced hellhounds, demons, vampires, and all manner of scary beasties in her time. One oversized cowboy with a chip on his shoulder didn't even cause her to bat an eyelash.

"Now, sweetheart, you're not wanted here, so why don't you just go on back to wherever it is you came from."

His gravelly voice reminded her of the sound her car made when she didn't add oil for too long. And the "sweetheart" grated on her nerves. She took a breath, calming her simmering temper and tried to use her most professional voice along with her sweetest smile. "This is the last time I'm going to warn you, Jeb. I have an appointment with Logan McAllister, and no one is going to scare me off." From her background check of Mr. McAllister, she knew Jeb was a former bouncer and Logan's horse trainer and sometimes security man.

If this is any indication of his people skills, he needs to stick to the horses.

His deep chuckle reverberated around her. "You've got spunk, I'll give you that, but you're no match for me and we both know it. So, this is the last time I'll ask you to leave before I help you out the door." His lascivious gaze slid over her like an oily caress. "And believe me, *that* won't be a hardship."

Dream on, big boy. I've been leered at by far scarier things than you.

Quick as lighting, Ariel grabbed Jeb's wrist. Twisting it back at a painful angle, she used leverage to drive him to his knees and then locking his hand up behind his head, she applied more pressure to keep him there.

The door in front of her flew open and a man right out of her fantasies stepped through and then stopped short as if he'd slammed into a solid wall. As if still trying to comprehend what he saw he stared at the scene in front of him openmouthed. Ariel took the opportunity to study him right back.

Six foot plus of golden muscular delight topped by gently waving sandy blonde hair and piercing blue-gray eyes the color of the sea after a storm stood before her.

Jeb's whimper brought her back from her male inventory. She glanced down to see her captive's eyes watering from pain.

"I tried to ask you nicely," she reminded him.

The intensity of the scrutiny from the blue-gray eyes burned through her skin until she glanced up. The passion swimming in the fevered depths hit her like a physical blow. It zinged through her, touching off small sparks of awareness throughout her body and causing heat to pool between her legs. She sucked in a breath, fighting not to drown in the sexual buffet of sensations assaulting her. Closing here eyes for a moment, she allowed two hundred years of training to return her to her calm center.

Ariel stood stock still as he completed his slow inventory. And if his hungry gaze was any determination, he liked what he saw. A flicker of pure female delight flowed through her until she reined it in.

Get your mind out of your crotch!

She'd even worn her business skirt and blazer to appear professional, but the way he looked at her gave images of him peeling her out of it to discover what secrets she hid underneath. That blew her whole professional image out the window.

"You must be Mr. McAllister," she said, breaking

him out of his inventory.

"Yes," he said finally and reached out to shake her outstretched free hand.

"I'm Ariel Knight. I believe we have an appointment?"

His lips quirked just enough to reveal the dimple in his left cheek. "Yes, I believe we do." He gestured down at Jeb still trying to break out of Ariel's leveraged grip. "Would you mind letting Jeb up?"

Ariel smiled, just a small curve of her lips, as she met his gaze. She wondered briefly what his stormy eyes would look like darkened with desire as he moved inside her.

Get a grip, Ariel. You're here to work, *not…play.* Her traitorous body reminded her it had been quite a while since she'd *played*, and it would be more than happy to nominate Logan McAllister to play *with*. She chided herself out of that train of thought and glanced down at Jeb. "Now, I'm willing to let you go if you promise to keep your hands to yourself. I really don't want to have to hurt you."

Anger flashed in Jeb's eyes and smoldered. She knew she'd just made an enemy, but in her job, she made many more of those than friends.

Jeb's ego was taking a beating, but from the pained look on his face, she wasn't overly surprised when he finally muttered, "Yes, Ma'am."

"Ma'am works much better on me than sweetheart," Ariel said. She released Jeb's wrist and stepped back so he could stand, keeping enough distance to maneuver in case he wanted to take another shot. But he only stood, rubbed his sore wrist and glared at her.

Logan, visibly trying to hide his smile, turned to his bouncer. "Thank you, Jeb. I think I can take it from here." Jeb looked between the two of them before nodding and turning to go.

Logan turned his attention back to Ariel and let his

eyes wander over her again as he motioned to his office. "Ms. Knight, after you." Normally, Ariel didn't appreciate the perusal, as if she were the all night dessert buffet, but for some reason, when Logan did it, it sent thrills shooting through her.

He pulled the door shut behind them and then gestured for Ariel to sit. "What can I do for you?"

Ariel settled comfortably into the chair in front of the desk, fixing an easy smile on her face, as he relaxed into his own office chair. "I take it by my warm reception, you weren't the one who requested this meeting."

Logan took his time answering. "I'm sorry about Jeb. I hope he didn't hurt you."

Ariel's left eyebrow lifted up in amusement. "I think I'll recover."

"My business manager's been attempting to hire a bodyguard for me." Logan leaned back in his office chair, steepled his fingers and stretched his long legs out under the desk. "He and I don't exactly see eye to eye on the issue."

Ariel leaned forward and her gaze seared into his. He seemed to have the power to mesmerize almost like a cobra. Ariel's heart tripped into high speed and slammed into her chest. "So, where do we go from here?"

He chuckled, an amused glint twinkling in his eyes. She could practically read his thoughts. He couldn't see her as a bodyguard but thought she might prove interesting in other aspects. Nothing she hadn't seen before. And when he said, "We could always discuss it over a romantic dinner." Ariel tried not to chuckle at the male predictability.

She smiled as a wicked thought took hold. He wanted to play. All right. She'd play. And when the kitty tossed the mouse into the air and hooked him with her claws, she'd decide what to do with him. "Do you always proposition prospective employees, Mr. McAllister?"

"Only the ones who take my breath away." A large

lopsided grin bloomed over his face. Ariel tried to hide her answering smile, but this was just way too easy.

"I've brought a list of references." She took a small envelope from her inside blazer pocket and placed it on the desk in front of him. "I'm sure you'll want to call them and check my firm's experience and performance."

Vivid thoughts of Logan personally checking her performance and experience flooded her brain, and she shifted in her chair as heat pooled low in her stomach. *You have a job to do! Keep your mind in the game and we can take care of the dry spell later!*

She glanced up in time to see his emotions and thoughts flow across his face as if they were written there. She wondered if Mr. McAllister played poker. If he did, she'd bet he lost a fortune at it. His thoughts were so transparent, she considered giving the guy a break. He still didn't think he needed any guard at all, let alone a woman. But Gabriel had asked her as a personal favor to take this job, so she'd convince Mr. McAllister it was in his own best interest one way or another.

He leaned forward and gazed into her eyes, not even bothering to pick up the envelope she offered. His frank gaze issued an unspoken challenge as old as time. She refused to back down, but kept her gaze steady on his—not that it was a particular hardship in this case.

He broke the standoff first. "Why don't you tell me a little about yourself, Ms. Knight?"

Ariel nodded once and shifted into professional promotions mode. "My three sisters and I own and run the Knight Security Agency. Each of us is trained in most forms of security and combat. Although we prefer to do the security well enough that the combat isn't often needed. It keeps the clients safer and we are less intrusive in their day to day lives."

Logan raised an eyebrow and looked intrigued, but

not by her or her sisters' guard skills, she was sure. His next question confirmed her suspicions. "I meant personal about you. You know, where you grew up? What do you like to do in your spare time? What are your favorite restaurants? What time can I pick you up? That sort of thing."

Very smooth, Romeo. How easy do you think I am?! Her body seemed ready to remind her, so she pushed forward with the conversation before it could. Her eyes glinted mischievously as Ariel leaned forward so she could whisper something to him over the desk. "Mr. McAllister, I'm applying to be your bodyguard, not your personal escort service."

Logan laughed as if she'd surprised him, then leaned back in his chair. A grin curved his sculpted lips. "I would never offend you by considering you any kind of personal escort, Ms. Knight. I was thinking more of a cozy dinner companion."

It was Ariel's turn to laugh. "You're persistent, I'll give you that. But then so am I."

He smiled, warming to the challenge. "I love that in a woman."

"I'll just bet you do."

She was surprised he wasn't swaggering with all the ego and confidence he portrayed sitting behind his big desk in all his gorgeous glory. She would've been able to work up some self-righteous fury had it not been for the fact she'd been drooling over him since the first time she saw him.

"There's a terrific steak and seafood house about twenty minutes away. We could continue our discussion over dinner." A smile blossomed across his face, making her inwardly catch her breath. She reassured herself that any woman still breathing would be affected by that lethal weapon.

Too predictable, McAllister. Time for the cat to move in for the kill. "Let me see if I can cut to the chase for you, Mr. McAllister." She stood and began to walk around the office, examining his songwriting awards and pictures, purposely invading his personal space, putting him on the defensive.

After a moment of obvious discomfort, he seemed to recover his composure. She smiled inwardly, enjoying their banter.

"Does that mean you're not up for dinner, darlin'? Or are you just afraid of me?" His voice, a deep Texas drawl, mocked her with the good-ol'-boy routine.

Ariel ignored the endearment and the question. "After two death threats, three break-ins, one act of vandalism and almost having your family jewels removed by a stray arrow, your business manager decides to hire a bodyguard. But you think you can take care of it yourself, so you hire bouncer man..." she gestured to the outer office where she'd encountered Jeb, "to get rid of any potential bodyguard candidates who show up. Am I getting warm?"

Logan's gaze hardened and he glared at her, the typical alpha man warning away another who invaded his territory. It amused her that *now* he chose to treat her like an equal—even if it was as a threat. "I *can* take care of it myself," he insisted, his male pride obviously smarting. But she noted the wince—probably from the memory of the rogue arrow narrowly missing his most prized body parts.

Ariel pierced Logan with a nonchalant look over her shoulder. "I can see how tight your security is. I batted my eyelashes out at the gate and was admitted without any ID check and no questions asked." She smiled and continued her perusal of his office.

The blue-gray of his eyes turned dark and deadly. "Now wait just a minute—"

She plowed on as if she hadn't heard him. "Then I gain admittance to the main house by talking recipes with your housekeeper. She's making peach cobbler tonight, by the way—apparently your favorite."

"So I need to have a talk with my staff about checking ID's. Is that all you've got?"

Ariel picked up a picture of Logan shaking hands with Reba McEntire at the Flameworthy Awards and studied it before answering. "No, I have more." She nodded at the picture. "Nice picture. I'm a big Reba fan."

He stalked around the desk, grabbed the photo and placed it reverently back in its spot on the shelf. "If you have more to say, get on with it." He crossed his arms in a defensive posture and then deliberately dropped them to his sides as if he'd just realized what he'd done.

Ariel turned to face him. He stood close enough for her to smell his cologne, which sent her senses churning. Soap, hay, horse and the musky scent of man—it suited him and made her think of dark, steamy nights under the stars with his work-roughened hands roaming over her.

His hostile look brought her back to reality. She needed to remember she'd invaded his territory and put him on the defensive. She couldn't afford to let her guard down now.

Why the hell do I keep reacting like a mare in heat with this man?

"Anyway," she continued when she had his attention. "Then I walk up the stairs to your personal office and your sole security, an ex-bouncer by the look of him, was disabled in less than five seconds." It probably wouldn't help his mood to know she'd studied his background extensively and knew exactly who Jeb and every other member of his staff were.

He stood still as a statue, his hands fisted at his sides, his beautiful eyes shooting daggers at her.

"But what concerns me most is when I sweet-talked your housekeeper into giving me a tour, I found several deliberate security breaches."

"Such as?" He stepped forward, his stony look demanding answers. Suddenly the lord of the manor, she knew security concerns were at the forefront of his mind for the first time in the conversation.

Ariel's expression softened, and she almost felt sorry for him. She searched his face before answering, and noted a quick look of vulnerability before he hid it behind his mask of anger. "I found taps on your downstairs phone and I'd bet money your office lines are tapped as well. I also found a deliberately cut wire in your security system. Specifically, the wire to the audible alert system. In other words, the lights are on and the alarm looks like it's working, but no sound to alert anyone."

He looked like she'd just kicked him in the crotch. His eyes were wide with shock, his skin tinged a little green around the edges. "Phone taps? Security system wires cut?" He ran both hands through his hair and tried to get himself under control. After a few deep breaths, he asked, "Anything else?"

She nodded. "The locks on the downstairs windows have been tampered with. None of them are operational, but you couldn't tell by looking at them. As soon as you open the window, they snap off in your hand. I'm sure there's more, but I didn't want to seem suspicious to your staff."

An ironic smile curved his lips. "Seems like you did everything but search my underwear drawer right in front of my staff and they didn't have a clue." He shook his head and paced around the small room.

"I'm good at what I do, Mr. McAllister. Let me help you. My clan and I can give you your peace of mind back."

"Clan?" Logan stopped in his tracks and his sandy blonde brows furrowed at the strange term.

"Sorry, that's what my sisters and I call ourselves." She knew he sensed there was more under the surface, but to his credit, he didn't dig further.

"Ms. Knight, I'll be frank with you."

"Please do," she interrupted, "and call me Ariel."

"Ariel," he conceded. "I'm not a chauvinist, but I don't know how comfortable I am with a bunch of women being my bodyguards."

She smiled indulgently, as if she expected him to say that very thing. Logan's eyes flashed at her expression, but he continued.

"Look, I appreciate your time, but maybe you have some men in your company who could come out? That way you and I could still work together in an advisory capacity?"

I'm impressed. At least you're honest about it.

Ariel smiled. "We are a company comprised solely of females. And every one of us is an expert at both security and blending in. You may look like a womanizer having four women around all the time, but you won't look like you've got a contingent of bodyguards." She sat down again and watched him patiently. "I'm assuming you prefer discretion."

Logan sighed. "We may not be Fort Knox here, but then again, we don't need to be. Regardless of what bull my business manager told you, I'm not some big Hollywood star. I'm a simple songwriter."

She startled at the dichotomy of the humble man standing before her now and the over-confident one from a few minutes ago. "The most sought after songwriter in Nashville, last I heard. And you don't have to be a star to be in danger, Mr. McAllister. I'm good at what I do, and as I said, I can help you."

She knew the death threats, the arrow, and even the break-ins had to have rattled him, but the revelation of the phone taps and all the rest might make him see reason.

"I don't think you have a choice, Logan. You've scared all the rest away." The deep voice came from the doorway.

*****

Both Logan and Ariel turned to see the newcomer.

"James…" Logan began. Ariel bolted to her feet, a stricken look marring her lovely features.

"You," she said. She rebuilt her composure in the span of a few seconds.

The change was so quick Logan wondered if he'd imagined the look of pain that rode across her face moments earlier.

"Hello, Ariel. It's been a very long time." James Wellington, Logan's business manager, stood as if prepared for battle.

He started at the wistful tone of James' voice and looked back and forth between the two of them. "Am I missing something? I feel like I'm interrupting a reunion."

Ariel's eyes flashed, and she continued to stare at James with a mixture of anger and bitterness. "Not unless you already know your manager is a soulless blood-sucker. I should have suspected something when an evening meeting was requested."

James's deep laugh rumbled through the room, but Logan noticed the edge of sadness. "Still have a heart of stone, don't you, Ariel?"

"We can discuss it at high noon tomorrow under the blazing sun if you'd like," she answered in a low, deadly voice. "Or how about over some Italian with heavy garlic in that nice little converted church downtown."

Logan realized whatever was between them must be pretty bad if she was comparing James to a vampire. What could James have done to alienate her so completely? Then he glanced at Ariel and saw the hurt behind her anger. Jealousy burned through him at the thought of James with the brunette angel before him.

Where did that come from? I've only just met her!

James walked fully into the room and took the chair

next to Ariel. "This has nothing to do with the past, so don't get your wings all in a ruffle. This is about Logan. He needs protection, and I think there's some dark and evil intent behind the threats."

Logan was about to point out the irony of calling the threats dark and evil, when Ariel spoke up.

"Some of the old brotherhood, maybe?" she asked, her expression still clearly skeptical.

James only nodded. "You and I both know Gabriel asked you to take this. Even if you don't trust me, I know you still trust him." James started to reach out to touch her hand, but she flinched away. "Don't put Logan at risk just to spite me."

Ariel's eyes flashed again, and her chin thrust up in a stubborn tilt, but she remained silent.

Logan furrowed his brow. It was as if they were both speaking Swahili and he didn't have the translation guide. "I assume by the conversation, you two know each other." What an understatement. "Would you care to let me in on it? And who the hell is Gabriel?"

The tension in the room skyrocketed, until finally James broke the silence. "I've never been one of your assignments, Ariel, and contrary to what you believe, I would never betray you."

"Yeah, I'll bet you only do that once every two hundred years or so, right?" She nodded curtly to Logan and stood. "I'll discuss this with my sisters, *and* with Gabriel. I'll be in touch." She turned on her heel and walked out of the office without a backward glance.

Both men watched Ariel's retreating form, then Logan turned to James. "What the hell was all that about?"

James smiled. "About? It's about the most fascinating woman I've ever met keeping you safe."

*****

Ariel slammed the front door of the house she shared with her sisters and threw her purse in the general direction of the hall table.

"Gabriel. We need to talk," she yelled into the air, then stalked toward the living room. She plopped down on the couch and kicked off her high heels as she heard one of her sisters pounding down the stairs.

"Ariel, what the hell is going on?" Kefira stood in the doorway, her red hair still wet from a shower. "None of us have ever dared speak to Gabriel that way!"

"That was before he set me up," Ariel growled. Her sister sat down next to her, a concerned frown marring Kefira's striking blue eyes.

"Who set you up?" asked Dara from the doorway, her long blonde hair pulled back into a stylish twist.

Ariel sighed. "Where is Odeda? I might as well tell everyone at once. *And*, I'd like everyone to be here in case I'm tempted to dismember a certain Archangel."

Ariel reached out with her mind to summon her remaining sister. Times like this made her glad God hadn't removed their telepathic link when She released them from their warrior status last year.

Odeda rushed into the living room.

"What's wrong?" asked Odeda as she sat down on the loveseat opposite the couch, waves of chocolate brown hair frothing around her.

Ariel glanced around at her sisters—her clan, and sighed. All of the original five hundred gargoyles were created at the same time. So, in the purest sense of the word, they were all sisters—created by the same hand. But they were also a clan, a traditional fighting unit, and the last remaining clan of the entire gargoyle race.

She blinked back tears and said a silent prayer of thanks for these three women. With all life had thrown at them over the centuries, they had always been there for each other. She knew this time would be no different. They would listen and help her through this, no matter how it turned out.

She would rather take on an army of shape shifters, zombies and Pharisees all at the same time than face James again. Now if she could just convince her sisters.

"I met with our new client this evening, and he really does need our help. He has taps on his phones, security alarm wires were tampered with along with several other issues. He's really a very interesting man...." *Sexy, frustrating, adorable, stubborn...and interesting.* "But, I don't know if I can take the job."

Dara turned toward her, her lovely face etched with concern, her blonde brows knitted. "Tell us what's wrong. I've never heard you say that about *any* job we've ever done. And that's saying quite a lot."

"Logan McAllister's business manager is...James Wellington." Her eyes burned with unshed tears and she blinked them away. She'd cried enough tears over James two-hundred years ago. She refused to give him any more.

"Wait." Kefira held up her hand in stop sign fashion. "You mean that lying bastard vampire, James, from when we took that assignment in England?" Her blue eyes flashed fire. "I knew we should have hunted him down and staked him through the heart while we had the chance. The bastard!"

Dara, always the voice of reason, spoke up. "Ariel made a conscious choice to let him go, and we stood by it." She laid a comforting hand on Ariel's shoulder. "Besides, he wasn't our assignment and we don't kill indiscriminately, Fi. Or have you forgotten that?"

"Hold on," Odeda broke in. "Let's cut through all the emotional crap. Ariel, tell us what happened at the client's meeting."

She filled them in and her anger returned as she

mentally relived her encounter with James.

Odeda whistled long and low. "Wow, did you really say all that vampire stuff in front of Logan?"

"He's a mortal," Ariel said stubbornly. "He'll just think I was speaking metaphorically."

"So, is James still hot?" asked Odeda with mischief dancing in her chocolate-brown eyes.

"Deda, one of these days I'm going to belt you in the mouth." Ariel pressed her palms to her eyes to keep the tears at bay.

"I think that answers my question," Odeda said and grinned, clearly unrepentant. "And what about Logan McAllister? I've seen pictures of him that could singe a girl's panties!"

Before Ariel could lie and deny she'd soaked her own panties at the mere sight of Logan McAllister, the room suddenly smelled like cinnamon and the air crackled with electricity.

"Now, maybe we'll get some answers," Ariel said under her breath, pointedly ignoring Deda's last question. She wasn't ready to examine her reaction to one Logan McAllister, which was actually very interesting before James showed up and ruined it.

Gabriel appeared, floating a few feet off the floor, in a comfortable sitting position. Once again, Ariel was stunned by the angel's surreal beauty. Even after seeing him daily for centuries, he still took her breath away.

A halo of light surrounded him, which glinted off his long blonde hair. All six-foot-eight of him was very well defined—the Creator had definitely been paying special attention the day She made Gabriel.

Odeda often described him as a walking wet dream, and no one disagreed. Eyes so blue, they looked like glittering sapphires glinted mischievously. And beautiful, sculpted lips curved up at the edges.

She looked around and realized the four of them had unconsciously stood when Gabriel entered the room. Nine hundred years of ingrained habit had Ariel kneeling down on one knee and placing her right fist over her heart in a sign of respect. Her sisters did the same. She may be angry with him, but there were some lines not to be crossed.

When Gabriel nodded, Ariel stood and faced him, her hands on her hips, while her sisters resumed their seats. "James Wellington." She said each word distinctly and glared at the angel.

Gabriel had the grace to look almost sheepish. "Ariel." He sighed and let himself float down onto the armchair, which sat to the right of the couch and the loveseat. "I asked you to protect Logan because he has lasting significance in the Creator's plan. I didn't think you'd have issues with James—after all, it's been two-hundred years."

"Bull," Ariel said, though curiosity snaked through her about what significance Logan represented. She knew better than to ask Gabriel, he would only share on his own timetable. She stalked over to stand in front of him. "I don't have a problem with the assignment itself. I have a *problem* with the fact that you didn't warn me James was involved." She groped for the words to explain what she was still trying to understand.

"You're right, Ariel. I didn't warn you, but that wasn't my decision to make."

"What?!" she sputtered. "You mean *She* told you not to tell me James was there? What possible reason could She have for putting me in that position?"

Gabriel's gentle laugh flowed throughout the room and a sense of comfort and contentment rolled over her, as it always did when the angel laughed. Irritated, she shrugged it off and continued to glare at him.

"You know better than that, Lioness of God. She

doesn't tell anyone the reasons behind Her decisions, not even me. No one but The Creator is capable of seeing all the nuances to Her plan, especially with free will wreaking havoc." Gabriel stretched out his long legs and crossed them at the ankle. "Besides, you've handled entire armies of undead, zombies and other beasties. I didn't think you'd have a problem with one lone vampire."

Ariel's irritation mounted. There was nothing worse than a smug angel. "So, you won't have a problem if we stake him?" she asked with a saccharine smile.

He sat up straighter, his severe frown causing his halo of light to dim. "Now, Ariel, there's no need for that. I never asked you to eliminate James. Frankly, there are worse beings out there."

Interesting. Gabriel actually defended James. She decided to push down this path further. "You wouldn't be trying to influence my free will, would you?"

"Certainly not!" Gabriel's scowl marred his beautiful features. He was clearly offended by the insinuation. "I was just attempting to point out that you've always had excellent intuition about good and evil in all its forms. But it seems like you're letting your personal biases cloud your judgment."

Kefira bolted to her feet and pushed Ariel out of the way. "Are you trying to tell me that lying bastard isn't evil? He's the undead, right? And I'm perfectly willing to help him become all the way dead!"

Ariel smiled at her sister's impassioned protection of her. Did Kefira realize she'd cursed in front of the angel for the first time ever? Even if "bastard" wasn't really all that racy. They were meshing with the mortal world faster than any of them realized.

Gabriel merely smiled and gestured to include everyone in the room. "All of you have an excellent ability to sense evil. Yet none of you ever warned Ariel when she entered into the relationship in the first place." He turned to Ariel. "And when you talked with him tonight, did your skin crawl as it does when you are in the presence of the truly evil?"

The words hit her like a blow. After she saw James rip a man's throat out and realized he was a vampire, she never once stopped to think if he was truly evil or not. But then again, the line seemed pretty clear when he had blood dripping from his chin.

"Remember, not everything is always as it seems. I think you four of all people, would have learned that by now." Gabriel gazed around the room. "Now, it's up to you if you take the McAllister job or not. After all, you were released from your warrior vows, and I only asked this as a favor among old friends."

Ariel smothered a snort of laughter at Gabriel's description of them as old friends. True, they all held great respect for the angel, but not once in nine-hundred years had he ever shared anything personal with them.

"Logan *is* very important in the overall plan. And he's also a challenge. You will no doubt have your hands full." Gabriel fixed them all with a smile that could melt any woman within one hundred miles. "From past experience, I know you all enjoy challenges—especially you, Ariel."

She ground her teeth. "I don't suppose you'd share why Logan is so important?" she asked, already knowing his answer.

Gabriel just smiled. "All will be known in due time."

Damn, how many times had she heard that old gem? But he did have her pegged correctly. She loved challenges, especially now that there were no more missions to keep them busy. And Logan McAllister *had* peaked her interest. Besides, she'd never run from anything in her life—except for James.

Maybe it was time to start fully enjoying her new mortal life. And Logan McAllister might be a great way to start. She placed her fist over her heart and nodded at Gabriel. "Her will be done."

CHAPTER TWO

Ariel stepped out onto the balcony off her bedroom wearing a low-backed tank top and comfortable jean shorts. She concentrated on the small fairy wings tattoo between her shoulder blades. The tattoo began to tingle, and suddenly her massive wings reformed and unfurled around her.

She rolled her shoulders to get used to the weight of the large leathery wings against her back, which had only been a tattoo for the last two months.

That was one of the big problems with modern-day America as far as she could see; too much radar and other monitoring to allow her clan ample time to stretch their wings.

She didn't miss the days when she had the wings twenty-four-seven. Those were also the days when her clan turned to stone from sunrise to sunset. But at least when you sleep standing up as a block of stone, there's no fighting for a comfortable prone position with wings that are bigger than the rest of your body.

No thank you!

She didn't miss it. The Creator released them after nine-hundred years of loyal service. She allowed them to walk in daylight and gave them the ability of glamour for their wings. Much easier to fit in with human society that way. And Ariel was eternally grateful.

Stepping lithely onto the railing, she breathed deeply and enjoyed the rich smell of earth and night. Then she said a silent prayer of thanks for allowing them to find a ranch with enough land where no nosy neighbors would be around to see the women return to their true forms.

She spread her wings wide and gave a few trial flaps to make sure they weren't overly stiff, then jumped off the railing and let the wind catch her. Immediately, she pumped her wings to gain altitude.

Her unused muscles protested, but after a few

minutes, they began to warm and remember what had come so naturally for so many centuries.

The cool wind against her face exhilarated her. Adrenaline pumped through her and she felt more alive than she had for months. She reveled in the way her wing tips cut through the currents to propel her forward. Tangy Texas night air whipped past her, billowing her hair and giving her the feeling of freedom flight always allowed.

All too soon, she sighted her objective. The McAllister ranch.

If Gabriel wanted them involved in protecting him, then she wanted some reconnaissance free of James' bias to go on.

Or maybe she just wanted to get a closer look at how Mr. McAllister lived. She'd recognized the spark of attraction with him immediately. Sparks she hadn't experienced since…well, since James. She remembered being surprised that after two-hundred years of not being affected by a man, merely being in the same room with Logan McAllister made her heart race and her palms sweat.

She was enough a creature of The Creator to know when She was trying to tell her something. But exactly what, Ariel wasn't sure. Then again, she'd gone with that theory with James, and look what happened.

The thought instantly irritated her. Even if James wasn't the evil bastard she believed—or so Gabriel said—she still didn't trust him. Good guys didn't go around ripping people's throats out and drinking their blood! And no one would convince her otherwise.

But, Logan…. His sandy blonde hair and ice blue eyes were etched into her mind, as was his cocky grin. She'd always been a sucker for a cocky grin. Okay, that and a nice ass.

She may be a former supernatural warrior, but she'd definitely developed human preferences.

Returning her thoughts to the task at hand, Ariel landed lightly on the roof of the main house and froze. She listened to make sure no one heard her. She wanted a discreet look around, not company. Padding silently around the perimeter of the roof, she glanced down at the ground to ensure no one was about. When she was sure all was quiet, she vaulted herself off the roof and landed silently on the ground, willing her wings back into their tattoo form.

Her tank top hung loosely in the back where her wings had stretched it out. *Yet another tank top ruined.* But it was worth it to stretch her wings now and then. She could always fly topless, she supposed, but for a woman with curves, it would be just as bad as jogging braless. *Not a pretty thought.*

She'd landed on the south side of the house, close to a stream that ran through the back of the property. She could hear nothing out of place above the gentle bubbling of the water over the rocks.

The wind shifted, and the smell of death and decay reached her. Ariel instantly came alert. Very few things in this world smelled like that. But she'd killed every single one of them at one time or another. She turned toward the putrid stench and crept forward silently.

Ariel listened intently and then peered around the back of the house. Every hair on her body pricked to attention. A ruffling sensation at her nape crawled along her skin like a rattler on its belly. Pure evil. The calling card of the vampire. But there was also something else out there she couldn't quite place.

I wonder if I'm sensing James? Ariel shoved the thought away. Gabriel was right, if she hadn't sensed this same thing when she met James earlier, he couldn't be truly evil. She wasn't sure exactly what he was in that case, but she'd save that dilemma for another time.

She crept along the back wall of the house until she

came to the steps leading up to the wrap-around porch and then she saw it.

A zombie trying to shuffle its way up the porch steps. No wonder she hadn't placed the smell. Zombies smelled different depending on their rate of decay and where they were originally buried.

Tattered remains of a suit clung in patches, and bones and teeth were clearly visible through the ooze of rotting flesh. A cheerful red tie flapped in the breeze looking like a cherry on a dung heap.

"Damn! Why does it have to be zombies? I hate killing zombies. I can't get the smell out of my hair for weeks!"

She ducked out of sight. Zombies weren't the smartest creatures. Probably due to their rotted brains. But she didn't want to draw attention to herself before she found the controller—most likely the vampire she sensed. Not to mention the rest of the zombies.

Where there's one zombie there are several—they always traveled in packs.

She sniffed the air to locate the others and found them out by the barn. Along with the vampire. Why is *there is always a vampire?*

He stood in front of a pack of more than two dozen zombies and spoke to them using very animated hand gestures, like well meaning but ignorant people use to talk to the blind.

From the looks of him, he hadn't been a vampire very long. He wore a leather biker jacket and his black hair swept back into a fifties ducktail. Since vampires of a few centuries were considered teenagers, this one was still a baby.

No wonder he'd gotten zombie duty. It was the KP of the evil food chain.

Luckily, he hadn't noticed Ariel—he seemed to be

having trouble getting his zombies to behave. They milled around bumping into each other and into him, while he kept pointing toward the house, mouthing "house."

Like fighting Laurel and Hardy on evil steroids. The thought popped into Ariel's head and she had to stifle the urge to laugh aloud at her own lame joke.

In the meantime, the zombie behind her finally navigated up the steps and swung a tattered arm, smashing through the glass on the door and losing his hand in the process.

It would have been funny if she weren't the only one here to stop them all.

The zombies out at the barn turned toward the noise and lumbered forward, finally accomplishing what the vampire apparently couldn't.

Ariel cursed under her breath. She didn't mind group fighting, she'd had worse odds, but with zombies, it would be messy.

Concentrating, Ariel willed her arm to change to stone. The familiar sensation of icy cold traveled up her arm making her shiver.

Adjusting her stance, as the arm was heavier in this form, she waved it experimentally. She briefly wished she'd brought her sword, but when she planned the evening, her agenda didn't include zombie chopping, so she'd have to make do.

Ariel bounded up the steps and backhanded the red tie zombie, watching its head fall off, roll across the porch and over the side as it landed with a wet splat. The decapitated body still tried to get in through the door, but it would have a harder time without the head since it would have to feel its way around.

That was the problem with using zombies, if they weren't fresh they fell apart too easily. And even though the various parts would continue to fulfill their mission, they usually weren't very effective.

She raised her arm to disassemble Mr. Red Tie further, but the other zombies closed in behind her before she had a chance. Fighting in close quarters was never easy, but she had to have more room to maneuver with this many enemies.

Ariel turned to face the first zombie coming up the steps. She delivered a hard roundhouse kick to the side of its head and then a front kick, which knocked the group back like rotting dominoes, giving her time to unfurl her wings and fly out into the yard between the porch and the barn.

She landed hard, rotating her body into a fighting stance as the shock traveled up both legs. The taste of adrenaline coated the back of her tongue, sharp, metallic and heady—better than the effects of alcohol or any drug.

Her wings rose around her giving her at least some protection and allowing her to fight only a few at a time.

Thankful her wings were tough, leathery and flexible, Ariel charged ahead in battle. Zombies usually didn't carry weapons, so they could pound on her wings or try to rip them, but that was about as effective as trying to rip tires with your bare hands.

Zombies pressed close all around her and she saw the vampire off to one side, leaning against the barn, a smirk on his pale James Dean face.

Asshole. I'll get to you next.

She didn't have to worry about him going for the house—since he definitely wasn't invited, he couldn't cross the threshold anyway. One of the "perks" of being a vampire.

The zombie in front of her, wearing the tattered remains of white sequined wedding dress, clamped onto her non-stone arm leaving painful furrows in the tender flesh. She immediately shifted the injured arm to stone, healing away the abrasions as if they'd never been. Then, using her free stone arm she lopped off the zombie bride's head and sent it rolling—wedding veil and all.

If she could remove most of the heads, they'd be forced to grope around.

Before she could take down more than two of the zombies in front of her, a shotgun blast sounded next to her causing her to jump. She whipped her head to the side in time to see the zombie to her right explode, or at least the head. She sheltered her face against the spray of bone and rotted flesh and then turned to see where the gunshot originated.

There on the porch stood Logan McAllister, his feet comfortably set apart, a pump-action shotgun cradled against his right shoulder like a familiar lover. As she watched, fascinated, he squeezed off another shot and pumped the shotgun, ejecting a spent shell. Then he fed another cartridge of double aught buckshot into the chamber. He looked like a man who knew how to use a firearm.

"Damn! Why couldn't he stay in the house?" she asked the nearest zombie, a nearly six-footer who resembled a Jack-o-lantern in that every other tooth was missing. In answer, it squeezed its rotted hands around her neck, an ever tightening vice that threatened to snap her spine. Without conscious thought, stone rippled along her neck, thwarting Jack's efforts to choke the life from her. She reached around to grab both of Jack's shoulders and ripped his arms from their sockets. Jack grunted, but the hands stubbornly refused to release her neck, so she left the arms hanging down like lumpy long necklaces.

"Don't you know when to give up?" She began to pry one of the hands from her throat, even as Jack tried to head butt her. His movements were clumsy and she sidestepped easily. One of the attached arms chose that moment to give up its grip on her neck, and she used the newly free arm to beat back the rest of his body.

The edge of her peripheral vision revealed the vampire making a beeline for Logan. Apparently, he'd been waiting for the zombies to flush Logan from the house.

"Oh no you don't, baby vamp." Ariel stretched her wings to take flight in an attempt to reach him, but a sea of rotten flesh impeded her ten-foot wingspan.

Icy panic surged through her veins at the thought of Logan at the mercy of the vampire. *When did I start feeling responsible for him? I haven't even officially agreed to take the case yet!*

He stood fifteen feet away, but she knew she'd never make it to him before the vampire did. "Aim for the heart!" she yelled at Logan and beheaded two more zombies, still using the zombie arm as a weapon.

"Clan! I need you at the McAllister ranch, now!" Ariel heard her sisters' frantic assent, so she returned her attention to cutting a path through the zombies so she could reach Logan. She made it within ten feet when another shot rang out. A large hole blossomed in the vampire's back, but since he didn't disintegrate, some of the heart must still be intact.

She saw only a small flinch cross Logan's face as he pumped the shotgun to eject a spent shell and fired point blank at the vampire's head. The right side of the vampire's face exploded, sending bone and cartilage flying out like shrapnel. Ariel winced as a piece of bone embedded itself into Logan's cheek. Blood poured down his face, but to his credit, he never took his hands off the gun. He pumped the shotgun again and aimed. But before he could pull the trigger, the vampire bared his fangs and lunged at Logan's crotch, knocking the gun from his hands.

What the hell? Since when does a vamp not go for the jugular?

Logan stumbled back as the vampire rounded on him and tried to orient himself with only one eye.

Depth perception has gotta be a bitch with half your face missing. Ariel pushed past another zombie and grabbed the vampire from behind, just as he lunged again for Logan. Fangs bared, he went in for the kill. The loud snap of fangs clacking together as they missed Logan's crotch—again—echoed through the night.

Realizing with half his remaining brain that Ariel was behind him, the vampire whipped around, a feral growl sounding low in his throat, his claws extended for attack.

Ariel willed her midsection to change to stone as the vampire raked his nails down the front of her body. He jumped back hissing in pain, a few of his fingers hung limp from his hand.

"A gargoyle," he growled, hatred burning in his eyes, his mouth barely working enough to form the words. "I thought you bitches died out centuries ago."

"The 'bitches' are alive and well. Sorry to disappoint you." Ariel thrust her stone hand through his chest, crushing the rest of his heart. His body disintegrated around her outstretched arm. She turned away quickly, to avoid breathing in any of the foul smelling ashes.

Another gunshot whistled past her and a zombie's head exploded off to her left. Her eyes ricocheted back toward Logan. He stood unsteadily against the back wall, but continued to methodically pick off zombies.

Ariel marveled at his composure. It wasn't every day zombies showed up in his back yard with a vampire who tried to kill him…or chomp off his balls. But no one would ever know it by looking at him. He seemed perfectly calm, his movements smooth and fluid. The deep-etched scowl and the slight tremor in his arms when he stopped to reload, was the only thing that betrayed his inner tension.

Ariel's head jerked to the right as a zombie grabbed her by the hair. It was her own fault. She'd allowed herself to become distracted by watching Logan. *Focus!* Pivoting for better leverage, she gripped the zombie's arm and snapped it in two, the hand still buried in her hair like a macabre barrette. The rest of the zombie tried to push past her and up to the porch. Dropping to a crouch, Ariel swung her leg around completing a sweep kick and knocked the creature's legs out from under it. It hit the ground with a squishy sucking sound.

With only two intact zombies left, along with several writhing pieces still doggedly trying to get to Logan, Ariel caught up to the zombie halfway to the porch steps. She executed a front kick and then smashed her hand into its cracked jaw knocking its head sideways. This one was fresher and his head sat ear-to-shoulder, still held on by some ligaments and tissue. His sight, now impeded, he began walking in a tight circle.

She punched him in the back with her stone hand. Impaling a zombie resembled sticking your hand in rotting waste. The stench wafted out in a brown, thick cloud. Her stomach pitched and rolled and she began to salivate, the first hint of nausea churning. She tugged hard on her hand. It sounded like slurping mud when she finally freed it.

The unmistakable sound of wings cutting through air signaled the arrival of her sisters, who joined the fray with relish. Ariel heaved a sigh of relief. Worried about Logan, she desperately wanted to check on him.

"You brought us out here to fight zombie parts?" demanded Kefira. "You could have at least left us each a whole one."

It had been almost a year since any of them fought like this. And as much as all of them were glad not to do it daily anymore, the rush of adrenaline and the thrill of the fight still pulled at them.

Ariel surveyed the yard. It looked like a used parts lot for Dr. Frankenstein. There were partial zombies everywhere, but only one fully intact—if you could ever call a zombie that. "Clean up the parts for me so I can check on Logan," Ariel yelled. She ignored the curses from her sisters and turned to walk toward the porch.

This isn't the way I wanted him to find out I'm not exactly human. But then again, I guess there isn't really a good time.

It wasn't one of those first date subjects—"Oh, by the way, I'm a gargoyle. Any non humans in your family?" Yeah, right, that would go over well. She knew she'd have to haze his memory, but she dreaded the condemnation and even the fear she knew would show in his eyes right now. She should be used to it after centuries of experience, but for some reason, she still wasn't.

*****

Logan collapsed against the wall, legs out flat in front of him, his pump-action lying across his lap. He gripped it like a lifeline to a time where things made sense.

When exactly did the world start going crazy? He tried to muster enough energy to care, but a slow numbness spread through his body as his adrenaline ran out. He slumped back against the wall. *How much more strange can things get?* After all, he just spent the last half hour fighting what he assumed to be a vampire and rotting mummies.

And then there was Ariel. She wasn't exactly what he pegged her as earlier in his office. A gargoyle, according to the vampire, but Logan wasn't sure what that was.

He noticed the tickle of something on his face and reached up to touch it. *When did that happen?* He ran his fingers over the sharp shard embedded in his cheek and winced. His hand came away wet with his own blood. "Terrific."

Movement caught his eye and he glanced up to see Ariel, massive grey-black wings billowing around her. The breeze played her raven hair around her face and his breath caught at the sizzle of attraction that shot through him. He noted with appreciation the thin tank top, which showcased the most amazing pair of breasts he'd ever seen. She looked like an erotic statue come to life undulating toward him.

Apparently, he was a man who found large wings attractive on a woman, because his body wanted to take her right here on the steps, even though his mind wasn't even ready to have him stand up. A laugh tried to swell up out of his throat and he swallowed hard to restrain it. It seemed his baser instincts weren't affected by a little death and mayhem.

Something wasn't right here. Maybe he'd just taken a hard hit to the head. Yes, a concussion could explain everything. None of this could really be happening. He didn't even believe in vampires, let alone mummies and beautiful women with wings.

He glanced at Ariel and shook his head to try to clear his vision.

His world tilted precariously. He slapped both hands to either side of his head to make sure it didn't fall off his shoulders and roll off the porch like one of the mummy's had. He'd hoped shaking his head would clear things up, not make him woozy.

He looked up at her again. She still had wings, and now that she stood closer, he had a nice view of tantalizing cleavage when she leaned over so she could be eye level with him. The light musky vanilla scent of her wafted out to tantalize his senses.

Damn, maybe this wasn't a bad vision after all.

"Are you okay?" she asked in a tentative voice.

Logan tried to nod and then groaned as pain shot through his head. "As long as I don't move my head, I think I'm fine—other than..." he struggled for how to list all of the unusual things he'd seen. He gave up and made a sweeping gesture with his arm to encompass his entire back yard.

She nodded, seeming to understand his discomfort. "Dara can take care of this." She reached out to touch his uninjured cheek. "She's our healer. We'll get you cleaned up and then we can talk."

"Dara?" He looked past Ariel and saw three women, all of them stunningly beautiful, all with wings, out in his yard picking up mummy parts and corralling them into a squirming pile. He wasn't sure what they were going to do when they rounded them all up, but he was glad they were keeping them away from the barn and his horses.

The pretty blonde looked up from her work as if she'd been called and jogged toward them. Her motion did wonderful things to her lush curves and he flinched as Ariel caught him ogling her sister. Because there were enough similarities besides the wings that he knew this must be one of the sister's Ariel referred to earlier. *At least whatever's happening, I'm surrounded by gorgeous female flesh!*

"Logan, this is my sister, Dara."

Dara pushed Ariel out of the way with the impatience of woman wanting to see to her patient and dropped down on her knees beside him. Her cool hands traced the shard in his face and concern etched her lovely features. But no sizzle of awareness flowed through him like it did every time he saw Ariel.

Turning his thoughts back to his yard, he said, "What are you going to do with the mummy pieces? How do you kill something like that?"

Ariel's lips curved up on one side, and Dara's concerned look turned to one of surprise. It seemed he'd said something interesting. Ariel gestured to the squirming pile. "Those are zombie pieces, not mummy. We'll have to burn them. We could use salt, but it would only stop them, it won't get rid of them."

He promised himself he would eventually ask all the questions running riot through his mind, but right now he just wanted to get a shower, some rest and a stiff shot of whiskey, in any order he could. "There's stuff in the barn to make a bonfire out of them or whatever you need to do. Just make sure no zombie fingers are going to get in to scare my horses. I've got a few about to foal soon."

"Don't worry, we'll take care of it." Ariel sat down on the top step and turned sideways so she could talk to him. "Is anyone else on the ranch besides you right now?"

He shook his head and then instantly regretted it. "No," he managed. "James is having dinner with some record producers, my housekeeper always visits her grandkids on Friday nights, my secretary won't be back from vacation until next month and it's payday, so my ranch hands, including Jeb, are in town at Whiskey River."

"Whiskey River?" asked Dara softly from under impossibly long lashes.

He turned to her and stopped short as his gaze fell into sea green eyes. Her long blonde hair played around her face in the breeze. She was classically beautiful and he couldn't resist just looking for a while.

"Whiskey River," Dara repeated, a small dimple to the side of her mouth giving away the fact she was trying to hide a smile.

"Sorry." Logan pulled his mind back to the subject at hand. "Whiskey River is a local honky-tonk—uh, country bar and dance hall."

"So, you're all alone out here tonight and everyone knows it?" asked Ariel.

"I guess so. But why the hell would anyone want to attack me?" He ran his hand through his hair in frustration. "Before an hour ago, I never knew half these things existed. And why they have an obvious fetish with my family jewels is beyond me."

The memory of the near miss with the arrow came back to him with painful clarity and he looked back and forth between the two women. "The arrow."

Ariel nodded. "That's right, you had a near miss with an arrow. Maybe it's time you told us exactly what happened."

Logan reached up to touch his throbbing cheek and Dara slapped his hand away so she could finish removing the piece of bone. "I was out hunting with Jeb and I stepped in a hole and staggered backwards. The next thing I knew, there was an arrow imbedded in a tree next to me where my crotch would have been. Jeb and I just figured it was a hunter with some really bad aim."

Ariel didn't comment, only nodded, her eyes boring into his. "That's what we're here to find out."

Logan's mind went warm and fuzzy and his eyes slowly closed of their own volition. "I haven't even had my whiskey yet. What the hell is going on?" he demanded of the world in general.

When his senses cleared, he sat in his living room in the recliner, and the four women and James ranged around the room talking. He bolted up as the lethargy left his body and he could move again. Unfortunately, his head still throbbed like his prize bull had danced on it, so he sat down again, hard.

All eyes swiveled to focus on him and conversation stopped.

"What the hell happened? Are the zombie pieces taken care of? I won't have my horses miscarry because of this."

He noticed the stricken look Ariel shared with her sisters, as if he'd just done an amazing trick. Then her composure reappeared like it had never gone, reminding him of their meeting in his office. Had that only been earlier today? It seemed like a million years ago.

"Logan," she said as if trying to sooth a spooked horse. She walked toward him and his mind began to warm and go fuzzy again.

He shook his head hard, the pain beating back the disorientation. He'd lost consciousness the last time this happened, he refused to do it again. Using every ounce of his determination, he pushed himself up to stand and faced Ariel. "Tell me what happened," he said through gritted teeth.

Ariel's mouth hung open, clearly in shock over something. But Logan struggled to understand what.

James stepped forward. "Logan, sit and we'll explain everything." James helped him back into the chair and then glanced over his shoulder at Ariel. "You've never failed before and now you've failed twice, I'd take that as a sign."

"Failed doing what?" Logan glared at each of them in turn. They were starting to talk in code to each other and it was damned irritating. "Look, I've been attacked by a mob of zombies and one very pissed off vampire. I think I deserve to know what the hell happened tonight."

Ariel stepped forward and took a seat on the footstool facing him. He noticed with disappointment, she'd borrowed a shirt to cover her flimsy tank top.

"You wouldn't have been attacked if you stayed in the house and let me take care of it."

His patience reached the end of the line. Too much had happened, without answers and without anyone including him. If they thought they were going to treat him like an invalid, they were wrong. This was exactly why he didn't want a bodyguard in the first place. "Hold it right there. I never hired you as my bodyguard and I don't recall you complaining when I was blowing holes in those things out there." He gestured toward the back porch and tried to ignore the warning pains shooting through his head from his shouting. "So, why don't you try telling me what the hell is going on rather than coddling me like some day-old calf?"

Ariel sighed and then finally nodded. "Okay, why don't we get some breakfast and then have a drink. I think this news will go down much better on a full stomach. You don't have any whiskey in this house, do you?"

A woman after my own heart.

CHAPTER THREE

Logan lay in his bed staring up at the ceiling. His head continued to throb, even though he'd downed a few painkillers with a belt of whiskey. His doctor left a few hours earlier after announcing he had a mild concussion that a few days of bed rest would fix. Of course, that was after a lecture about the wisdom of trying to ride an unbroken horse at night.

Logan's pride smarted over that one. Thanks to James, now the doctor thought he was an idiot as well as clumsy with his horses.

Logan sighed. It wasn't like they could tell the doctor he got his injuries from a rogue vampire. Then Logan was sure his diagnosis would've been very different. Maybe he should've listened to Ariel and just trusted Dara's opinion. She was sure a hell of a lot easier on the eyes than his ancient doctor.

He closed his eyes and tried to relax. The events of the evening were still sinking in, and he struggled with why he could so easily accept all he'd been told. Wouldn't a sane person reject all of this out of hand? And if so, what did that say about him?

After a four a.m. breakfast, he spent a few hours hearing all about the overall war of good versus evil, myths based in reality and underground races such as vampires, zombies, were-creatures and gargoyles. He'd listened calmly, told everyone he needed to get some rest and then hastily retreated to his room.

He wished rest would come. So far, all he accomplished was a thorough hour-long study of his ceiling fan and a few very vivid fantasies about Ariel, both with and without the wings. His body had responded by giving him the longest running hard on he'd had since high school.

He sighed and tried to relax.

He thought he heard the sound of faint giggling. He

looked around his room, trying not to move his head too much, but heard nothing. *Must be imagining things.* He closed his eyes and willed himself to fall asleep.

The cool breeze from the fan played over him, and he could smell the crisp Texas pre-dawn just outside his window. He stretched and kicked off the rest of his covers, enjoying the way the breeze caressed his bare skin.

The giggling sounded again. Now that he was more aware, it sounded like little bells would if they could laugh. He pried open his heavy eyelids and looked down his body to where he'd heard the sound.

A small face looked back at him from behind his morning erection. A second of shock and disorientation held him frozen. He pushed up in bed—hitting his head on the headboard and dislodging his small visitor. He let fly his favorite round of curses.

The giggling sounded again, and he pulled the blanket haphazardly over him to cover his nakedness. He saw a blur fly up and then settle on top of his covers. When the blur cleared, the face was still there, attached to a miniature voluptuous, naked body.

She had long blond hair, which flowed about her independent of her movements, pert breasts that bounced invitingly as she laughed, and luminous eyes of liquid lavender.

She reminded him of a Barbie doll. Only the Barbies he'd seen never made him wish he were Ken-sized. And…she had gossamer wings between her shoulder blades, which flicked back and forth lightly like a cat idly flipping its tail.

What is it with me and women with wings?

She giggled again, amusement dancing in her expressive eyes. "You like my wings, man-thing?"

Her voice held the same bell quality as her laugh, like tinkling which came out in the form of words. "How did you know what I was thinking?" Logan demanded. "Who the hell are you?"

"You didn't have to cover up your nether parts because of me," she said, pointing to the tented sheet where his erection remained on full alert. "Too bad the men of my kind aren't as well endowed as that!" She tittered and then winked at him. "And I'm so glad the mean vampire didn't bite it off."

A blush crept up his neck into his face and he pulled another blanket over him to help reduce the tent effect. "You didn't answer my question. Who are you? And how did you know about the vampire?"

She waved expansively. "I'm Alonna. Your kind would call me a fairy. And fairies know all kinds of interesting things."

"A fairy," he repeated. Well, that certainly explained the wings.

She preened her wings and turned so he could see all of them, including her pert little bare backside. "I'm flattered you like them." She looked back over her shoulder and gave him a smoldering look he could interpret on a woman of any size. But even if he didn't already have a woman with wings to fantasize over, this situation would be strange and surreal.

She threw back her head and laughed. "Oh, man thing, you do entertain me." She flew closer to him and sat on top of his thigh swinging her feet lightly over the side.

"Why are you here?" Logan asked finally.

Alonna cocked her head, studying him. "I bring prophesy and insight into human dreams. But as a favor to my giant cousins, I bring it straight to you. Especially since you don't pay attention to the dreams I've already brought you." She snorted decisively, letting him know he was ignorant for ignoring them.

"Giant cousins? Prophesy and insight? What are

you talking about?" Logan had seen many strange things lately, but figuring out a riddle first thing in the morning while his head throbbed was asking a little much.

She puffed her breath out fluttering her hair and moving it away from her spectacular miniature breasts. She smiled at him knowingly, and he tore his gaze away.

A tinkling laugh flowed through the room. "Man-thing, don't feel bad. Men of every species like to look." She waved in a dismissive gesture. "My giant cousins are the gargoyles. Years ago they saved me from being raped by a vampire—a full-sized one!" she said with hands on her tiny hips. Her eyes reflected her horror at the thought.

She wagged her finger at him. "And I'm forgiving you for hurting Ariel, since you had no meanness in your heart." She sighed, the movement doing wonderful things to her tiny breasts. "You are just a man-thing, after all."

Logan stiffened and tried to rack his brain for what she meant. "I never hurt Ariel," he insisted. "At least I don't think I have."

"Not yet, but you will." She pursed her small lavender lips and studied him.

Logan scowled. Terrific, it had finally happened. They judged men on *future* actions. It was just a matter of time. But, he couldn't imagine hurting Ariel in any way. "I wouldn't hurt her on purpose."

"Isn't that what I just said?" she demanded with a long-suffering look. "Pay attention, man-thing. I have others to deliver to this night, you know." She stared at him until he nodded his head that he understood.

"Your prophesy—and mind it well—is this. If you raise the son of your blood, he will become a champion for good. If you raise the daughter of your destiny, she will swallow the world in darkness. If you cease to exist before your fated time, the son of your blood will avenge you with great rivers of dark blood and the heavens will shine on him."

"What the hell is that supposed to mean? I don't have any kids—blood, destiny or otherwise."

"That is for you to figure out, man-thing." She stood and turned to go. Then she turned back to him and held up her index finger in warning. "But, be warned. Do not share this prophesy with anyone, or it could change the direction of your fate and all will be lost."

Logan sat up straighter and hissed against the pain in his head. "Wait," he called after her. "You said you trusted the gargoyles. Can I share it with them?"

She turned and studied him for a moment and then flew back to him to stand on his chest. She reached down a tiny hand and placed it over his heart—her cool touch burning through him like fire. "The one who touches your heart, but no other. And even then, there is risk."

She walked up his chest and placed a small kiss on his bottom lip. "Good bye, man-thing. I'll visit again in your dreams." She glanced pointedly down at his crotch, still covered in blankets, and sighed. "If only I were bigger." And then she vanished as if she were never there.

*****

A brisk knock sounded against his door and Logan smiled. He'd know James' knock anywhere. "Come on in, James." Finally, someone he knew wasn't associated with anything but normalcy.

James opened the door and crossed to Logan's bedside. "How are you holding up?"

Logan heard the affection in his friend's voice and saw concern etched across his rugged features. "As well as can be expected, I suppose." He sat up, propped a second pillow behind him, and leaned back.

He studied James for a moment. His friend looked tired, almost haggard. Logan had never seen James like this before, but his clothes belied his fatigued state. James looked like an ad for men's casual wear in his black jeans and perfectly pressed button down shirt. "Have a seat, I know you well enough to know there's something on your mind. Why don't you tell me what's bothering you? It will be a nice change to think about something 'of this world' for a while."

James pulled the chair closer to the bed and sat down. He seemed to be gathering his thoughts. His features were drawn and for the first time, Logan sensed fear from James.

What's he afraid of?

Logan had known James for nearly ten years and he'd never seen the man concerned, let alone afraid. He found himself uncomfortable with this new James, and wanted to help put him at ease. "James." Logan noticed he wouldn't meet his gaze. "We know each other too well for you to be worried about talking to me. Hell, you've pissed me off more times than I can count and we're still friends, aren't we?"

James sighed. "You're the best thing that's ever happened to me. You're my best friend in the world and I consider you my family."

He nodded. James had become the family he never let himself have after his mother died. His aunt and uncle tried their best, but Logan spent most of his life making sure no one got too close. James had somehow gotten past his internal walls, and he would always be grateful.

James sat up a little straighter and looked Logan in the eye for the first time since entering his room. "Unfortunately, this *is* in the category, 'not of this world.'" James looked down and shook his head as if garnering his strength for what would come next. "I've got a past I'm not very proud of, and since you've heard all the other strange things tonight, it's time I came clean with you."

Logan's brow furrowed. How could the events of

tonight and what happened to James have any relation to each other?

Ice ran thorough his veins as he remembered the banter between Ariel and James in his office. Ariel had done everything but call James a vampire to his face. But she hadn't meant it literally—had she?

James watched him carefully for a few moments then squared his shoulders. "Do you remember when Ariel told you the gargoyles were created in eleven-hundred?"

Logan's palms broke out in a sweat and bile rose in the back of his throat. He wasn't sure he wanted to hear this. But he swallowed hard and nodded.

"Well, the Dark One—always one to twist God's works, decided to create a race similar to the gargoyles, but evil. Since he doesn't have the power of creation, he took evil men and turned them into what later became known as vampires."

"James…" Logan began, shaking his head and ignoring the pain. He didn't want to hear the rest. Somehow, he knew whatever came next would change his perception of the world even further, and he didn't know if he could take anymore tonight.

James stood and began to pace the room, but continued as if Logan hadn't spoken. "I was one of the original men turned." James stopped pacing and looked at him as if searching his face for a reaction.

Logan's first reaction was denial. He'd known James and spent the better part of ten years with him. He wasn't an evil man, he would bet his life on it. And from the look on James' face, Logan knew there was no hope James was joking.

"But I've seen you out during the daytime, I know you're not fond of garlic, but you eat it and you went with me to my cousin's wedding last year—in a church. So how the hell do you expect me to believe you're a vampire?"

"I'm a very old and very powerful vampire. I can do any of those things within reason. Although Ariel's taunt about meeting at high noon had some bite—the high noon sun would probably disintegrate me, while varying degrees of exposure during the rest of the day would only burn me severely."

Logan sat silent for a moment, trying to come to terms with his long-time friend being a vampire, because his gut told him it was true. Then another thought entered his mind that chilled him to the bone. He looked up at James. "Do you know why I was attacked? Do you know the vampire we killed tonight?"

James shook his head. "From Ariel's description, this was a baby vamp, only half a century or so old." He met Logan's closed gaze. "I would never do anything to hurt you. I swear on my life I know nothing about these attacks. I've been trying to protect you on my own, but I needed help."

Logan took a moment to let this new information sink in. He knew James well enough to accept he was telling the truth. And now curiosity took over. "Do you drink blood?"

"I have to in order to survive, but I'm powerful enough to eat human food as well, even though it's not very good for me."

"Human blood?" Logan asked, not sure if he wanted the answer.

At James' nod, he fought back a shudder. Only hours earlier, a vampire had nearly ripped off his crotch. He couldn't imagine James attacking anyone in that manner.

"I know what you're thinking," James said. "And there have been times in my life I've hunted humans and I've killed. But most of my blood comes from willing donors."

"Willing donors? Who the hell would offer

themselves up like that?" He laid his arm protectively across his crotch. Thankful the baby vamp, as James called him, had missed.

James scrubbed his hand over his face and looked embarrassed. "Many people in the Goth movement like to play at being vampires and like to exchange blood during sex. But even with those, I fade their memories so they don't get suspicious."

"So that's why the world at large doesn't know there are vampire, gargoyle and zombie fights going on a daily basis around the globe." Logan's thoughts wandered back to earlier in the evening with Ariel. "Wait a minute." He looked up at James. "Ariel tried to fade my memories, didn't she?"

James nodded. "Twice, and neither time worked. So you're meant to retain these memories for whatever purpose."

Logan's emotions ranged from betrayal at Ariel for attempting to take his memories from him to smug male satisfaction that it didn't work. He knew it probably had nothing to do with his male constitution, but he was happy about it nonetheless.

He looked up at his friend. "Sorry, I've been peppering you with questions. If I let you finish, you'd probably answer them all. So you were telling me about when you were created." He gestured for James to continue.

"The newly created vampires were given great powers and expected to wreak havoc on the world. But mostly to make the humans fear all things supernatural—including the gargoyles."

James resumed pacing, as if moving his feet helped him get the words out. "But after the first five years, I couldn't do it anymore. I was an evil man during my mortal life—I stole, cheated, lied and womanized. But there were always lines I wouldn't cross, things I wouldn't do even then."

Logan saw the anguish on his face. "Like what?" he heard himself whisper.

"Cold blooded murder of good men, rape, torture, things like that. Although I'll admit, I've killed my share of evil men."

"So what did you do after the five years?"

Logan noted the relief that flowed across James' face at his lack of judgment. James crossed to the chair and sat. "I walked out into the daylight. We were new vampires then and couldn't even handle the early morning or dusk. I wanted my existence to end." James looked past Logan and seemed to be reliving long ago memories.

"But when I stepped out into that first ray of sun, I didn't experience lancing pain, only comfort and peace...and I smelled cinnamon." A small sad smile curved James' lips.

"Cinnamon?" he asked, incredulous.

James nodded. "The air always smells of cinnamon before the angel Gabriel appears. At first when he appeared to me, I thought he was God, come personally to strike me down for all my sins. But the angel explained to me that while I'd done evil deeds, my heart wasn't truly evil, and I still had a conscience. And if I chose of my own free will, I could be a good man, even in the body of a vampire." James made a sweeping gesture with his hand to indicate his body.

What would a second chance at life be like? Logan couldn't even imagine.

"Anyway, I became a spy of sorts. Gabriel didn't tell any of the gargoyles about me in fear they would treat me differently and give away my true purpose to the other vampires. In the meantime, I accepted assignments to spare certain people or to steer my kiss to other targets."

"Your *kiss*?" interrupted Logan.

"A kiss is a group of vampires. Sort of like a gaggle of geese." James grinned at the description.

Logan considered. He'd been right about James, he *was* a good man. So why were he and Ariel at such odds? Unless she still didn't know. "How did you and Ariel meet?" Logan asked, selfishly hoping they were never lovers.

James sighed and leaned back in his chair looking weary for the first time Logan could remember. This was definitely a night for firsts.

"I was hoping you didn't want to know about that." James held up a hand to stop Logan's objection. "I was hoping, but you have the right to know since she's going to be guarding you."

Logan wasn't sure what he wanted to hear. Jealousy burned through him and he ruthlessly buried it. After all, anything that happened between James and Ariel had been before either of them had met him.

"I met Ariel in 1804 in London. She and her clan were doing assignments in the area, and I'd moved my kiss there for better targets, and to begin to infiltrate the mortal government."

"Infiltrate the mortal government?" Logan asked in disbelief.

James chuckled and ran his hand through his hair. "You'd be surprised how many congressmen, senators and even presidents and prime ministers are not exactly human."

Logan wasn't sure he wanted to delve into that right now, so he asked the next question on his mind. "You and Ariel were created in the 1100's and you didn't meet until the 1800's?"

James frowned suddenly. "There were five hundred gargoyles created, so Ariel and I were in very different places for many years. My kiss killed most of the local gargoyles and the local humans did the rest. You see, we'd done our job well, and the humans were leery of anything supernatural, including those sent there to protect them."

James rose and walked over to the window. He stood looking with his back to Logan, his arms crossed over his chest.

"Ariel and her clan are the last four of the original five hundred gargoyles created. That's why God released them from service. They'd fought faithfully for centuries." James glanced back over his shoulder to smile at Logan. "Anyway, when I met Ariel, she was the most beautiful and exotic woman I'd ever seen. She captured my imagination." He trailed off and stared out the window for a few minutes in silence.

Logan wasn't sure he was going to continue, but finally, James cleared his throat and turned toward him again. "We fell in love. But then, she didn't know who or what I was. I was doing some work for Gabriel, so she figured I was trustworthy."

Logan realized how difficult it must have been for James to have a foot firmly planted in two different worlds. Each identity so dangerous that trusting anyone with the whole of it could get him killed. He glanced up at his friend. "You weren't trustworthy?" He pushed himself up into a more comfortable position.

"I wasn't even on an assignment that night, but I saw some human servants about to rape and kill a young innocent girl."

Logan interrupted. "Wait," he held up his hand, palm out. "Human servants?"

"Human servants are humans who wish to become vampires. We use them as easy food, or even sex slaves. Most of them were evil men and women, hoping to gain vampire powers, which in time, if it suited the vampire's purposes, they would."

Logan nodded and gestured for James to continue.

"Anyway, when I saw the two human servants about to rape and kill the girl, I attacked them. That's when Ariel came in. I was in the process of ripping one of their throats out." James sat down heavily in the chair looking like the weight of the world sat upon his shoulders. "I'll never forget the way she looked at me. But then she finally knew what I was. I saw the knowledge, the betrayal and the revulsion in her eyes. So when she ran away, I never went near her again."

Logan tried and failed to picture James ripping anyone's throat out, so he pushed it from his mind. "She still doesn't know?"

James shook his head. "And I'd appreciate it if it stayed that way."

"But..."

James held up a hand cutting him off. "I made a promise to Gabriel when I first gave him my oath, centuries ago. I won't go back on it now. God granted me my life, and what She chooses to do with it, is Her decision. Besides, whatever was between Ariel and I is long since gone. I'm sure she's moved on."

"She? God is a woman?" Logan tried to wrap his mind around this new piece of information. It gave the phrase "God's sense of humor" a whole new twist.

James smiled. "God is actually both and neither. But She prefers the female form. The scribes of the bible, obviously male, as well as the male dominated church perpetuated the maleness of God. When in actuality, if She appears to anyone, it's in female form."

Logan sat staring at the far wall. He'd have to mull over the new feminine face of God later. Right now, he was still trying to come to grips with the shift in his perception of James.

The entire decade he'd known James, he never saw him on a date or even out with friends. He glanced at James with a purposely stern expression on his face. "You know, I never saw you take any of the female groupies off by themselves, and I'll admit I did wonder a time or two about you. I was starting to think you were sweet on me. Glad to hear you were just pining for a female with sexy black wings."

And I'm jealous as hell that Ariel loved you.

James laughed. The first truly happy sound he'd made since entering Logan's room. "Don't get me wrong. I will always love Ariel. She was my first taste of love, after all. But I found someone after her who I loved even more. Someone I would walk through fire for, or even defy God Herself. But unfortunately, I didn't realize that until I'd lost her.

"I've had more life than any man has a right to ask for, and I've had my share of good fortune. I just want to make sure you have the time to live yours."

CHAPTER FOUR

Fear marched up Logan's spine in icy little pinpricks. The enclosed space of the cabinet pressed close around him along with the smell of the softener his mother always used in the laundry. He rubbed his face against the velvety softness of his mother's best bath towels and tried to curl into a more comfortable position. But it was hot inside the small cabinet, and he wiped his sweaty palms on his pajama bottoms.

Confusion and fatigue warred inside him, and he scolded himself when a yawn forced itself out. He'd promised he would stay awake until his mother came for him.

His mother had grabbed him out of bed and shoved him in the linen cabinet, telling him to be as quiet as possible and to cover up with the towels and sheets so no one could find him but her. That seemed like ages ago, and he was afraid something had happened.

Fear still pricked at him, but concern for his mother had him peeking out of a thin gap in the cabinet door to make sure no one was in the hallway. He crawled out, careful to leave the door open in case he needed to dive back in, then crept out into the hall to the head of the stairs.

Voices—angry voices cut through the night and his blood iced over as he heard his mother whimper. He turned to run to her and the smell of cinnamon permeated the air.

He looked up and saw a beautiful blonde man reaching for him. And when the man's hand touched Logan's head, all his pain and worry melted away.

Then he was in bed, and someone warm and soft pushed the hair back from his face. She smelled like vanilla and her hand against his face felt like heaven. A sense of peace and comfort infused him. Next, he saw a beautiful brunette walking toward him, her large wings billowing around her, her eyes beckoning to him. Another whiff of vanilla permeated his senses and Logan opened his eyes.

Deep blue eyes, the color of the sky before a storm stared back at him. There was concern etched in them, but also a sweetness that called to him.

His mind was fuzzy, and he knew the woman before him couldn't be real. She was too lovely, too perfect. The full mouth beckoned to him, so he reached up to take. He noted the quick look of shock when he pulled her under him and delved into those soft lips. He took for only moments before she melted against him and twined her arms around his neck.

Her kisses were tentative at first, but then she gained confidence and explored on her own, causing the urgency to ignite between them. Logan pressed his body fully against her soft curves and his fingers itched to touch and possess. The silky brush of her soft shirt and jeans against his naked skin sent erotic shivers through his body, and impatience had him slipping a hand under her shirt and cupping her lace-covered full breast. She moaned into his mouth and his erection hardened to the point of pain.

She writhed under him, her busy hands exploring his back and pulling him tight against her. He cupped the weight of the breast in his hand, and then traced his fingers down along the rounded curve of her hip. An urgency to bury himself deep inside her gripped him.

Slowly, the realization that there was a real woman writhing underneath him percolated into his blood-deprived brain.

Ariel?

He'd fantasized about these curves from the moment he first saw her.

He held a slice of heaven in his arms and wanted to treasure every second. But grabbing her while coming out of a recurring childhood nightmare wasn't a great way to start something like this.

He tried to savor one last kiss before pulling away, but then she wrapped her long fingers around his throbbing erection and sent all his best intentions soaring out of his head. He heard his own gasp and then his chains of control strained almost to the breaking point. He clawed at her clothes until she was completely bare. His body demanded he plunge inside her softness, but he pulled back and turned his attention to savoring every luscious curve.

When he took one full breast into his mouth, she gasped and held his head close as if she never wanted him to stop. Her nipple pebbled against his tongue, and he teased her with a light graze of his teeth until she whimpered with need. He moved his attention to the other breast until she was panting, and he knew she wanted to explode.

She tasted dark and exotic, enticing his senses and scattering his thoughts. Logan trailed his hand down slowly to cup her and then slipped one finger inside. Immediately, his head swam as need slammed into him. Wet heat clamped around his finger and Ariel bucked against him searching for release.

Before he could think, he shifted and slipped inside of her, burying himself completely.

A groan filled his ears, and he wasn't sure if it was his or hers. Inside, she was velvet heaven and welcoming heat and he took a moment to savor. The light vanilla scent of her filled his senses as he moved within her. He stopped to look down into her stormy blue eyes, and caught his breath.

There was desire there, but also something else he couldn't quite place. Sanity seeped back into his brain and the impact of everything he'd done closed in on him. He'd ravaged her without a word and now he'd buried himself inside her. He'd surfaced from a dream needing comfort, but there was no excuse for this. Even if he had fantasized about her almost non-stop.

When he started to shift away, she took his face in her hands and pulled him down to her. Her lips met his, and the heat they built between them flashed again. Her tongue explored the inside of his mouth as her hands roamed over his body, until finally, Logan melted against her, all his doubts like dust on the wind.

Ariel shifted and he knew she wanted to be on top. Logan spanned his hands around her waist and rolled off her, still buried deep. Their positions reversed, he watched in awe as she settled herself more comfortably on top of him. She leaned over to place her hands on either side of his head and then began to move.

Her raven hair fell around her pale shoulders, porcelain in the early morning light. Her full breasts moved invitingly in front of his face, and he couldn't resist taking one into his mouth. Ariel moaned and clamped tighter around him, her breathing labored.

Logan knew she was close and wanted her to come, wanted to watch her face while he pleasured her. He took her full hips in his hands and each time she came down, fully impaled, he pulled her hard against him, making sure she took him deep. Soft sounds of urgency slipped out of her throat and she moved faster, her blue eyes boring into him, her lips parted in ecstasy.

She clamped around him, ever tighter and he hardened further inside her, causing them both to gasp. Their movements became more insistent and the slap of flesh against flesh and panting breaths, louder.

Ariel cried out, pulsing around him in rhythmic waves. Logan's climax pushed beyond the point he could control it. Ariel continued to ride him through her own spasms until his explosive release spurted deep inside her.

For a long moment, the world came screeching to a halt and time remained suspended. There was only Ariel—her scent, the sound of her labored breathing and her wet heat on top of him, surrounding him.

Ariel collapsed against him and Logan wound his arms around her, enjoying the way she sank into his embrace and the way her body still quivered with the little aftershocks of good sex. No one had ever felt quite so perfect in his arms before.

"Well, Ariel, I can see why you were resistant to protecting Logan." James' angry voice boomed from the doorway.

Ariel stiffened and then slid off him. She pulled up the sheet to keep covered, and sat up to face James.

Logan's protective instincts kicked in. James might be his friend, but whatever had been between he and Ariel, was obviously over. James would just need to come to terms with how things were now. "Close the door, James," Logan said in a menacing tone.

James narrowed his eyes at Ariel. "I guess I should have figured you'd sleep with any man you spend more than twenty-four hours with. It would have saved me years of regrets."

Logan saw Ariel wince and then square her shoulders. "My sex life stopped being your business as soon as I found out you lied about your place in the food chain. I could fuck everyone you've ever met and it still wouldn't be your concern."

James glowered and then slammed the door with a wood-splitting crack.

Logan heard Ariel's gasp and knew she was close to tears. He sat up and gently rubbed her bare back over the fairy wings tattoo, the skin over the iridescent colors velvet to his touch.

"Ariel," he said softly.

"Don't," she said, her voice breaking. "I can't talk about this right now."

She jumped out of bed and Logan let her go. She

fought the sobs welling up inside her as she pulled on her clothes in record time and then slipped out of his room without a backward glance.

"Damn," he said as he slipped out of bed and reached for his jeans.

His temper on full boil, he went to find James.

*****

Gabriel sat on top of the dresser in Logan's room and frowned. He'd have to have a word with James. His destiny and Ariel's didn't lie together.

Gabriel turned back to see Logan angrily pulling on jeans and smiled. Sometimes it was nice being able to observe humans without their knowledge. Angels didn't have genitalia, so he'd never been particularly interested in sex, but he could see what a terrific gift it was for God to bestow on humans. And useful too.

"I'd say this was a successful evening all the way around, Gabriel. But I'm still jealous of my giant cousin." Alonna perched on Gabriel's shoulder, her shapely nude legs crossed at the ankle. "That man-thing has some niiiice equipment. Why doesn't She ever endow our males like that?"

He laughed and watched Logan pull on a shirt. "Because then you'd never be out doing your job," he teased.

Alonna harrumphed and crossed her tiny arms over her bare breasts. "I'm going to make sure to give James nasty dreams for being so cruel to Ariel!"

"Now, Alonna. James is hurt and jealous. His faithful service will be rewarded in time, so go easy on him." *Besides, I'll make sure he doesn't derail The Creator's plans for Ariel.*

She glared over at him, clearly unconvinced. "If I must," she conceded and then turned her attention back to Logan. "Is the creation of the child of blood now complete?"

He nodded. "And if all goes well, they will fall in love before the child of destiny is brought into the picture. Otherwise, I'm afraid all is lost."

*****

Logan pulled on his boots and stood. His anger at not being able to find James all day had quickly turned to irritation and worry when he couldn't find Ariel either. Dara and Odeda assured him she would be with him tonight for his monthly concert. She had spent the day at Whiskey River to ensure they knew the layout well enough to protect him.

Meanwhile, he'd spent the day like a schoolboy pining after a crush. She infused his thoughts and left her lingering scent indelibly etched inside his mind.

But his waiting was finally over. Logan smiled, his blood quickening in anticipation. It was time to leave, and she wouldn't be able to hide from him much longer. He picked up his guitar and stepped outside. Odeda was already comfortably ensconced in the driver's seat of a sleek black sedan looking like a leather-clad sex goddess. He smiled. As gorgeous as she was, his body didn't respond to her the way it did to Ariel's understated sexuality.

Odeda stepped out of the car, her chocolate brown eyes dancing with mischief. "Logan, what do you think of our sex-mobile?" She waved her arm to encompass the car.

"Sex-mobile?" he asked warily. He liked Odeda, but she loved to push the envelope and to try to embarrass him. And as much as it disconcerted him to admit it, she often succeeded.

Kefira walked out of the house behind him. "Since you're going to look like you're bringing your own harem, Deda dubbed our lovely bullet-proof sedan, the 'sex-mobile.'"

Logan stopped short. He'd been going to Whiskey

River ever since high school, and he'd never once shown up with a woman. He'd left with his fair share of beauties, but never brought one. That would have somehow shown his intent to possess a single woman, and he'd never in his life had any desire to limit himself to just one—until now.

Wow...when did that happen?

The thought surprised him, but didn't bring the racing panic it always had before. Only smug male satisfaction at having found the woman he wanted to possess. Now he just had to ensure the chosen woman was on the same wavelength.

He laughed. "And I'll be bringing four of the most beautiful women anyone has ever seen. What an entrance we'll make." He placed his guitar case gently inside the trunk and closed the lid. "You four are going to cement my bachelor love-'em-and-leave-'em reputation, you know."

"Don't worry. We'll still try to make you seem tantalizingly available." The sultry voice he'd been listening for all day sounded from behind him, only it was more breathy and tentative than he remembered. Heat flowed through him and he turned to look at her.

The sexy half-smile on her face froze when his eyes locked with hers. The world fell away and there was only Ariel. He kept drowning in her deep blue eyes. The nine hours since he'd seen her had stretched like a lifetime. Before he knew it, he'd closed the distance between them and taken her in his arms. Her lips were hot and greedy against his, her skin warm and tempting.

Her arms twined around his neck and the silk of her hair flowed around his fingers. Logan lost himself in a sea of sensations. His universe revolved around Ariel...only Ariel. He knew he could lose himself for all time—right here, with this woman.

A sigh of longing brought reality slowly back into focus. Logan reluctantly pulled back from Ariel, but kept his arm firmly around her waist.

"Damn, I've never had anyone kiss *me* like that!" Odeda said to Kefira, her eyes sparking with interest and envy.

Logan saw a flicker of pain in Kefira's eyes. "I have," she murmured before slipping into the front passenger seat and closing the door. He glanced at Ariel, who shook her head, warning him not to ask. Logan nodded, but vowed he'd ask later. Everyone important to Ariel had suddenly become very important to him.

"Are you guys ready? Dara is meeting us there." Odeda glanced toward the car where Kefira disappeared. A worried frown creased her face for the first time since Logan had met her.

"We'll be right there," Logan said, his eyes still locked with Ariel's.

He waited until he heard the car door click shut to speak. He wasn't about to lose the moment. "Ariel..."

Ariel placed a finger against his lips, silencing him. "Don't. I'm sorry about the way I left earlier. There is a painful history between James and I, but it's done."

Logan kissed her finger and then took her hand in his, removing it from in front of his mouth. "Is that why you avoided me all day?"

She dropped her eyes and a sheepish smile curved the corner of her lips. "Not exactly," she said with a weak grin. "I was also trying to work out how I felt about...well, everything."

Logan placed his finger under her chin and lifted, so she would look at him. "So what was the verdict?" Even after the searing kiss a moment ago, he was surprised to find himself nervous about her answer.

Her blue eyes searched his and Logan held his breath waiting for her response. When she finally did speak, her voice was just above a whisper. "I've decided I don't like spending the day avoiding you. Especially since I wasted nine hours we could have spent in each other's arms."

Logan exhaled sharply in relief. "That's damn good, because I feel exactly the same way." But before they moved on, he needed to make sure of one thing. "What about James? I'm sorry if this will be awkward, but I don't see any way around it. He's not just my business manager, he's like family."

Ariel nodded and seemed to choose her next words carefully. "James and I were involved a long time ago. I admit, there are some unresolved issues between us, and I'll have to make peace with James in my own way. But you'll both have to give me some time to figure out how to approach it."

Logan saw the pain in her eyes when she talked about James and the bolt of jealousy hit hard from the knowledge that only love could leave that lasting a scar after two-hundred years. Part of him was tempted to tell her the truth about James, but he held back. He assured himself it wasn't only for selfish reasons, but because he'd promised James he'd keep his secret. "We'll work it out," he said, wishing he could put all his uncertainties to rest.

Ariel's face bloomed into a smile and she grabbed the collar of Logan's button-down shirt and pulled him down to her. As she melted against him, her mouth fused with his, he promised himself he'd find a way to make peace with James. James was his family, and if he had anything to say about it—Ariel was his future.

The car horn honked impatiently and they both jumped like guilty children. Ariel laughed and the happy sound flowed around him, reminding him for a moment of Alonna, the fairy.

"We'd better go, or we'll be late. And sometime, I still want an explanation of what kind of a dream you were having when you grabbed me this morning."

Heat rushed into Logan's face. He wasn't sure which one embarrassed him more, the childhood nightmare or the erotic visions of Ariel. He decided a change of subjects was best, especially since thoughts of Alonna brought back a vision of Ariel with her wings billowing around her.

He opened Ariel's car door for her and then slipped inside next to her. Looking around the car at the three stunning women, he said, "So, what happened to your wings?"

Kefira glanced back over her shoulder and laughed. All traces of her earlier sadness completely gone. "Right now they are a small fairy-wings tattoo on our backs."

"But I'm sure you've already seen at least one of them," chimed in Odeda, who smiled at him in the rearview mirror.

Logan remembered the small tattoo between Ariel's shoulder blades from this morning and itched to ask to see her sister's, curious if they were all the same, but held himself in check. Asking to see what's under her sister's shirts seemed a bad way to start the evening—even if it was an innocent request. "Very handy," he said and instantly wanted to smack a hand to his forehead for acting like a teenager on his first date.

Kefira laughed. "I like this one, Ariel. And if he doesn't work out, he's easier to get rid of than a nine-hundred-year-old vamp."

*****

Ariel stood just to the right of the stage at Whiskey River and sighed as yet another man tried to catch her eye. She itched to announce that the next man who came on to her would have his eyeballs ripped out through his nose. She couldn't watch out for potential threats to Logan while every man in the place was trying to charm his way into her panties. Besides, she was trying hard *not* to think about the man who had already charmed her *out* of hers this morning. She needed to concentrate on keeping him safe.

All the male attention seemed to irritate Logan. In fact, every time a man approached her, a distinct scowl found its way onto his handsome face. But she understood his sentiment. Every time a woman came up to flirt with Logan, she had to fight the urge to pull Logan away and say "mine!" like a five-year-old claiming a favorite toy.

She sighed, cleared her thoughts and let her mindset flow into her familiar protector mode. She'd done it so many times in her long life, it was like slipping on a familiar and favorite outfit. Her face set into her familiar blank "bodyguard" mask, she began to survey the bar.

They'd arrived an hour ago, before the little bar started to fill up. Now there was standing room only, all the way from the stage to the large oak bar against the back wall. The dance floor remained open. The scuffed hardwood freshly shined surface stood out, since it looked like the only thing freshly shined in the whole place. Other than that, men and women were stacked shoulder to shoulder like cowboy sardines. They were so close, Ariel wasn't sure how they raised their beers to their lips without elbowing someone's eye out.

The lights were dimmed low and the atmosphere smoky, but the different neon signs hung strategically around the bar gave off fuzzy multicolored sections of light. Ariel's favorite was a purple lizard wearing a red cowboy hat and holding a bottle of tequila. As the neon flashed and changed, the lizard drank the tequila and a small worm swam around inside his neon belly.

She heard a breathy laugh and glanced over to see a local radio DJ drape herself over Logan's shoulder. An urge to rip the shiny blonde locks from her perfect head gripped Ariel, and she reined it in hard. Let them flirt, especially when she knew Logan would be in her bed tonight and not Miss DJ Bombshell's. "Keep drooling ladies, he's all mine," she said under her breath.

"If you give off any more territorial vibes, you're going to disintegrate the entire bar," Kefira complained inside Ariel's head.

"Then they'd better keep their distance," she thought back. *"Anything out of place?"*

Her sisters checked in one by one to report all looked like a normal night at a country bar in the middle of Texas. Not that any of them besides Odeda had ever spent an evening in a country bar in Texas. But Odeda assured them all looked good.

Ariel turned to make sure everything on stage was set, and Logan locked gazes with her. The impact hit like a fist to her heart. The air seemed to shimmer between them and she couldn't get enough breath into her lungs. Would it always be this way when they were together, the air sizzling with awareness? She returned Logan's smile and then reluctantly looked away to resume scanning the bar.

"Damn, that man can smile," Odeda said inside Ariel's mind. *"I wonder if he has any brothers."*

A soft strum of a guitar distracted Ariel from answering Odeda. The noisy bar fell silent—the sudden change almost deafening. She looked out over the crowd to see every eye trained on Logan. Ariel knew he was popular here, but the rapt expressions bordered on hero worship.

Small town boy makes it big.

Another strum—louder this time, then a gentle cascade of notes from the piano and an easy soft beat from the drums heralded a ballad.

Ariel watched as Logan stepped close to the microphone, took a breath and began to sing.

The first note stabbed through her like a knife—with a velvet edge. Her mouth dropped open. Logan was a famous songwriter, but Ariel now knew he could very easily be a country music *singer*. His voice was a soft caress of rich tenor, but he also had a touch of a throaty, sexy baritone. She shook her head to clear her senses and finally started hearing the words rather than just the sound of Logan's voice reverberating through her like a forbidden caress.

> *What I wouldn't do…to get you to forgive*
> *I wish you could step inside my heart*
> *You'd see your name carved deep*
> *…so deep I can't survive without you*
> *I'm not asking you to forget, only to understand*
> *I'm just a man*

Ariel couldn't imagine any woman not offering forgiveness after hearing Logan's voice stroke along her skin. And even though she had nothing to forgive him for, a softening around heart toward this amazing man showed her she was far from immune.

It had been a long time since she'd allowed herself to feel this way for anyone. A stab of regret and pain lanced through her as thoughts of James surfaced. What would her life have been like if James hadn't lied to her and betrayed her? Ariel shook her head. No use dwelling on things she couldn't change.

Ariel chided herself for getting sidetracked. She heard the chorus swell in the background and saw several couples heading hand in hand for the dance floor. Lovers and love songs. She smiled as she realized she wished she and Logan could be out there with them, holding each other close.

She scanned the room again. Everyone besides the dancers was held in rapt attention, listening to Logan. Ariel had to admit—he had a gift. It wasn't only the words to the songs he wrote, but how he sang them. Listening to him gave her the sensation of living inside his song.

Kefira echoed her thoughts. *"Why isn't he recording his own songs?"* she said in an awed tone. *"I've never heard anyone sing like that."*

Ariel could only nod, even though she knew Kefira couldn't see it from across the room. She found it impossible to look away from Logan. He turned his head and locked eyes with her as he sang the last line.

I'm just a man...

The last note trailed away and only when applause thundered inside the small bar did Logan break eye contact with her. The loud clapping broke through the spell Ariel found herself caught in, and she blew out a breath of frustration. She was going to put Logan in danger if she acted like a lovesick teenager.

If she hadn't already given her word and taken this case, she would back away and let her sisters deal with Logan. But that was the cowardly way out, and she'd never taken it before now.

Amazing, almost a thousand years of dealing with the most evil beings in the known universe, and one handsome songwriter scared her enough to make her consider breaking her word.

The next song began, a fast two-step, which had couples whirling and twisting around the dance floor and bystanders stomping and clapping their hands. Logan's voice was beautiful and haunting. But now held a hint of the sexy, mischievous man she'd come to know.

Ariel resisted tapping her foot in time to the music. It wouldn't do to have the bodyguard bumping along with the beat.

She glanced over at Logan and suddenly, Ariel wanted sex. Hot, steamy, illegal in forty-seven countries sex. Something wasn't right. Logan definitely turned her on, but this emanated from somewhere else.

Every breath she inhaled rubbed her suddenly engorged nipples against her silk bra and made her want to weep. Wet heat pooled between her legs and soaked her panties, and every nerve ending begged to be touched, caressed and traced. Staggering under the onslaught, she gripped the side of the stage with one hand and dug her fingernails into her other hand until the sexual urges receded.

Sometimes being supernatural sucked. It made her more sensitive to the negative energy of every otherworldly being's output. Ariel guessed God made the gargoyles that way to help them track down the other species when needed, or alternately to better protect the humans in the crossfire.

And there was only one being which exuded sex like this.

"*Keep an eye out for a succubus!*" Ariel hurled into her sister's minds. It could be an incubus—the male flavor, but she had a hunch it was the female variety, since Logan was the most-likely target.

"*No shit!*" swore Odeda inside Ariel's mind. "*I haven't been this hot in four-hundred years!*"

Ariel shook her head in disbelief. Odeda liked to brag about her torrid affair with Charles II, King of Scotland to anyone who would listen. After a few centuries, hearing about it got old. And apparently, none of the men in the last four centuries could compare. But it seemed like good King Charles had just been dethroned.

Getting back on track, Ariel scanned the crowd and was surprised to find none of the crowd seemed affected. She knew gargoyles were more perceptive of otherworldly vibes, but the crowd should be showing some signs—unless... "*She's got to be powerful, watch your backs!*"

If the crowd wasn't affected, the succubus planned to target someone specific, but Ariel doubted she and her sisters were the sudden targets of a succubus with bi-sexual tendencies. They tended to be extremely heterosexual and let their incubus counterparts target females.

Logan's song was in full swing, but Ariel needed to be close to protect him. She'd rather ruin his show than his life. She stepped out onto the stage and stopped short.

Logan's face was red and sweat dripped from his forehead, soaking into his T-shirt. Ariel glanced down to confirm her suspicions and noticed his tight jeans were even tighter around the crotch than before.

"*Logan is being targeted. Find her!*" Ariel started toward Logan as the chorus rang out.

Several women in the front row began to take off their panties and bras and hurl them onto the stage. Ariel cringed as a moist pair of blue bikinis landed on her arm. She brushed them aside as if they were a snake that suddenly materialized out of thin air.

Ariel made it within ten steps of Logan when five women launched themselves onto the stage, surrounding him. The last words of his song were lost in a tangle of arms and legs and Ariel tasted metallic fear on the back of her tongue. She was too late.

CHAPTER FIVE

Logan saw Ariel step onto the stage toward him, and he almost wept in gratitude. Something was wrong—*very* wrong, but he knew Ariel would be able to make sense of it. He kept singing, because he wasn't sure what else to do, but also because he trusted her to watch his back.

Everything had been going well until a few minutes ago. The crowd went crazy over his new song. They were dancing and stomping to the music, when suddenly, he wanted sex.

Not just horny, he wanted sex with the same urgency a dying man in the desert would want water. He *needed* sex.

His erection was so hard and tight, he thought it would literally explode at any moment. Each breath he drew in to sing, sent agony zinging through him as the expansion of his abdomen tightened his jeans around his already painful flesh.

Sweat dripped down his face and he blinked at the sting of the salty liquid. Something hit him in the face, and he opened his eyes to see a leopard pattern bra sitting haphazardly on top of his guitar. Bras and panties in all colors blanketed the stage.

Not knowing what else to do, he kept singing. The singers always got this kind of attention, but this had never happened to Logan—at least not when he wasn't in a one on one situation.

He glanced to the side and saw Ariel striding toward him. Shock flowed across her face and he followed her line of sight to see what had surprised her.

All he saw was a blur of bodies before his guitar was ripped from his hands and he was on his back under a moving mound of soft female flesh. At least he assumed they were all female from the distinctive curves and the smell of sultry perfume.

Panic gripped him as rough hands roamed every inch

of his body and his body's reaction reached a fever pitch. He knew the only thing that would end his torment would be an ice pack or removing his package altogether—mere sex could never quench the need roaring through him. He began flailing his arms and legs in a futile attempt to break free.

"Logan!" He heard Ariel's strained and urgent voice call out to him.

Before he could draw breath to answer her, hands grabbed him under his shoulders and he was yanked backward a few inches. In the next instant, a searing pain ripped through the inside of his right thigh. His own cry of pain echoed in the enclosed space, and he noticed the trickle of hot liquid on his leg.

My God, I'm bleeding.

He had a moment to panic and then bodies flew off him, until Ariel's face filled his vision. There was a crease between her dark eyebrows and concern clouded her eyes.

"Logan, are you hurt?" She ran her hands over him as if to ensure everything was in working order. Her cool hands only served to heighten his already fever-pitched lust, and he fought the urge to whimper.

He started to speak, but his throat went scratchy and dry. He cleared it and tried again. "My leg…"

Suddenly dizzy and very weak, his vision wavered and Ariel's face swam in front of him. He heard a thick ripping sound and a second later, it registered in his foggy brain that Ariel had ripped open his jeans to check his leg.

He sucked air in through his teeth, making a hissing sound as she pressed down against the wound and unspeakable pain lanced through his body.

"Logan."

He heard his name and realized his eyes had drifted closed. It took all his willpower, but he pried them open and looked up at Dara.

"Logan, you've lost a lot of blood, more than I can

treat in front of this many people. Ariel will get you outside to the car and then home—I can treat you on the way."

He turned his head to the side and tried to see past the wall of bodies surrounding the stage. "Where's..." His throat wouldn't work, but he desperately wanted to see Ariel.

Dara smiled down at him. "Don't worry, she's close."

Dara reached across his body to retrieve something from her medical kit and brushed across the front of his jeans. He couldn't help but whimper. He was so aroused, every nerve in his body hurt. Even air against his sensitized skin sent anguish zinging along every inch of his flesh. He closed his eyes and gritted his teeth against the onslaught.

"Where are they?"

Logan heard James' booming voice and opened his eyes. Dara pointed backstage and James strode purposely in that direction.

A few seconds later, there was a hollow thump and then all the pain and lust drained out of Logan like air rushing out of a popped balloon. He sighed in relief as his entire body finally relaxed. Even the throbbing pain in his thigh lessened to a dull ache compared to the full body assault of a minute ago.

He winced against a sharp stab in his arm and then Ariel's face wavered in front of him. He tried desperately to say something to her, to ask her not to leave, but his mouth wouldn't work and his eyes were closing again, of their own volition.

"Go to sleep, Logan. I'll be here when you wake up."

He struggled against the warmth seeping into him, but in the end, it was too much for him to fight.

*****

James burst backstage like a contained explosion. There were two succubae still conscious, and one lying on the floor, her severed head sitting a foot away from her body. Kefira and Odeda were trying to get the two conscious ones to say who hired them for the attack on Logan. They each had a succubus kneeling in front of them, their arms twisted behind their backs at painful angles.

"We'll be killed if we speak," protested the redheaded succubus.

James glared around the room at Odeda and Kefira, who glared back at him with bored contempt. He turned to the succubus who'd spoken. "And what do you think will happen to you if you don't?" he queried. He leaned down eye level with her and deliberately let his incisors grow long and sharp.

She flinched away and hissed. Succubae were a kind of sex demon who seduced men and compelled them to have mindless sex, orgasm after orgasm until they were literally dry husks. The succubae gained nourishment by taking the men's fluids into their bodies through the sexual contact.

A most painful way to die, since once the man ran out of semen, the rest of the body's fluids soon followed. James had once found a succubus after a kill—she'd been covered in the victim's blood and other bodily fluids he didn't want to think about. But she'd drained him so fast, her body hadn't had time to assimilate the fluids. The demon version of gorging.

James snapped his teeth together close to her face and watched her eyes go round with fear. "You know what you do to those men? How painful it must be for them to know they are dying with every orgasm, but unable to stop. To feel their bodies waste away?

"I'm an ancient vampire—one of the originals." James let his index fingernail grow out into a deadly looking sharp claw. "I can suck you dry, or..." He sliced a long bloody furrow down her cheek, the stench of rotten blood filling the room. "I can slice you so full of holes, you'll bleed out on the floor. And since you can't die unless your neck is broken and your head severed, or if you are burned— I can leave you as a lifeless husk for eternity with all your feelings and thoughts intact."

She whimpered and shrank away from him.

He whirled to the other succubus, this one a brunette. "Release your hold on Logan, now," he commanded.

She closed her eyes, but the pull of her powers remained. In one fluid movement, his razor sharp index finger claw sliced her head from her shoulders. It made a thunk as it hit the floor and rolled so it stared up at the redheaded succubus still held on her knees in front of Kefira.

James still felt the succubus' pull, but weaker now. "Release him, or I'll follow through on my promise."

Black tears began to stream down her face. "I cannot. Do what you must, but even that is less than what my Master will do if I disobey him."

James sighed. He'd really hoped to scare her into compliance. He needed her alive to find out who hired her. He could bite her and force her to do his will, but he still wouldn't be able to read her mind.

Succubus blood, poisoned by decay, would instantly kill a lesser vampire or even disintegrate most being's flesh. As an ancient, he was immune. But that didn't mean he relished the thought of drinking in their foul tasting blood. However, he had to swallow some—make it part of him, if he was to control her mind.

Steeling himself for the foul taste, he bent her head back at a cruel angle and struck fast and hard like a snake. The dark chunky fluid almost made him gag as it flowed over his tongue, but he forced his throat to swallow twice before he released her and let her fall limply to the floor.

Someone tapped him on the shoulder and he turned

to see Odeda holding out a shot glass full of amber liquid and a bar towel.

"A little Jack Daniel's chaser to get the taste out of your mouth?" she asked with a knowing smirk.

"Thanks," he muttered as he wiped his mouth with the bar towel and then downed the whiskey. The burning of the alcohol disintegrated the foul taste of the blood, but still left him with the vampire version of heartburn as his body tried to assimilate the foul stuff.

He turned to the remaining succubus and prodded her with the toe of his boot. "Release Logan," he commanded. Immediately, the pull of the succubus subsided and he heard Logan's sigh of relief, even from backstage.

He turned to face the two sisters. "What happened?" he demanded. "How could you let Logan almost be killed?"

Kefira stalked up to him, her full five-foot-five inch frame vibrating with indignation. "You can take your questions and kiss my ass, James." She poked a finger into his stomach for emphasis, which was at her chest height. "While we were here protecting Logan, you were off licking your wounds because Ariel pricked your immense vampire pride."

He opened his mouth to retort when he realized that arguing with Kefira, while satisfying, wouldn't give him any answers about what happened. He took a deep breath and then tried again in a calmer voice. "My apologies for arriving late. But right now, I'm concerned about Logan. And if you tell me what happened, maybe I can help."

Kefira sniffed with obvious distain and glanced over at Odeda. After what he was sure was a mental conversation between the two sisters, Odeda nodded to Kefira.

Kefira crossed her arms in front of her, fire still sparking in her eyes. "You're going to have to quit disappearing. You miss what's going on."

Odeda ignored Kefira and turned to James. "They

targeted Logan specifically, so we couldn't pick them out of the crowd until they turned on their sex-vibes." She tossed her mane of wavy brown hair to get it out of her face and continued. "Then they rushed the stage and mobbed him. Ariel tried to pull him out from under them, but one of them bit him in the thigh before we got him free."

James nodded. "Why the thigh?" he asked more to himself than the sisters. "Succubae are terrific assassins because they know so much about human anatomy. But they never do anything without a purpose."

"The bitch bit him in his inferior gluteal artery." Kefira broke in, her red brows drawn together, her lips thinned with temper. "He almost bled out before Dara could slow the bleeding."

James sighed. "But I don't see what could be gained by hitting that artery—there are easier ones to puncture which will bleed out faster."

"You bit *her*." Kefira pointed at the fallen succubus. "Can't you pull the information out of her mind?"

James shook his head in frustration. "That's actually a myth we like to perpetuate, but it isn't altogether true. I can control her—make her do what I want physically, but I can't read her mind or make her tell me something she's been ordered not to. That's one of those vampire myths from the Count Dracula movies."

Odeda puffed out a breath, which ruffled her hair. "Too bad we don't have Count Dracula instead of you then. So, where does that leave us?"

Kefira gasped. "Wait a minute." She looked back and forth between them. "Ariel mentioned the vamp who controlled the zombies tried to strike at Logan's groin, instead of his neck. So either that has some significance, or the whole supernatural world suddenly has a fetish for Logan's crotch."

Odeda crossed her arms over her impressive

cleavage. "I don't see what they have to gain by attacking his Johnson."

James' brows furrowed in confusion and then an idea hit him that chilled him to the core. "Unless they are trying to keep him from reproducing, for some reason."

The three exchanged worried glances.

Odeda looked down at the last living succubus. "After we put her on ice somewhere, we need to put in a call to Gabriel."

*****

Astor, James' vampire first lieutenant and company vice president looked up as James walked in through the large oak doors of his office. *About time James decides to grace us with his presence.*

Aloud, he said, "James, so good to finally see you. We were beginning to think you'd abdicated your position." James was the head of the Wellington Talent Agency, his entire vampire kiss employed in various, and sundry positions throughout the company. No better way to integrate into the human world than to hold the power of their entertainment.

Nothing would make Astor happier than to have James step aside and leave everything to him. That was one of the reasons he'd taken this assignment in the first place.

James glanced at Astor, clearly ignoring the jibe. "Where are the others?"

Astor leaned back in his swivel chair and sighed. "Several are offsite meeting with clients. I'm here holding down the fort and I've got an appointment this afternoon to meet with a new client."

"Good. So, things here are going smoothly?" James walked to the sidebar and poured two fingers of Jack Daniels into a glass.

Astor's brow furrowed. "Other than some of the kiss taking on too many human servants, yes. But I'm taking care of it since you haven't been around. Just leave it to me."

James raised both eyebrows. "Are you having problems handling things here while I'm otherwise engaged, Astor?" He punctuated his question by raising his glass. "If so, I can have Edward step in. I'm sure he can handle the added responsibility if you can't."

Astor bit back an acid retort. "That won't be necessary. I'm more than capable of handling things here in your absence." He ground his teeth as he waited for James' reaction. The last thing he needed was to be replaced in the hierarchy. Then his real master, Nicholas, would ensure he didn't live to see the next moon.

James finally nodded and turned back toward the bar.

Astor pointed toward James' drink. "I don't think I've ever seen you imbibe when clients weren't around to see. Is something wrong?" He stood and watched as James downed the burning liquid and scowled.

"Logan was attacked at Whiskey River. I had to bite a succubus to see who sent her."

Astor grimaced and held his envy in check. If he had bitten a succubus, he'd be dead. But unfortunately, James was extremely powerful and wasn't affected. Power always seems to be wasted on the weak and stupid. No wonder James' ancient rival wanted Astor to infiltrate. James cared more about the human than his own kiss. "That explains why you'd drink *that* stuff." He nodded toward the alcohol. "I've heard succubus blood is foul."

"And chunky," James said under his breath as he set the glass down on the sideboard and gestured to the conference room. "Shall we catch up before I need to go back out?"

Astor started toward the conference room. "Of course. So, did you find out who sent the succubus?" he asked, hoping he didn't sound too anxious. His existence would be short-lived if James ever found out who hired her and traced it back to his involvement. The ancient who'd hired him had stumbled upon the prophesy and had been frantically searching for the mortal it described ever since. Once they'd determined Logan's involvement—it was easy to piece together the identity of the ancient force for evil who would betray his kind to swing the pendulum toward good.

Now if James would just cooperate and let him know if the child of blood had been created, they'd know if it was safe to kill Logan or not.

"No," James said as he settled into a plush chair inside the conference room. "Not yet. But I'll keep trying."

Astor straightened his tie and took a seat across from him. "Maybe I can help. I do have some extra time in my schedule and I'd be happy to take some of the pressure off you."

James' heavy gaze settled on him like a shroud. He tried his best to retain a look of bored indifference as James' eyes narrowed and studied him.

"Since when do you have any interest in helping me protect Logan? The last time I mentioned he was having problems, I believe you referred to him as my pet meat popsicle."

Astor resisted the urge to squirm under the scrutiny. His very existence depended on James believing him. "And my opinion hasn't changed. I merely think if his problems were finished, you'd have more time to spend with the business for the good of the entire kiss. Not that I can't handle it, but the human servant overpopulation has begun to cause some problems, and has brought some unwanted attention." He leaned back in his chair and crossed his feet at the ankle, careful not to scuff his Italian loafers.

James leaned forward in his chair, his voice taking

on a dangerous soft edge. "Then handle it. Do you question my loyalty to the kiss, Astor?"

Astor forced himself to chuckle and unflinchingly meet James' gaze. "Of course not. I only want to do what's best for the kiss as a whole. And I know you've had to spend more and more time with…Logan." He hastily amended his 'pet meat popsicle' nickname.

Astor forced himself to hold James' gaze as the tension level in the room skyrocketed until it was difficult to draw breath. Not that he needed to draw breath to live, but nonetheless, the oppressive sensation unnerved him.

Finally, James said, "I decide what's best for the kiss, Astor. Not you. If I deem it important to protect one of our clients, whether they are vampire, human or were-creature, it's none of your concern." James leaned back in his chair, stretching his long legs out in front of him. "Unless you desire to challenge me…"

Astor couldn't help but cringe at the implied threat. James was an ancient and no matter how weak of character he was, he was too powerful for Astor to defeat, let alone challenge openly. Astor's best bet for the future would be to wait until James' rival killed him and then gave the kiss into Astor's good keeping. He closed his eyes and tipped his head to the side, revealing the long line of his exposed throat, showing obedience and trust. "Of course not, Master." He invoked the ancient title due James as leader of the kiss. It wasn't used in common practice, purely because it would be hard to explain to the human population.

One second James was leaning back in his chair and the next his teeth snapped a hairsbreadth away from Astor's neck. Before Astor could think, he found himself flinching back against the chair with James' laugh echoing around him.

Astor opened his eyes to see James leaning over him, his hands resting on either arm of Astor's chair, bracketing him in. "I know all too well that you hunger for power, Astor. If you wish to leave this kiss, I'll allow you to apply elsewhere. But keep this in mind, I run this kiss in order for us to be successful in the coming centuries. *That* is the key to our survival. Not continuing the ancient power struggles, which kept us hunted throughout history. Our success is contingent upon our ability to blend."

Astor forced his throat to work. "Yes, Master. Understood." He waited until he heard the front door close behind James before he allowed himself to relax. "Damn you, James. I want to look you in the eye while Nicholas kills you slowly."

*****

Logan lay in his bed staring up at the ceiling—again. This was the second time since he'd met Ariel that he was flat on his back because of some supernatural beastie who wanted him dead. Or, at least emasculated. He shuddered as he thought about how close he'd come to losing his family jewels. About half an inch, he noted as he looked down at the two angry red bite marks marring the inside of his right thigh.

He glanced around to make sure the door was firmly closed, and then pushed himself up to lean against the headboard. Bending over, he spread his legs wide and inspected himself to make sure everything was unharmed and where it should be. Having satisfied himself that all was well, he relaxed back against the pillow and let out a sigh of pure male relief.

His thigh continued to throb, even though he'd downed a few painkillers with a belt of whiskey. He realized with a laugh, it was becoming his cocktail of choice lately. He was glad everyone had finally gone downstairs. It hurt to have the sheet over him, and the bite was too close to his groin to make wearing underwear comfortable, so once again, he was naked. He was never a modest man, but having four gorgeous women around *when* he was naked, pushed his limits. It might be every man's fantasy, but not when it was only one on one you were interested in. And also not when three of them were the sisters of the woman with whom you'd like to have the one on one.

Logan sighed and tried to find a comfortable position. The ride home was still a blur. When he awoke in his own bed, Dara had already replaced his lost blood and told him he would heal in a day or two. Since he'd seen no IV equipment, he'd been too afraid to ask how. Not when there was a vampire somewhere on the premises. If Logan were lucky, he figured he'd never know.

"Not as happy to see me today, man-thing?"

Logan jumped and then groaned as his movement caused sharp pain to radiate out from his injured thigh. He glanced up to see Alonna sitting at the foot of his bed, on top of his sheets and covers. He pulled the pillow from behind his head and hastily shielded his crotch from her probing gaze. "I really wish you wouldn't sneak up on me like that, Alonna."

"Not that it isn't still impressive in its resting state," she said, still staring as if she could see right through the pillow. "But I did like looking at it the other way."

Logan didn't know what to say, so he kept quiet.

Alonna waved a hand in front of her, causing her blonde hair to flutter around her frantically. "No matter. I'm sure it had quite a scare tonight. I don't blame it for hiding." A bright smile bloomed across her face and she raised her eyes to his.

"Did you have a purpose, other than to discuss my genitals?" Logan asked.

Alonna stood and then flew up to perch on top of the pillow. She sat down facing him, her knees bent, her legs spread wide. "I came to see how you were doing," she said with a sexy pout.

Logan registered the perfect miniature folds of her sex, moist and open. His body began to respond and he decided staring over her head would be a good idea.

She smiled as the pillow undoubtedly shifted with his reaction. "You don't like what you see, man-thing? Men are always saying size does not matter. Is that not true?" Miniature eyelashes batted over her liquid lavender eyes.

Logan realized she was teasing him and lowered his eyes, but only just far enough to meet hers. He realized he was on boggy ground. Women of any size knew how to load questions, and he had become quite adept at sidestepping the obvious male trap. "Alonna, in this case I think the size difference might be too difficult to overcome. But I think God made you this size on purpose to make men of every other proportion wish they could be compatible."

Alonna's eyes danced with pleasure. "Oh, man-thing, you are good for my giant sister. Take care of her well." She closed her legs and stood. "And try to stay away from the beasties. I think Ariel would miss your manhood if it were severed." She gestured toward the pillow under her feet. "And it would be a shame if you were unable to pass on your seed someday."

Logan's blood drained from his face. *Son of my blood. Daughter of my destiny.* "Wait, is that why everyone is out to castrate me? Because they don't want me to be able to have a child?"

Alonna's liquid lavender eyes sparkled. "It is not for me to explain prophesies, man-thing. I can only deliver them. I came by purely to check on you, remember?" She crossed her arms over her bare breasts. "But heed what I have told you. Have you told the one who holds your heart?"

Surprise slapped Logan in the face. Why hadn't he thought to tell Ariel? Because he'd barely just figured out she was the one who'd touched his heart, he realized. Not that they'd had any time alone that he wasn't intent on doing other things besides talking. The prophesy seemed far removed from everything else that had been going on.

"Not that I can give prophesy advice, mind you. But if I were a man-thing in a situation such as yours, I would trust the one who held my heart to help me...and to keep my secret."

Logan could tell she was giving him direct help, which could get her into trouble. He grinned down at her. "And of course as a man-thing, I would be smart enough to think of that advice on my own and without help from you."

"Exactly," she agreed, a smug smile curving her lips. "Now, I have a gift, if you'll trust me."

Logan narrowed his eyes at her. "What kind of gift?" Alonna seemed trustworthy, but the mischief dancing in her eyes made him wary.

"I can heal your wound," she said, her smile now as wide as Texas. "But, you'll have to remove the pillow."

Logan was instantly skeptical. "Why do I have to move the pillow?"

She stamped her tiny foot. "Man-thing, do you pride yourself on being so difficult? I must touch the wound in order to heal it." She turned her back to him. "But, if you want to continue to suffer in pain, I guess I'll go." She began to walk toward the edge of the pillow, her tiny hips swaying provocatively.

Logan's thigh throbbed harder as if to say, "take her offer." What did he have to lose? She'd seemed trustworthy so far. And if she'd really been sent here to make an attempt on his life, she could've done that while he was sleeping. "Alonna, wait."

She turned and glanced at him expectantly.

"I'm sorry, I didn't mean to seem ungrateful. I'd really appreciate it if you healed me."

She smiled and flew off the pillow to perch on his

knee. "That's more like it. Now move the pillow." When he did, she rubbed her tiny hands together and devoured him with her eyes.

Logan tried not to squirm. He'd had plenty of women see him naked, but not even the most blatant had looked at him like this.

Alonna walked up the length of his leg and when she reached his wound, knelt down to examine it. Her nearness made his body react, and he noted she watched in fascination, as his erection grew full. Logan was tempted to cover himself with the pillow again, but he couldn't without smothering Alonna.

"It's just as I thought, man-thing. The succubus has left her poison within you. It must be removed by magic. That is why I offered my gift. It would be a shame to have such a wonderful specimen turned into a dry lifeless husk."

Logan tried to ignore the erection which stood stiff and proud between them. "What will happen if the poison isn't removed?" he asked, not sure he wanted to hear the answer.

"It will slowly fester inside you and you will become something of an incubus yourself in time. It would take much time or more bites, but it would happen."

Some of the blood returned to his brain from that shock of reality, causing his erection to soften.

"My, it is a timid thing, isn't it—easily scared." She laughed. "Don't worry, Alonna will fix everything. Just don't move, this may hurt."

Logan was stunned to see her lean down on all fours and kiss each bite mark in turn. "That's it?" he asked as she stood to go.

"That's only the beginning. You may want to summon Ariel. It will be painful while the poison works itself out. I would stay, but I cannot bear to watch such as this." Her tiny brows knitted and her pert lips turned down into a worried frown as she disappeared.

"Terrific, there's always a catch." He sighed. How could he call Ariel from up here? Almost immediately, pain began to build inside his thigh until a feral scream filled his ears. It sounded like something inhuman, and he was shocked to realize it came from him. He only had a moment to draw another breath before the pain spiraled ever higher, giving him no chance to recover from its onslaught. He fought for breath as scream after scream ripped from his throat.

CHAPTER SIX

Dara rushed into Logan's room, her sisters and James close behind her. Logan lay naked on the bed, still screaming and writhing in pain. The screams started only moments earlier, and they sent cold sharp fear spiraling straight to her gut. She knew well the dangers of a succubus bite. She'd been given a great gift of healing, but poison from this type of being was beyond her. She'd been about to call for Gabriel when Logan's first screams sounded.

Dara saw the stricken look on Ariel and James' faces and took charge. She wouldn't let their fear for Logan get in the way of her doing everything possible for him. "Everyone take a limb and hold him down, so I can figure out what's wrong."

Ariel and James each took a leg with Odeda and Kefira holding his arms. Logan was held motionless by their superior strength, but his head still thrashed wildly, the screams becoming more desperate. Logan tried in vain to grit his teeth against another scream, and Dara's heart twisted inside her chest at her inability to stop the pain.

She took a deep breath and stepped forward so she could examine his wound. What she saw made her gasp aloud. Putrid smoke rose from Logan's thigh wounds and grey-black pus bubbled up in greasy belches. Dara wiped at the pus with the tail of the sheet and the cloth began to smolder and smoke in her hand.

"Damn," she swore and ran toward the bathroom. She needed water to flush the pus away so she could see the wound and keep the foul stuff away from Logan's skin.

She grabbed a handful of towels and then searched frantically for something to put water in, but only found a large bottle of hydrogen peroxide. "Might help keep that crap off his skin," she murmured rushing back to her patient.

"What's happening?" Ariel demanded.

Dara shook her head as she pulled a towel under

Logan's leg. "The poison is being forced out of his leg, but I'm not sure why." Dara unscrewed the cap off the peroxide and met Ariel's worried gaze. "Hold him tight, this may hurt even more." She tipped the peroxide bottle so that a steady stream fell onto his wounds.

When the peroxide stream hit the succubus poison, it began to bubble and sizzle like a frying pan full of fajita meat. Logan's thrashing hit fever pitch until finally, mercifully, he passed out, his body falling slack.

"Logan!" Ariel cried out.

"It's okay, he just passed out. The pain became too much. Maybe this will finish before he wakes up, and we can spare him any further pain." When the last of the peroxide drained from the bottle, Dara tossed it aside and waited until the bubbling subsided. Then she took a towel and wiped the wound clean. She saw two perfect lavender lip prints where Logan's wound used to be.

Tossing a towel over the wound and hoping no one besides her saw Alonna's handiwork, she took action. "Everyone out except for Ariel. All we can do is watch and wait, and we'll need to conserve our strength in case we need to take shifts with him."

"I'm not leaving him," James insisted, not meeting anyone's eyes. "If I had been at the bar rather than off sulking, this may not have happened."

"We can protect him as well as you can," Ariel bristled.

James glared back at her. "I can see that," he said and gestured down at Logan's still form.

"Enough," Dara snapped. She needed to get everyone out of here before they started asking questions about Logan's wound. "James, no one is blaming you—you know as well as we do that you wouldn't have sensed the succubus threat any earlier than we did. We all want Logan to be all right, and the best way you can assist me is to get the hell out and let me work."

James seemed about to argue further, but then merely nodded. His face was all hard lines and angles when he reached down to brush his fingers across Logan's forehead. "Take good care of him," he said, his voice almost a whisper. Dara suddenly couldn't breathe, almost as if all the air was sucked from the room. Her heart twisted inside her chest at the depth of emotion this ancient vampire had just shown for Logan. No wonder Ariel never guessed James was a vampire—the man simply was not evil. Dara would bet her life and even the lives of her sisters on it.

Before she could think about what she was doing, she reached out and took James' hand in her own. The contrast of the large brown fingers against her own creamy white skin was striking. "I'll do everything within my power for him."

James stared down at their entwined hands for a moment, an unreadable expression chasing across his features. Finally, he nodded and then disappeared from the room, followed reluctantly by Odeda and Kefira.

"We'd better hear what's going on soon," warned Kefira.

"You'll just have to trust me," Dara thought back. Kefira nodded and pulled the door closed behind her.

Ariel turned to Dara. "What's going on? And why all the secrecy?"

In answer, Dara picked up the towel off Logan's wound and revealed the telltale lip prints.

"Alonna!" Ariel leaned closer to examine the prints, but Dara had already seen that no wound remained.

Alonna had saved Logan's life, but Dara didn't know why. It wasn't that Alonna was evil, but for her to intervene for a mortal, one of the prophesies must be involved.

Ariel finished inspecting the wound and looked up at

Dara. "You were smart to hide this from everyone. The more people who know, the more chance it could change the outcome."

Dara sighed. Alonna had never before gotten involved, which meant this was big. "Maybe Gabriel will be able to help us figure out what the prophesy is."

Ariel shook her head. "No need, Alonna wouldn't do this," she gestured to the twin lip prints, "without Logan's consent. She's already told him and most likely warned him not to tell anyone for the same reason you just kicked everyone out."

Dara pulled the goo-covered towel out from under Logan's leg and rolled it in a ball. She'd have to take this out to the barn and burn it the same way they'd burned the zombie parts. It wasn't worth the risk to let someone else touch the caustic poison. "You're probably right, but I think you should be the only one to speak to him about it. I'm going to try to pretend I don't know anything about it. Otherwise, I'm putting the prophesy at risk too. I'll trust your judgment if you need me involved once you find out what it is."

Dara turned to go, but Ariel's hand on her arm stopped her.

"Thank you for everything you've done for Logan."

"I would give my life to see you happy again." She pulled her sister into a hug. "Two hundred years is a long time to hurt."

*****

Ariel stepped into the bedroom next to Logan's and pulled the door shut behind her.

"Are you going to tell us what all the secrecy is about?" Kefira asked.

Ariel sighed. She should've known it would be almost impossible to keep anything from her sisters. She turned to see Kefira sitting on the bed, Indian Style, her blue eyes intense against the deep red of her hair. "Fi, I can't tell you," Ariel said as she pulled open her suitcase and took out the silky white teddy she slept in.

"So, Logan is involved in a prophesy," Kefira stated.

Ariel's head snapped up and then she laughed. "I should know better than to try and keep anything from either of you."

"Yes, you should. We know each other too well for that. Don't worry, we'll step lightly, but you should have told us." Kefira wagged a finger at her. "The risk of us changing the prophesy is moot next to us second guessing ourselves because we don't know everything."

Ariel pulled her shirt over her head and then slipped off her jeans. "You're right, I just don't want to take chances with Logan's life."

Kefira bristled. "I would never put someone in our care in danger—or at least not more danger than they were in when they came to us."

Ariel dropped her bra and panties into the suitcase and stepped into the teddy, fastening the snaps at the crotch. "I didn't mean to infer that you would, Fi. It's just...." She trailed off, not sure what she was trying to say.

Kefira unfolded her legs and stood, laying a hand on Ariel's shoulder. "It's just that you're in love with him and are leaving yourself wide open to getting hurt."

Ariel met her sister's worried stare. "I'm not sure if I'm in love with him, but I'm happy for the first time in two centuries. Can't that be enough for now?"

Kefira dropped her hand at Ariel's defensive tone. "I just don't want to see you get hurt again. You know what kind of a playboy he is, and I don't want you to be the flavor of the month."

Ariel's temper snapped. "Just because Dagan betrayed you doesn't mean Logan will do the same to me." Ariel instantly regretted her words as pain filled her sister's eyes. If she ever saw Dagan again, she'd rip his heart out for the pain he'd inflicted on Kefira.

Ariel remembered only too well the dark days after Dagan told Kefira he never wanted to see her again, and then later when she'd lost the baby. But then God never mentioned that when they were released from service, they could get pregnant. And even beyond that, turning to stone would cause them to abort. It was just part of what they did for nine centuries. Ariel reached out and when Kefira stepped away, dropped her hand to her side.

"You're right," she said, her voice thick with unshed tears. "But in this instance, I think caution would be best. I don't want any of you to have to go through what I did." Pain still rode across Kefira's features and she crossed her arms over her chest. "I need to go check the perimeter. Are you going to bed?" she said, refusing to meet Ariel's gaze.

Ariel tried to think of something to say, but nothing she could ever say would erase her sister's pain, so she just nodded. "I'm going to watch over Logan."

"Just make sure you watch over yourself, as well," Kefira said before she strode to the door.

*****

Logan woke to the smell of musky vanilla caressing his senses. As awareness returned, he realized he spooned Ariel's scantily clad form in front of him, his nose buried in the lustrous cloud of her hair. His body woke faster than his mind, as was evidenced by his throbbing erection already cradled against the crack of her shapely ass. He breathed deep and let Ariel's familiar scent imprint itself in his memory. After all, this was the first time he'd woken up with her. *But I swear it won't be the last.*

He ran his hand down Ariel's side, caressing the curve of her hip and enjoying the soft warm skin and silk under his calloused fingers. He had a moment to worry if his fingers were too rough for her before she stretched back against him like a cat.

"Mmm, good morning," she murmured, her voice thick with both sleep and desire.

"Sorry about my hands. Playing guitar means calloused fingers. I hope they aren't too rough."

In response, Ariel grabbed his hand and pulled it up to her breast. "I love your hands," she whispered. As if to prove it, her nipple pebbled to a hard peak beneath his touch.

She wiggled back tighter against his erection and he groaned aloud. The friction of the silk against his engorged flesh almost pushed him past reason. He had to hold himself back from taking her hard and fast—he'd already done that their first time out. Logan promised himself this time he'd show her what she meant to him and worship every inch of her.

"You're going to kill me, Ariel," he said through gritted teeth, his control straining.

She chuckled and reached behind her to run a hand over every part of him she could reach.

Logan smiled. If she wanted to play, he was definitely game. He gently pulled her hair away from her neck and placed a row of open-mouthed kisses against her nape. When she gasped in pleasure, he renewed his efforts and kissed a line down her shoulder and along her back. At the same time, he caressed her stomach with his right hand, searching for sensitive spots.

Logan slipped the teddy strap off her shoulder and chased its path with his mouth. As erotic as it was to feel her through the silk, he wanted her naked and warm under his seeking hands. "Off," he murmured as he continued to kiss in the wake of the spaghetti strap. He smiled as she slipped out of the garment with practiced ease and tossed it on the floor.

Pushing her over onto her stomach, he lazily traced the fairy wings tattoo with the tip of his finger. It was made up of vibrant colors and looked almost like Alonna's gauzy wings, but in a thousand shades of color and texture. But under his fingers, there was only warm, silky flesh. He replaced his finger with his tongue and she moaned into the pillow as he traced a hot wet line along the edge of the right fairy wing.

Then he began to systematically explore the rest of her with hands and teeth and tongue. Before he'd made it down to her waist, she was already writhing with need beneath him.

"Logan...," she pleaded.

He smiled against her waist. "I'm not done with you yet. I haven't even finished the back, and then there's still the whole front."

She groaned, her hips already bucking against the mattress, her body searching for release.

Logan reverently glided his hands over her rounded ass. This woman had the most magnificent backside he'd ever seen. He would gladly spend hours caressing and exploring it, but so much more of her still awaited him. When he laved and then nipped the back of her right thigh, she buried her fingers in the sheets in a death grip, the motions of her body still begging him to give her the release she sought.

But Logan continued his single-minded exploration of her. The wonderful indent at the back of each knee, the delicate ankles and the dainty feet, which held so many sensitive spots, that when they were explored, she gasped. When he'd thoroughly explored her back, he flipped her over and gasped at the results of his handiwork.

Ariel's skin was flushed with desire, her nipples engorged and dark coral, her blue eyes flaming with desire. He could smell her arousal thick inside the room, a primal scent that any man recognizes. He couldn't resist skimming a hand along her inner thigh to the apex of her legs to sample the wet heat awaiting him. She gasped again when he feathered a finger against her swollen outer lips and then groaned when he pulled his hand away so he could begin to worship the front of her as he had the back.

He wanted to uncover every secret and mark this woman as his. Brand her with his body and his touch until she could think of no one but him—ever.

Logan knew he should be shocked at the thought. But since he'd met Ariel, it was as if he'd recovered a missing piece of himself. Something he never even knew was missing until she filled it and made him complete. He'd never believed in love before, and definitely hadn't believed a woman existed who could hold his attention for more than a few hours at a time. But here she was, entwined around his heart, and he would gladly lay himself bare for her.

Ariel bucked under him as he nipped at her softly rounded stomach and continued downward. The thought of tasting her hardened him further and made him groan aloud. The first swipe of his tongue against her swollen outer lips was more than he'd ever imagined. Ariel gasped against the sensation, and spread her legs wider to give him greater access.

She tasted like musk and honey on a sunny Texas afternoon, sweet and addicting. He gently traced her folds with his tongue until she shuddered, he smiled and continued to lave her clitoris. It was a hard nub, just begging to be tasted and he gave it his full attention. Taking it inside his mouth, he sucked and was rewarded with a moan, her hips thrust against his face. He continued to suck and lave his tongue over the small nub, enjoying the needy sounds spilling from her throat.

"Logan...," she said, her voice strained and breathy.

Continuing his ministrations, he slipped a finger inside her heat searching for the sensitive spot, which would push her over the edge. Her body tightened around him and she thrust herself against him repeatedly. Logan knew she was close and smiled to himself in pure male satisfaction. He was the one driving her to this mindless state—he, Logan McAllister. This woman was his. He pulled his mouth away from her and she sobbed from the loss of sensation. "Do you want to come, Ariel?" he asked. His voice sounding harsh in his own ears.

"Logan, please…," she begged.

He inserted another finger and returned to alternately sucking and laving until she was perilously close to the edge once again. Then he eased back just far enough so his breath would still brush her sensitive flesh. "Answer me, Ariel. Do you want to come?"

"Yes, please, yes," she squirmed under him.

He returned to his ministrations, his fingers mimicking what he wanted to do with her next, his mouth firmly latched around her engorged clit. When she began to pant, he grazed his teeth lightly over the sensitive flesh and she exploded. Ariel cried out and clamped around his fingers like a vise. Logan couldn't wait any longer, he removed his fingers and crawled up her body and buried himself deep inside her.

She was still rhythmically pulsing around him, at the end of her orgasm, when Logan began to move inside her. She wound her arms around his neck and moaned long and low. "Logan…."

"Yes, baby, I'm here," he said and leaned down to take her mouth in a gentle kiss. He knew she could taste where he'd just been on his tongue, but if she minded, it didn't show. She pulled him harder against her and met him thrust for thrust, her tongue still dancing with his.

Logan pulled back to look into her eyes. He wanted her to look at him while he took her. She stared back at him, her Kerry blue eyes, dark with desire and something else he couldn't quite place.

God, but she felt amazing. He'd never made love without a condom before and the skin to skin sensation was indescribable next to what he'd experienced in the past. But then again, he'd never made love before, it had always been just sex.

A fleeting thought ran through his mind about protection and pregnancy, but the thought of Ariel pregnant with his baby made him ache with longing. He never knew such a thought would make him desperate to come inside her, to make his want a reality.

"Ariel," he whispered and gazed into her eyes. "You're mine, tell me. Tell me you're mine."

He saw her eyes sharpen, her mind fighting through the haze of desire to make sense of what he asked of her.

Logan kissed her, thoroughly and completely, branding her and leaving her breathless. When he finally pulled back and looked into her eyes again, he saw again that elusive expression he didn't know how to place. The demands of his body were mounting and an urgency to possess her like no other man ever had flowed through him. "Tell me, Ariel," he said thrusting inside her and fighting for control as she continued to tighten around him. "Tell me you're mine while I come inside you. Tell me."

"Logan, please...."

He knew she was close, he changed the angle and thrust deeper and harder. Her eyes dilated, the black eating away at the dark blue. "Ariel...," he insisted.

"Yes, Logan—yours. Only yours," she said as she began to convulse around him.

The words seemed to trigger his own release, and the world shattered and exploded as he emptied his seed inside her.

*****

As the haze of afterglow cleared, Ariel's mind settled slowly back into reality. Logan lay on top of her, with their bodies still joined. She closed her eyes and enjoyed the comforting weight of him against her pelvis, and the way the crisp hairs of his chest scratched against her breasts every time he took a breath. She and James never had the luxury of this type of after sex cuddling. After all, those were the days she still had her wings 24x7. Not too conducive for on-your-back sex, let alone savoring it afterwards. So, this was the first time she'd felt the weight of a man on top of her. *I could definitely get used to this— especially with this man.*

"Get used to it later," Kefira's voice chided inside her head. *"James said he senses something evil on the property. Deda is going to check it out."*

"Doesn't anyone respect a private moment?" Ariel thought back sharply. *"Have Deda keep me posted."*

Ariel opened her eyes to find Logan watching her, a lopsided grin showing through his morning stubble. She reached up to brush an unruly blonde lock of hair away from his forehead.

"Let me guess, your sisters were talking inside your head," he said, the grin never wavering.

"How did you know that?" she asked.

He leaned down to run his stubble lightly over the side of her face causing her to giggle. "Because you always look so serious when they do."

Ariel was mortified that a giggle had escaped her. She was a gargoyle warrior, she didn't, under any circumstances, giggle. "Hey," she said pushing his face away with her hands. "No tickling," she said trying to regain her composure.

"Just wait until I give the rest of your body the same treatment."

The look in his eyes was pure dark male desire and lava flowed through her veins at the thought of him paying such thorough attention to her body again. She realized duty called even if she was tempted to stay in bed for the rest of the day and take him up on his offer. Besides, she didn't want her sisters interrupting an even more inopportune moment. "Can I get a rain check on that?" she asked. "Kefira said James senses something evil on the property. Deda is going to check it out. And besides, we need to talk about last night."

Logan nipped her bottom lip playfully. "Work, work, work, nag, nag, nag," he said in between kisses. "Okay, you win. But that will only give me time to come up with more things I'd like to do to you."

Heat rushed through Ariel's body again and he hardened inside her. She started to give in, but then remembered Kefira would be waiting for them downstairs. "Rain check," she said, pushing him upwards. "Before you erode all my willpower."

Logan laughed and rolled off her. "As long as I know I affect you as much as you do me, I'll take the rain check and count the minutes."

Ariel leaned over the side of the bed, found her teddy and began to untangle it.

"So, what did you want to talk about?" Logan asked, lying on his side, his head cradled in his wide palm.

Ariel had to pull her mind back to the topic at hand. He looked too damned tasty laying there with nothing but a thin sheet between them. "Why don't you tell me about the prophesy?" At Logan's guarded look, she said, "I know Alonna was here last night. The only reason she would show so much interest in you would be because you were involved in a prophesy."

Logan seemed to deliberate for a few moments, and then a wide smile and a look of relief washed across his face. "Okay, but she told me to tell you and no one else."

"I understand. It's dangerous when too many people know about a prophesy. My sisters all know you're probably involved in one—all the signs are there. But I won't share the actual prophesy with them if Alonna thinks we shouldn't."

Logan nodded. "I don't remember it word for word. But it had to do with the son of my blood and the daughter of my destiny. If I raise the son, I got the impression it was a good thing. But if I raise the daughter, then evil would prevail."

Ariel's heart compressed at the thought of Logan having a daughter or a son. That would mean he'd have to sleep with someone else. She'd worked for God for too many years to think She'd leave her in the dark if she was a key player in a prophesy of this magnitude. "Can you remember the actual wording? Sometimes that's very important," Ariel pressed.

Logan's brow furrowed in thought. "There was something about if I cease to exist before my fated time, the son would avenge me with rivers of dark blood and the heavens will shine on him."

Ariel let out a breath she hadn't realized she'd been holding. "Well, that's good." At Logan's confused expression, she continued. "That means if the side of evil tries to bump you off early to avoid the whole prophesy, the son will avenge you and good wins."

Logan sat up, his eyes dark. "But it also means if they bump me off before I make this son, then the whole prophesy is null and void, right?"

Ariel remained silent. What could she say? If this weren't Logan she was talking to, she'd tell him to get busy on making the son in question. But the thought of the large calloused hands caressing another woman made her blood run cold.

"So, on that cheery note, why don't we both get dressed and see what Kefira wants," Logan said as he swung his legs over the side of the bed and stood.

Ariel's breath caught in her throat. He was truly magnificent. All tanned skin, blond hair and muscle. Her worry over the last few minutes vanished in a wash of female hormones. She thought about giving his body the same thorough treatment he'd given hers and sighed. *Focus, Ariel.*

She looked up to find Logan grinning at her.

"See something you like, darlin'?" he asked, deliberately using the nickname he'd used on her in the office that first day.

Ariel's cheeks heated, but she forced herself to meet his gaze squarely. "Yes, I was admiring your new tattoos."

Logan's puzzled look lasted a few seconds before he followed the line of her gaze down to his thigh where two perfect lavender lip prints replaced the bite marks from last night. "Damn!" he swore. "Are they permanent?"

He looked so scandalized that Ariel had to laugh. "Yes, but before you get mad at Alonna, you need to know she doesn't bestow healing lightly. You could have died from the succubus poison."

Logan moved over to the mirror on the back of his bedroom door to take a closer look at the new permanent decorations. "But they're so damned girly," he protested. He turned to look at Ariel. "Wait, now I remember. The wound was smoking and oozing…," he trailed off as the full memory of the evening hit him. "That was the worst pain I've ever experienced in my whole life."

Tears stung the back of her eyes. "I know, I was so scared we wouldn't be able to save you." She stared hard at the floor and tried to blink back the watery signs of weakness.

Logan crouched down in front of her, put a finger under her chin and lifted her face to meet his gaze. "There's no need for tears. I'm a lot harder to get rid of than all that."

Ariel's eyes chose that moment to betray her and

overflow. Full, hot tears made a wet path down her cheeks. The full impact of the realization that she would never be able to make this man hers hit her. The prophesies were decreed by God. Ariel knew better than to hope this one wouldn't come true in some fashion. She tried to turn away, to hide, but Logan gripped her chin.

"Don't ever be ashamed of how you feel, Ariel." He leaned in to kiss her salty lips. "It took me a long time to find you, I don't want to lose you either."

Ariel's emotions swirled. She told Kefira she wasn't in love with Logan. But did she mean that or was she just trying to shield her heart? She wasn't sure, but she now knew she couldn't let this go too far, or this time she'd be crushed even worse than when James betrayed her. She squared her shoulders and returned Logan's steady gaze. "I'll admit, I was really worried. But Logan, I'm not sure exactly what we have between us. We've only known each other a short time. Can't we just enjoy what we have right now?"

Logan silenced her with another kiss. "I know you've been hurt, I saw the pain in your eyes when James walked into my office that first day. But I've been unknowingly waiting for you my whole life. I'm willing to wait until you get comfortable with the idea."

She pulled back away from Logan and crossed her arms over her chest. "What idea am I supposed to be getting comfortable with?" she demanded, hating that she sounded defensive.

Logan reached forward, rubbed his stubbled jaw against her neck and chuckled when she shivered against him. "Whatever idea you'd like to—as long as it involves the two of us spending lots of time together."

Ariel pushed him away and put up every emotional barrier she had. "I think we're great together—in bed. There's no use romanticizing it. I think you're attributing more to this than there might be because of the situation."

She saw hurt flicker in Logan's eyes, quickly replaced by a nonchalant stare. "No problem, sweetheart. Whatever you want."

Ariel felt like a heel as Logan began pulling on his jeans and shirt. Just like that, all the closeness and the intimacy evaporated. She sighed and pulled on her teddy. "I'll go get dressed and meet you downstairs in ten minutes. Do you think we can be civil about this? After all, we've made no promises between us."

Logan turned to face her, his blue-grey eyes hard as steel. "Absolutely, darlin'. After all, we just barely met."

The verbal knife slid deep. She'd brought this on herself. If distance was what she wanted, it looked like he was going to give it to her. She just hoped she wasn't already too far-gone, but she feared her heart was already his.

CHAPTER SEVEN

Ariel stood outside the stables waiting for Kefira and Logan. Deda had contacted her while she was getting dressed to say the danger had passed, but Logan needed to see what she'd found. Ariel knew it was cowardly, but she asked Kefira to wait for Logan. Anything to delay having to face him for a few more minutes.

Whatever Odeda found took precedence over her own wounded heart. She figured if she said it enough times, she might actually start to believe it.

Ariel closed her eyes, took a deep breath and let it out slowly. *I can do this. I've faced death millions of times, so why is the thought of hurting Logan to save myself pain so much worse?*

She heard the scuff of boots and turned to see Logan and Kefira walking toward her.

Kefira looked first at Ariel and then at Logan before speaking. "I'll just go and make sure Jeb's got the horses saddled for us."

"*Traitor!*" Ariel yelled into her sister's mind and grimaced when all she heard back was laughter.

"Ariel." Logan tipped his cowboy hat to her in an oddly mocking manner. "So, where are we off to?"

Before she could answer, Kefira and Jeb walked around the corner leading three horses behind them.

"Don't worry, Jeb," Kefira said archly. "Ariel can ride a horse even better than me." Kefira had embarrassed Jeb earlier in the day by riding a horse he'd deemed unbreakable to all the ranch hands. Kefira had won $200 and the respect of all the men—except for Jeb.

Jeb scowled in response and then handed the reins of a large chestnut gelding to Ariel. "Scout can be a bit frisky, so be careful with him."

Ariel ignored Jeb's obvious displeasure and slipped into the saddle. "I'm sure I'll be fine, Jeb. But thanks for worrying about me." It seems Jeb still hadn't forgiven her for the scene in the office. Some men just couldn't handle a strong woman.

"If it's urgent, why aren't we taking the Jeeps?" Logan asked.

"Sorry, boss," said Jeb. "The boys took both into town for supplies. It will have to be horses or one of the street vehicles."

Logan shook his head. "No, don't worry about it, Jeb. The horses are fine." Logan mounted his own dark bay thoroughbred, Ransom, and turned to Ariel expectantly.

"Kefira, I need you at the gate, can Ariel spare you?" Ariel heard Dara say inside her head.

"It's freaking Grand Central Station around here," she muttered. And now she would be alone with Logan on the ride out to Odeda. She stifled a sigh. "Kefira, go ahead and see what Dara needs. If she can't handle it, it must be big. Keep me informed."

Ariel tuned out before Dara could elaborate on the front gate issue. She had enough problems to deal with, and she had faith her sisters would handle anything that came up.

Kefira winked at Jeb and jogged back toward the house, leaving the stable master scowling after her. Kefira never resisted taunting someone who begged for it.

Ariel studied Logan. He looked like a man born to sit in a saddle, just a handsome extension of the beautiful, sleek horse. She had a sudden mental flash of how his hard naked body felt against her own and heat flooded her cheeks.

"Ariel?" he asked, sidling his horse closer to hers. "Is there a problem?" he asked with a knowing smirk.

She swallowed hard and tried to turn her thoughts to more G-rated subjects. She'd pushed him away this morning and insisted all she wanted was sex, now she'd have to live with the results. "Fine," she croaked out, her throat dry as sand. "We should get going. Odeda's waiting." She flicked

Scout's reins and he surged forward.

Ariel clamped her thighs around the horse and let him set their pace. She pushed everything from her mind except the Texas greenery which rushed by them. She enjoyed the sting of the wind on her face and the adrenaline high of a good, hard ride across the countryside.

It had been almost eighty years since she last rode a horse, but she could never forget how. It had been too much a part of her life for centuries.

She heard Ransom and Logan close behind her and knew they would overtake her in seconds. Ransom was a sleek horse, built for speed, while Scout, a little stockier, had some cow horse somewhere along his family tree.

But that didn't stop Ariel or Scout from giving Logan and Ransom a race. Competition was a great motivator, and besides, as long as they raced, they couldn't have any more strained conversations or smug innuendo.

Scout slowed as they came up over a small ridge and Ariel saw Odeda. Deda's horse, tethered to a nearby tree, strained against his reins, shying as far away from the grisly scene as his reins would allow him. Odeda knelt down in the closely cropped grass, looking at four obviously dead cows.

The hair on Ariel's nape ruffled and icy pinpricks marched up her spine. This site reeked of evil.

Terrific. And I wondered how today could get better.

Ransom tried to buck and shy away from the spot, but Logan reined him in. "My God, what happened here?" Shock and outrage warred in his voice.

Ariel nodded at Logan's reaction. Nothing like this had happened on the ranch before or he wouldn't have been so surprised. Not that she doubted his honesty, but sometimes people left things out, and Ariel needed all the information if they were going to protect him.

Without turning toward them, Odeda said, "That's

what we're going to find out. You may want to tie the horses over with mine. They can sense the evil and it's making them skittish."

After tethering Scout, Ariel swung down out of the saddle and walked toward Odeda. "Deda?" she asked, when her sister still didn't turn toward her. Ariel stepped around into Odeda's line of sight and only then saw the deep furrows sliced down her sister's breast and stomach. "Why the hell didn't you tell me you were injured?"

Odeda snorted. "It's not like I'm dying. I just need to heal."

James rushed to the two women, his eyes round with disbelief. "Oh my God! We need to get her to a hospital or call Dara."

Ariel helped Odeda stretch out on the grass-covered ground. "There's no need. She can heal these wounds on her own."

"What did this?" Ariel asked.

Odeda rolled her eyes skyward. "What's left of it is dead. Now if you don't mind, I really need to heal."

"Go ahead, I'll watch over you," Ariel said to her sister. White, cold stone began to flow over Deda's body until her sister resembled a lovely reclining statue.

She noticed the rapt fascination with which Logan watched. "The furrows are still there," he said.

"She has to turn to stone first and then heal. Give her a few minutes." As if triggered by her words, the furrows began to fill in and smooth out before her eyes.

She heard Logan's boots scuff against the grass on the ground next to her. "What does it feel like?" he asked in a curious whisper.

"Which part? The turning to stone, or the healing?" Ariel noticed Odeda's body begin the transformation back to flesh, so she glanced up at Logan.

"Both."

"Turning to stone is a cold like no other. Your mind is intact and functioning, but your body is immobile and vulnerable. As for the healing…" She searched for the right word to convey the sensation she'd experienced numerous times throughout her life. "Well, it burns and tickles at the same time."

Odeda sat upright and touched a hand to her ruined leather jacket. "Damn! I just bought this."

Ariel stood and extended a hand to help her sister up. "Nice to see your priorities are in order. Logan will buy you a new one. He's paying us well for this job." She shot Logan a smirk over her shoulder.

"A purchase I'll be happy to subsidize," he said and then turned his attention back toward the cows for the first time since they'd arrived.

The three of them stood staring down at the grisly scene. The four bloated heifers lay on their sides, arranged in a circle, hooves out. The pattern reminded Ariel of a giant bovine pincushion. Each black and white cow had their throat ripped out, and dried blood smeared on their sides, proclaiming 'no new seed' in ancient Hebrew. "Seems a bit redundant, don't you think?" Ariel asked.

"Especially since they've had all their sex organs mutilated," added Odeda.

Logan's brows furrowed and he looked back and forth between the two women. "Why, what does it say?" he said, indicating the side of the closest cow.

"It says 'no new seed' in ancient Hebrew," supplied Odeda. "Someone isn't being too subtle, and they also have no imagination. But I'd hazard a guess they want to make sure you aren't using your male equipment for its intended purpose." Deda pointedly stared at Logan's crotch, a smug smile playing over her face.

Logan shot an accusing glance at Ariel.

"She didn't tell me the prophesy, but it doesn't take

a rocket scientist to figure out the obvious signs they've been leaving." Odeda glared at Logan, daring him to call her a liar.

"Deda, you're not helping," Ariel warned when she noticed Logan's mouth firm into a thin line.

Odeda flashed her dazzling smile and shrugged. "Sorry, I have a great sense of the ironic."

"You have a great sense of *something*," added Ariel under her breath.

Logan walked around the circle and knelt down to examine the scene. "So, why did they disfigure the udders?" he asked. "They aren't exactly sex organs." He looked up at the two women. "I mean, if he was trying to get a message across to me, why not mutilate my prize bull?"

Ariel shrugged. "The bull is closer to the house. I'll bet these were easier to get to without alerting any of us." The only thing that gave off this much evil and liked to disfigure genitalia was a rokurokubi. "Damn."

"If you're thinking 'kubis did this, you're right," said Odeda. "When I broke its neck it disintegrated, but the other two escaped. I can ask Gabriel if there's been an increase in population, but I haven't seen any of them in a few hundred years."

Logan stood and faced the women. "What's a kubi?"

"A rokurokubi is a Japanese goblin. Another creation of the dark one." Ariel circled around to stand next to him and knelt down to examine the shredded udder. "See these teeth marks here?" She pointed to a set of five imprinted teeth, which looked like a little oval of marks left behind on someone's sandwich after they'd taken a bite.

Logan leaned down to examine the spot she pointed to. "Wait, those look human." He looked at Ariel, disbelief plain on his face.

"Exactly," broke in Odeda. "The 'kubi can pass for

human, and do whenever possible. Some of them even take human spouses and hide what they are. They drink blood and eat people, but will settle for animals if they are trying to remain undetected. Sort of like politicians with better table manners."

"Deda," Ariel warned.

"So when I came upon them chomping on the udders, it was a pretty safe bet they weren't your next door neighbors come for a visit."

"But why chew up the udders?" Logan asked, clearly trying to come to terms with the macabre scene.

Ariel stood. "Because rokurokubi can't reproduce. They're sterile. So, anything else that can, angers them."

"Then why aren't they extinct?"

Odeda brushed some grass from her pants. "The dark one makes more 'kubi's out of humans. I've never heard what offense they commit to be consigned to this fate though."

"Great, so what does this tell us?" Logan asked. He stood and turned his back on the mutilated carcasses.

"That whoever is after you doesn't necessarily want you dead." Ariel studied Logan's back, trying to gauge how well he was taking this. "Like Deda said, this is another warning about you reproducing."

Logan faced her, his jaw clenched. "I'll get the ranch hands to clean up the cattle."

Odeda stepped forward. "I've already called a priest. This site will have to be cleansed of the evil before any of your other animals will even come near it. I'll get the ranch hands to help me after the priest is done."

She gestured in the general direction of the house. "You'd better go see what Dara and Kefira are doing. Dara rarely asks for help, it could be big. I tuned out when they were discussing it because I was busy here, but keep me in the loop."

"Thanks, I will." Ariel pierced Odeda with a stern stare. "And, Deda, do me a favor and don't seduce the priest this time."

*****

Logan swung into his saddle before turning to Ariel. "She seduces priests?"

The horses walked side by side at an easy pace. Ariel reached down to pat Scout's neck in an absent gesture. "Well, Odeda seduces everyone. But Gabriel told us man imposed the celibacy restrictions on priests, not God. God meant for all men to take a mate. So, Deda has since dedicated herself to helping to relieve them of their burden of celibacy, much to Gabriel's irritation."

Logan shook his head. He wasn't Catholic, but he always wondered about the celibacy rule, himself. "So why doesn't Gabriel just forbid it if it bothers him?"

"That's not how it works. God made a promise never to impede our free will, and the rule extends to all Her minions."

Logan would have to ponder the idea when he had more time. He'd been angry at God since his mother died, but he could see where leaving man free will would complicate things.

But that still meant God let bad things happen to good people. And it was definitely within His—Her, he corrected, power to stop it. But then again, how could She without affecting free will? It was a dizzying concept.

And on a more personal note, what about the attacks? Was this God's way of punishing him for being angry with Her for twenty-five years? He had absolutely no intention of having a child purely to fulfill a prophesy. His mind replayed the scene earlier when he'd actually hoped Ariel would get pregnant. He pushed the thought aside. It was probably his karma that he finally found a woman he could spend the rest of his life with, and she only wanted him for sex.

"Logan?"

He started as he realized Ransom had stopped walking and he had been staring off into space. He glanced at Ariel. "Sorry—lost in thought." The breeze shifted, and Ariel's vanilla scent wafted over to him. He breathed deep and sighed. How many years it would take him to forget her scent and how she'd curled against him earlier in bed?

"Why do you always smell like vanilla?" He purposely grinned at her and waited for an answer. If all she wanted was sex, then he would take away all the memories of her he could before she tired of him and moved on. Had any of the women he'd dated over the years felt the same way about him?

Slowly, Ariel's shoulders relaxed. That clearly wasn't the question she expected.

"It's my shampoo." She frowned and looked suddenly uncomfortable. "But I didn't realize it was so strong." She picked up a hank of her hair, brought it to her nose and sniffed.

Logan turned in the saddle to face her. "It's very subtle, and it's been driving me crazy since I met you." He reached out and rubbed a strand of her hair between his thumb and two forefingers, enjoying the soft silky flow through his fingers. "Don't even think about changing it."

Shock registered on her face and slowly turned into a wary mask. "And I just thought it did great things for my hair." She clucked to Scout and the horses began to walk side by side again.

She glanced over at him, under her long dark lashes. "Logan, about this morning…."

"Don't worry about it," he said cutting her off. If sex is all you want, then I'll make sure you get plenty." Logan forced himself to grin at her. "It's definitely not a hardship for me to supply it."

Ariel studied his expression for a few moments before answering. "So, you're not mad at me?" she said, sounding almost disappointed.

"Why should I be mad? A beautiful woman wants my body. I'm just going to enjoy the ride." When Ariel said nothing but just continued to study him, he said, "That's what you want, isn't it?"

"Yes. Of course it is. We barely know each other." She sounded like she was still trying to convince herself and not just him.

"Ariel, I've been attracted to you from the first minute. Something just clicked between us and I know you felt it too." He tipped his straw cowboy hat up away from his face with one finger and struggled to put into words what he'd noticed about her over the past week.

"But even beyond that, I admire the way you are your own person, the way you stand up for yourself and the way you see the best in people. If you'll let me I want a chance to get to know you better. And I promise, I'll keep it at the level of friends…with privileges, of course."

Ariel laughed aloud at his comment. "Friends with privileges, huh?" A smile blossomed across her face and she nodded in agreement. "I'd like to get to know you better too, Logan. As long as it doesn't interfere with my job here."

"Agreed," he said and let them fall into a companionable silence. Logan refused to think about what would happen to his heart when she chose to move on. But he pushed the thought from his mind. He wouldn't waste their time together worrying about what was to come.

Logan stared out over his ranch and let the familiar sights and sounds comfort him. There were cattle grazing off in the pasture to their right and horses strolling beyond the pasture fence to their left. The smell of sweet Texas grass and manure scented the air and the gentle mooing of his cattle made him smile, as it always did.

"Logan," Ariel began. "About what James said the other day...."

"James was angry and jealous and had no right to say anything like that to you." Logan was surprised at the hard edge in his voice.

Ariel faced Logan and met his gaze. "There's a lot of history between James and I. We ended our relationship badly, and I think there are still some unresolved feelings on both sides."

She looked away and stared out across the pasture toward the horses. "I'm just sorry you got dragged into it. James tried to hurt me and he did. But I want to make sure you know I'm not in the habit of—" She trailed off, looking uncomfortable.

"Falling into bed with every man you've known a little over twenty-four hours?" he asked, mimicking James' words.

Ariel looked over at him and her inviting mouth quirked up on one side. "Exactly. In fact, the last man I 'fell into bed with' was James."

Logan stared and then noticed Ariel watching him. "But, that means, you haven't...for two hundred years?" he asked incredulously.

He hid a smile as he watched Ariel's chin thrust into a stubborn tilt.

"It's the age of technology, you know. Women are perfectly capable of getting along without a man."

"Whoa." Logan held up his hands in a defensive gesture. "I didn't mean to insult you. You're the most beautiful woman I've ever seen and you can actually hold a man's interest for more than a few hours and..." Logan trailed off as he realized what he said. "I mean—"

Ariel narrowed her eyes and glared at him. "And you figured I wouldn't be independent enough to keep my legs together if some handsome man came along to charm me out of my panties?" she asked archly.

"No, not exactly like that." Logan scrambled to get his thoughts in line. When had this conversation taken such a dangerous turn?

"Then how, exactly?" Ariel asked from behind a tight smile.

Logan knew she was needling him and breathed a silent sigh of relief that she wasn't really angry. But he tried to put what he was thinking into words anyway. "You know how when you meet someone for the first time, you set them at a certain attractiveness level?"

Ariel tightened Scout's reins around her hand. "I suppose."

"Well, as you get to know that person, their attractiveness factor will go up or down, depending on their personality. You know, someone only marginally attractive will become more attractive if they have a great personality and a sense of humor, whereas someone drop-dead gorgeous will become less attractive if they are self-centered and petty."

Ariel seemed to be thinking about what he said. Then she threw back her head and laughed. "You know, I've never thought about it quite that way, but you're right." She tucked her hair behind her ear and out of her face. "So, I guess you paid me a backhanded compliment by saying I can hold someone's interest for more than a few hours?"

Logan smiled at her. "It was definitely meant as a compliment."

Ariel looked down at her saddle. "I'm sorry, Logan. I didn't mean to be so quick to think the worst of you. You'd think a few hundred years would dull some of the aftermath of what happened with James and me. But I guess if you don't deal with something, it can stay with you."

Logan noticed the look of pain flash across Ariel's

face and a knife turned in his gut. He wished he could break his promise to James and tell her everything as it really happened. Anything to remove the anguish in her eyes.

"I'm sorry you were hurt," Logan said and sidled Ransom closer to Scout. He reached out, took Ariel's left hand in his right, and brought it to his lips. "I have no control over the past. All I can do is make sure *I* never hurt you."

Logan caught his breath at the raw vulnerability in her eyes. He'd make damn sure never to put that look there because of something he did.

He stopped short as he realized it was the first time he ever wanted to protect anyone other than himself in a relationship. He wasn't sure if he should be happy about that or terrified. But with Ariel filling up his senses, happy won out.

The horses had slowed to a stop and Logan used pressure from his thighs to move Ransom closer to Scout. Taking off his hat, he leaned toward Ariel. After a moment of hesitation, she leaned toward him as well.

Logan's pulse quickened like thundering hoof beats inside his head. The anticipation of drowning in her kiss thrummed through his body. His lips were close enough to hers that her breath feathered against his skin and he inhaled her soft vanilla scent.

All he had to do was lean in and he could lose himself inside her luscious mouth. He reached up with his free hand, cupped her cheek and leaned in to close the last wisp of distance between them.

A shrill shout reached his ears and Ariel jumped back like she'd been bitten.

A ball of lead settled in his stomach. He recognized that voice. And he'd just promised Ariel he'd never hurt her. But if all she wanted from him was sex, maybe she wouldn't care. In a backward way, he hoped she cared very much.

He turned his head to look over at Ariel. She was looking at him, the question clearly in her eyes. He opened his mouth to explain, but wasn't sure what he could say that wouldn't make him sound exactly like what he was. Or at least what he was before he met Ariel.

Impeccable timing as usual, McAllister.

"Logan." The shout sounded again and ice churned through his veins. Charity Taylor. Damn, damn, damn.

CHAPTER EIGHT

Ariel saw guilt fill Logan's eyes and her heart sank. He'd been seducing her and she'd fallen for it. Even after all her bravado about just wanting sex, she'd been softening toward him and had almost told him so.

You were always a sucker for pretty words.

The happy shout sounded again, and Ariel turned to study the woman jogging toward them. She was tall, probably a few inches more than Ariel, even without the extra height the heels of the designer cowboy boots added. Her blonde hair tumbled around her to end near her waist. Large luminous green eyes sparkled with happiness on a flawless co-ed face.

She had the figure of a supermodel, encased in form fitting designer jeans and a clingy silk top, which matched her eyes. A perfect candidate for men to use as arm candy.

For the first time in her life, Ariel wondered what it would be like to be so thin. She never doubted her own attractiveness before, and she didn't like how it felt now.

She recognized Charity Taylor from television and several country music magazines. An up-and-coming star who was up for the Horizon award at this year's CMA's for best new country artist.

Inwardly, Ariel groaned. The tabloids had linked Logan and Charity romantically for the last few years. But when Logan hadn't mentioned a girlfriend, Ariel had just written it off as tabloid gossip.

That's what I get for assuming.

"Logan," gushed Charity. "I've been looking all over for you." She stepped forward and placed a hand on Logan's thigh in an obvious show of ownership, while looking Ariel up and down critically. Charity raised her eyebrow in a look of disdain and turned her back on Ariel, effectively dismissing her.

"I thought about just killing her at the gate, but I

was hoping you'd get on with that kiss before she interrupted," came Kefira's voice inside Ariel's head.

"Charity." Logan picked her hand up off his thigh and held it for a moment before releasing it. "I wasn't expecting to see you." Ransom pranced closer to Scout—no doubt sensing his rider's nervousness.

A smile lit Charity's face, so dazzling it rivaled the sun, and made Ariel want to vomit. "Now, Logan, don't tell me you forgot our date?"

Ariel slid her gaze from Charity to Logan to see his reaction.

Logan closed his eyes and sighed, his mouth firmed into a thin tight line. "The awards event. I'm sorry, I totally forgot. It isn't until next week."

Ariel watched Logan squirm under both women's intense gaze. She almost felt sorry for him—almost.

"I figured we could go to Whiskey River tonight, and listen to the new songs you're playing," said Charity with a definite purr in her voice. "We'd also have time to talk."

"Whiskey River was *last* night and I don't think I'll be going back for a while." Logan laid his hand protectively on his thigh where the two bite marks had been. "You should've called, Charity." Logan put his hat back on and stared down at her. "Lots has happened since the last time I saw you, as you can probably tell by the security guards."

Charity looked up at him under lowered lashes, her mouth puckered in a designer pout. "I was hoping to surprise you, Logan." She glanced over at Ariel and then back. "You always used to like my surprises."

Nice, she doesn't even care why he needs security guards. And she obviously hasn't been around enough to know. Maybe they aren't as close as Charity wants me to believe.

When Logan didn't answer, Charity turned her

attention to Ariel. "You must be one of Logan's new bodyguards." She studied Ariel up and down making sure her expression let Ariel know she didn't approve of what she saw. "I met your sisters out at the gate and you're all—built about the same."

Ariel's temper flashed. Enough was enough. Logan obviously had a past with this woman, and she was here staking her claim. If Charity Taylor thought she was going to do battle with Ariel and win, she was mistaken.

Ariel pasted on a saccharine smile and drew upon the other tabloid gossip she'd heard. "Yes, my sisters and I are blessed with bodies that don't require store-bought boobs, liposuction and a nose job."

Charity narrowed her eyes, irritation plain on her lovely face. "How dare you!" She turned her mock outrage toward Logan. "Are you going to let the hired help speak to me that way?"

"Ariel and her sisters are much more than hired help and they saved my life. You'll speak to them with respect, or you're welcome to leave, Charity."

Ariel faced Logan, ignoring the satisfying way Charity's face turned red.

After visibly fighting her temper, Charity smoothed her face into a serene mask and turned to nod toward Ariel. "Well, then I suppose I should thank you for taking care of Logan."

Ariel didn't buy the fake sincerity for a moment. *I notice she didn't even ask why his life was in danger. What an evil bitch!*

Logan turned his attention back to Charity. "You've caught me at a bad time. Why don't you head home and I'll call you before the charity event."

"I really need to talk to you *alone*, Logan." Charity glanced at Ariel and then fixed her gaze back on Logan.

Logan appeared impatient, the guilt and

uncomfortable tension all but gone. "Charity, we haven't been alone in two and a half months. I'm sure whatever it is can wait a week."

Charity's eyes misted and her gaze became soft and vulnerable.

You missed your calling, honey. You should've been an actress.

Ariel resisted the urge to roll her eyes.

"Logan," Charity began and flipped her long blonde hair back over her shoulder. "I'm pregnant."

A hard bolt of nausea roiled inside Ariel's stomach. She noticed her mouth had dropped open and she firmly closed it. A glance over at Logan confirmed he was just as shocked. His mouth *still* hung open and all the blood had drained out of his face, leaving him pale, his eyes impossibly wide.

Then finally, he took a deep breath and turned to Ariel. "Would you mind taking the horses in? Charity and I need to talk."

*****

Charity watched as Logan dismounted and handed the reins to his pudgy security guard. She couldn't believe Logan McAllister had been about to kiss the tramp. Logan was an Adonis, and this...*bodyguard* just wasn't in the same league. Probably just a groupie who wanted to be able to say she'd screwed Logan. But then half of Texas could lay claim to that particular achievement. Logan had never been too picky about where he dipped his pen. Oh, what a flair he had with that particular pen though.

That was why this was going to work out exactly as she planned.

Logan pierced her with a suspicious stare and she effortlessly pulled out her mask that said "innocent, hurt and scared." If it was one thing Charity was good at, it was manipulating men. It was so pitifully easy since she made sure she had a body they would drool over and they never thought with their upper brains. "Please stop looking at me like that," she said and added a hitch to her voice.

Logan's look instantly intensified. "How far along are you?"

She looked into Logan's eyes and used her best 'I'm-innocent-take-care-of-me' look. "Two and a half months."

Logan's jaw tightened and his eyes narrowed. "Why wait two and a half months to tell me?"

Charity pushed a wayward strand of hair away from her face. "I wasn't sure for a few weeks and then, well—we'd grown apart and you were finding excuses not to see me anymore." She pursed her lips in her practiced Charity pout.

A flash of guilt swam through Logan's eyes before he hid it. A smile of triumph almost blossomed across her face, and she had to bite the inside of her lip to maintain her strained expression. Logan was a sap when it came to "doing the right thing." He'd been raised with a backwoods country boy attitude, which would serve her purposes just fine.

"You still should've told me earlier." Logan pushed a hand through his hair and then tensed. "Are you sure it's mine?"

Charity's temper sparked. Why didn't he just buy this and let them move on. She wanted to get to the part where he fucked her brains out and bought her expensive jewelry. She knew he'd already seen past her innocent act, so she dropped it and moved on to the next tactic. "How can you ask me that?"

"Look, cut the crap—you and I both know the virginal act is for on stage. Are you sure it's mine?" he repeated, pinning her with his stare.

Charity crossed her arms in front of her chest and

glared up at him. "Yes, it's yours. I haven't been with anyone else since you."

Logan raised his eyebrows and let his skeptical expression show.

She sighed and leaned back against a nearby tree. "I'm serious, Logan. I've been in recording sessions since I left here, and I haven't had time for any extra-curricular activities."

Logan's face paled and he was silent a long time before he finally spoke. "We always used condoms, we were careful...how did this happen?"

She huffed, her patience straining. Logan had always been the one to insist they use a condom or she could've trapped him long ago, legitimately. "They are only ninety-nine percent effective. I guess this," she placed a hand against her flat stomach, "is the one percent."

She reached out to touch his cheek. Damn, Logan was a sexy man—it wouldn't be a hardship to fuck him on a regular basis to keep up her end of the marriage bargain. Besides, once they were safely married, she would also have the corner on the market of his songwriting abilities and her own career would take off.

Logan flinched, but didn't pull away.

"Come on, Logan." She stepped closer to him, just close enough for the tips of her breasts to brush his shirt. "I may be a lot of things, but I wouldn't lie about a baby." She kept eye contact and held her breath. *I know that country-boy sense of doing what's right is lurking in there somewhere.*

"Son of my blood," Logan murmured under his breath.

Charity hid her shock and pretended she hadn't heard him. So, he knew about the prophesy. That could only help her. She'd have to pay off the doctor to say she was having a boy when the time came and then deal with the consequences when the child was born. Because she was sure one of her vampire lovers—because she'd slept with the whole kiss to complete the ritual—had given her a daughter, the daughter of Logan's destiny. It would all be worth it when they made her a vampire and she got to keep her youth and beauty forever. And besides, Logan was a sentimental sap. Once he was attached to the child, he'd never abandon it, prophesy or no.

"Charity, look me straight in the eye and tell me this is my baby."

When Logan put his hand over her stomach, she had to fight the urge to smile. She knew she had him. She allowed her eyes to mist over and she sniffed just enough to be believable. "It's our baby, Logan. We're going to be a mommy and daddy."

Logan closed his eyes and leaned his forehead against hers. As he'd heard Ariel say on several occasions, he whispered, "Your will be done."

*****

James stood under the hot shower spray and let the water knead away his tension. Between Logan's attacks, Ariel and the problems within his kiss due to his recent absence, he was glad vampires couldn't have heart attacks due to stress. He sighed and poured a healthy dose of shampoo into his hand. The normal scent of musk from the shampoo scented the air and he thought he detected a hint of...cinnamon.

He whirled to look behind him, but saw no one. There was only one being who could get past his wards without James sensing it and who always smelled of cinnamon. James slowly cracked the sliding door on the shower and sure enough, Gabriel sat cross-legged on top of his vanity.

"Good morning, James," Gabriel said as if they'd run into each other at the local coffee shop and not in the middle of James' steam-filled bathroom.

In an automatic gesture, James tried to kneel on one knee and place his fist over his heart, while still trying to balance a palm-full of shampoo in his other hand. Since his six-foot-six frame and broad shoulders already filled the small shower stall, there wasn't much room left to contort them into a kneeling position. After a few tries, he looked up and caught Gabriel trying to hold back a laugh. He glowered at the angel, which only served to cause Gabriel to throw back his head and laugh aloud until he was holding his middle and rocking back and forth on top of the vanity.

Finally, James settled for just placing his fist over his heart and bowing his head. Figuring he'd completed the respectful greeting, he pulled the shower door closed and finished soaping his hair. "What can I do for you, Gabriel?" he asked over the sound of the water, still trying to ignore the angel's continuing chuckles.

"I'm sorry James, there are so few times you catch a vampire trying to kneel in a shower stall—you just have to enjoy it when it happens."

Fucking smart-assed angel.

"Now, James, there's no reason to start impugning my character," Gabriel said, amusement still plain in his voice. "Besides, I think it's rubbing off on you from the gargoyles."

At the mention of the gargoyles, James scowled. He and Ariel had avoided each other as much as possible since he'd caught her and Logan in bed together. And they never talked about what happened. Although he supposed it wasn't any of his business any more. His heart hurt all over again at the thought of Ariel in someone else's arms.

"James," Gabriel continued. "I wanted to discuss that very thing. Ariel is not your destiny. She is for Logan now and your destiny lies along a different path."

The words hit him like a blow. He knew long ago

that he'd lost Ariel and had to honor his commitment to Gabriel and to God. Seeing her with Logan now brought back the loss all over again. And after losing Jaclyn too…

James finished rinsing off the last of his shampoo and turned off the water in a rush, almost breaking the handle. When he opened the shower door, Gabriel held a towel out for him. He took it and began to dry off, not meeting the angel's eye.

"I know you think life has been unfair, James. But your destiny still awaits you. Jaclyn and Ariel were only visits along the way."

James grunted. "Life doesn't have to be fair for the likes of me. I was grateful for the opportunity to become more than I was." He slung the towel around his hips and tucked it together so it would stay up, then finally met Gabriel's piercing stare.

"Life isn't fair for anyone, Dark Redeemer, but I think The Creator has gone out of Her way to be generous to you in the past. You should trust Her with your future." The angel stood and gestured for James to precede him into the bedroom. "Please, continue your grooming ritual. We can talk while you finish."

James shook his head at the age-old term and walked to his closet to pull out clothes for his upcoming meeting with his kiss. "I wasn't questioning Her fairness to me, Gabriel. I know I deserve none and She's been more than generous with the life I've led. However, regrets do hound me about the two women I've loved and lost." He turned to look over his shoulder at Gabriel, who reclined on his bed, leaning back against the pillows, his hands cradled behind his head.

James resisted the urge to cringe. He wasn't homophobic, but the sight of a man he knew every woman in the universe would lust over lounging on his bed while he was trying to dress was a little unnerving.

Gabriel's lips quirked, then he continued. "You did have the great fortune to love, and love truly. Some men never find that—even those who lead pious lives."

James pulled on Armani slacks and the first shirt he could grab. Gabriel always had a way of making him feel selfish and petty. He knew his life of evil had earned him the notice of the Dark One and his status as a vampire. However, he also knew that he'd only been an evil man for thirty-three years and he'd been a good vampire for several hundred. Shouldn't that count for something?

Gabriel sat up and looked at James with compassion in his gaze. "Yes, of course it does. Jaclyn and Ariel were part of your destiny once, but no longer. Her plan has woven you in tightly so that you touch many lives. Your eventual destiny will come, James. Trust in Her."

James sighed and scrubbed a hand over his face. "I have and I do. Sometimes the human emotions overwhelm me. I can deal with the vampire emotions of hatred and violence better than I can deal with the pain and loss from the human ones."

"Maybe it's closure that you need." Gabriel stood and walked toward James. "Go to Ariel, take her in your arms. Kiss her and see if you love her as you once did. I think you'll find that time has changed you both."

A macabre laugh bubbled up out of his throat. "That's a sure way to get my bollocks cut off and fed to me, you know." He shook his head and studied Gabriel's face to see if he was serious. "Kissing a gargoyle without permission was risky even when we were together. Now, it's positively suicidal."

Gabriel smiled, his cerulean blue eyes glinting with mirth. "You're a vampire, James. One of the most fearsome creatures on Her planet and yet you're afraid of a mere woman?"

James knew Gabriel was baiting him. It seemed the

angel gained enjoyment out of needling his charges to see how they would react. James refused to give him the pleasure this time. "Ariel is anything but a mere woman. And if she were mad enough, I wouldn't put it past her to stake me herself. Although, I can see her guilt catching up with her later." James smiled to himself. "I hope."

Gabriel slapped James on the back and laughed. "You are one of my favorite charges, James. When you first came to me, I used to be able to prick at your massive vampire/male pride and watch you lash out. I think you've become almost domesticated over the last three or four-hundred years."

James ignored the comment and sat on the end of his bed to pull on his shoes. "So why are you so keen to have me go to Ariel?" He fixed the angel with a steely stare until another smile bloomed across Gabriel's face.

"Let's just say it will put things in perspective for both of you. And besides, I need you close to Logan this evening. After your vampire social, anyway."

James was shocked for a moment that Gabriel knew about his meeting, but then Gabriel knew everything. "Is something going to happen to Logan tonight? Do I need to go to him now?"

"Something has already happened to Logan, but it's not life-threatening. At least not yet."

James bolted to his feet, one Italian loafer still dangling from his hand. "If Logan is in danger, you should have told me sooner!"

"Calm down. It's nothing like that. Trust me. Logan's well-being is important to me, as well." The angel motioned for James to sit and continue putting on his shoes. "And there's no reason to hold the succubus. She will not tell you what you wish."

"I was afraid of that. I'll have the kiss kill her quickly. There's no need for her to continue to suffer."

James ran his hand through his damp hair and glanced up as he realized Gabriel continued watching him. He raised a questioning brow.

"Such compassion for a being of evil?" Gabriel queried.

"You've taught me that compassion for any being is well placed. I just wish we could find out who is behind the attacks. I'm afraid they will eventually succeed just from pure persistence."

Gabriel cocked his head as if listening to a voice only he could hear. "Yes, My Lord," he murmured and then turned his attention back to James, his blue eyes sparking. "Dark Redeemer, the one you seek equals your power, and it will eventually come down to a choice between yourself and the one you hold most dear." With that, the smell of cinnamon permeated the air and the angel disappeared from view.

"I hate it when he spouts prophesy and runs. It always means it's going to be really bad."

*****

Ariel stepped out into the hallway and ran into a wall—a human wall she recognized immediately. Squaring her shoulders, she raised her chin and met Logan's troubled gaze. "Hello, Logan."

He grabbed her elbow and steered her across the hall into his office, pulling the door shut behind him. "Ariel," he began and then stopped as if groping for what he wanted to say.

She took a deep breath and crossed her arms over her chest. "What can I do for you?" Inwardly, she winced as she remembered he had asked her those very words in this same office not long ago.

"I wanted to try to explain." He looked flustered, his sandy blond hair standing up in sexy waves, no doubt from having his long, tapered fingers thrust through it repeatedly.

"Explain what?" she asked as calmly as possible. "We had a nice time together. And now it's done."

Before Ariel finished speaking, his long strides had eaten the distance between them and he glowered over her. "Damn it, Ariel. We had much more than a nice time and you know it. If you'd open that stubborn stone brain of yours long enough to admit it."

Her chin thrust up stubbornly on impulse. "Whatever happened between us is obviously in the past. Now that the child of your blood is here, your destiny has arrived and mine lies along a different path." Her heart broke in two at the words, but she forced her expression to remain serene.

He studied her for a moment and she feared he'd seen a flicker of her regret. He sighed and stepped away from her. The sudden loss of his proximity made her long to run to him and feel his strong arms around her one last time.

"I wish I could dismiss us as easily as you can," he said softly and leaned back against his desk. When he finally met her eyes, he said, "Charity and I had sex, but you and I made love, and I'll never be able to forget you." He closed his eyes and sighed. "But you're right. My destiny has arrived and I have a child to think about now."

"Do you believe the child is actually yours?" The words were out before she could think better of them. She winced internally but schooled her face not to display her feelings.

Logan didn't appear shocked at the blunt question. "I do. I can't explain it, but I have a gut feeling this is the way things are supposed to happen. And I already feel a connection with the child." When he caught sight of Ariel's skeptical look he shook his head. "I know what you're thinking. Charity isn't exactly a one-man woman. I can't explain it logically, but I believe her."

Ariel opened her mouth to object to his blind belief

when he interrupted her. "Besides, I did some checking and she's been in constant recording sessions for the last few months according to her business manager. Just like she told me."

Ariel remained skeptical but reminded herself that she didn't know Charity as well as Logan. *And apparently, he knew her well enough to knock her up!*

She closed her eyes to allow her temper time to cool. When she finally opened them, Logan was watching her.

Her fingers itched to brush the frown from his face and skim over the crisp five-o'clock shadow, which peppered his cheeks. She fisted both hands until her nails bit into the soft flesh of her palms. And she willed the tears that burned in the back of her eyes to wait to fall until she was alone.

An uncomfortable silence hung inside the room and she knew if it didn't end soon, she'd give into her urge to run into his arms. She cleared her throat. "I've assigned Dara to protect Charity and the baby. Since she's a healer, I figured that would be best." *She can also watch the little bitch because I don't trust her one little bit. And at least she can be objective—or at least more than I can.*

His head snapped up, his eyes wide with shock. "Is that all you have to say to me?"

"No, Odeda will be watching over you for the next few days while I fly out to Nashville to perform a pre-security check on the awards show site. I leave in the morning."

Logan's eyes swam with regret and hurt and Ariel bit her tongue to keep from telling him what she really wanted to say. *I love you! I can't live without you...*

He straightened and stood. "Have a good trip," he said softly before he turned and left.

As soon as the door clicked shut behind him, Ariel gave her tears free rein, curled up in Logan's massive desk chair, and let the sobs come.

*****

James nosed his candy apple red Aston Martin into his private parking space and shifted uncomfortably. As a talent executive, he had to look the part, so he'd bought this little sardine can of a car to impress clients. However, it was uncomfortable as hell to fold his six-foot-plus frame into and he always felt like a sideshow freak trying to get out of the damned thing.

He much preferred his jet black PT Cruiser which was safely ensconced inside his garage at home. It was a little embarrassing driving it. However, it was extremely roomy inside and got terrific gas mileage on the freeway. Or at least that's how he rationalized it. In truth, it was just fun to drive and fun was something he made sure to enjoy whenever he could. The kiss would never let him live it down if they knew, so it would forever remain his guilty secret. Ancient vampires just didn't go around driving a *cute* car. It wasn't good for the image.

After slamming the door and pushing the button on his keychain to activate the alarm, James turned toward his offices, briefcase in hand. He opened his senses, and he knew he had a visitor. An ancient evil presence…Nicholas.

"Damn," he cursed under his breath. If he hadn't been distracted by extricating himself from the tin can that passed for his car, he would have noticed earlier.

Another of the original ancient vampires turned the same time as James, Nicholas could be the poster boy for the bad-assed vampire. His philosophy was to subjugate the food supply—namely humans, whereas James' philosophy was to blend in to avoid unwanted notice and thus survive. The last James heard, Nicholas had gone into acting, currently doing a few action movies that enjoyed mild success at the box office purely because Nicholas was willing to bare everything to the cameras.

James squared his shoulders and walked through the front door of Wellington Enterprises feeling as if he'd stepped into an enemy's lair rather than his own offices.

Astor met James just inside the door. "Nicholas Branson is here to see you."

"So I gathered." James continued walking toward his office knowing Astor would rush to keep up. "Why didn't you call me before letting a powerful rival into our lair?" James laid his briefcase on his desk and turned to look at Astor who visibly paled.

"I figured you'd be pleased, Master. Nicholas Branson is an up and coming star and sought out our agency for representation."

James sensed Astor's lie immediately. He let his lips curve into a smile before allowing his vampire speed take over. In the next instant, he gripped Astor by the throat, pinning the man's body up against the far wall, his feet dangling helplessly, his hands clawing at James' steely grip.

When James spoke, he made sure his voice stayed at normal conversation level. Calm always sounded scarier in his opinion—and scarier was definitely what Astor needed, if not death. Until James figured out what he was up to, it wouldn't be wise to kill him. *Keep your enemies close.*

He leaned in close to Astor's ear. "Nicholas is the biggest stickler for vampire law and customs I've ever known. It's just not done to invite yourself to another's lair unless you are specifically invited under a flag of truce. The Master vampire is the only one who can offer such a truce. As much as you dislike the fact—*I* am the Master."

James twisted his grip tighter until Astor's eyes bulged out of their sockets as if they were about to pop, and the cartilage in his throat made a satisfying crunch. "Not to mention, Nicholas had to be invited over the threshold by someone here on the inside. Which I'm assuming would be you." James stared into Astor's eyes for a long moment, letting the younger vampire wonder if he was about to die.

"Don't ever lie to me again, Astor. Or I'll be more than happy to turn you into dust. That is if I don't decide to kill you in the next few hours just for sport." With that, he let go his grip and Astor crumbled to the floor.

James returned to his desk and opened his briefcase, removing his files for the day. "In the meantime, I think I'll go see to our guest." He looked down to see Astor still struggling with his healing windpipe while he lay sprawled on the floor. "Make sure you're available in case I...need something violent to fill my afternoon."

James turned his back on Astor and headed toward the conference room. James knew Nicholas would be aware of him. Nicholas would have sensed him as soon as he was within a few miles. James had gotten in the habit of only using his senses in close proximity. There were just too many bodies within a radius of a block, let alone several miles. It wasn't practical to be constantly on alert—it tended to dull the fight or flight response for when it was actually needed.

James stepped through the conference room door. Nicholas sat on one of the plush leather couches, his legs crossed at the ankle, his right arm resting along the back of the couch. Time hadn't changed him much. He'd gone back to his natural black hair rather than the grey at the temples he'd used the last time James had seen him, and he now wore an Armani suit. Much different from back in the 1800's in England. In fact, it was Nicholas' human servants he'd been in the process of killing when Ariel had seen him all those years ago. James bit back a sigh and stepped farther into the room.

"Nicholas. To what do I owe this intrusion?" he said as if inquiring about the weather. James continued across the room and lowered himself onto the couch opposite Nicholas.

"Intrusion?" Nicholas asked, feigning surprise. "I hardly think seeking representation is an intrusion, James." He smiled, his perfectly capped teeth almost too white against his tanned face.

"Come now, Nicholas. Let us not play games." James draped his right arm over the back of the couch mirroring Nicholas. "You and I go back a long way. Your charm and gift of bull may work on Astor, but you and I know the ways of the world better than that."

Nicholas threw back his head and laughed. The rich sound flowed around the room and James could see on a purely professional level how audiences would eat up his film persona. But God save any groupies who got too close. Nicholas would literally suck them dry over time. He would promise immortality to many, however, he didn't believe in moving the hunted up in the food chain to hunter.

"James, I've missed you. It's been what? Two-hundred years?"

James held up his hand stop sign fashion. "What do you want, Nicholas? *After* you ask my forgiveness for this invasion." He couldn't afford to let the affront pass, or he would appear weak. And appearing weak within vampire society wasn't only bad for business, it was fatal.

Nicholas smiled, his dangerous nature peeking through the civilized mask he wore for the humans. He inclined his head in a gesture of respect. "My apologies. Since Astor was ignorant of the ways of our people, I admit I took advantage of his lack of knowledge. But all I want is representation, James. You're the best and I always use the best."

"I'll deal with Astor. However, if you exploit any other points of ignorance within my kiss, I'll consider it a personal challenge. Are we clear?"

Nicholas held his hands open in a gesture of subjection. "There's no need to start a war over such a small incident. Again, I apologize for the intrusion." His eyes twinkled and showed him clearly unrepentant. The words were enough for vampire formalities and Nicholas knew it. James bit back a sigh. And the mortals thought their politics had nuances.

James studied Nicholas and then nodded. Of course, he knew Nicholas lied through his fangs. Nicholas wouldn't exploit another vampire's kiss unless he planned to test the defenses before he challenged. Something was afoot and James knew he had very little time to find out just what.

"Why don't you tell me what level of representation you're looking for? I'll consider it and get back to you?" James stared Nicholas down until the visiting vampire had no choice but to look away or declare a challenge.

Nicholas finally broke eye contact briefly before meeting James' gaze again. "I'm sure you're aware of my acting credits to date. I want my career to soar for the next thirty years or so until I have to reinvent myself again. Since I don't have the aging problem other action heroes have, I definitely have an edge."

"True," James agreed, switching easily into professional manager mode. "But you need to be careful. You can be an active sixty-year-old. Much beyond that and we'll have to stage your death and fade you out gradually." No matter what he told Nicholas, he couldn't accept the representation and they both knew it. It would allow Nicholas too much unrestricted access into his kiss's affairs, which would be asking for a war. Nicholas knew as much, so why was he here? James knew he had to figure out that very thing before whatever Nicholas planned came to fruition.

Nicholas leaned forward looking like an eager predator about to pounce. "So you'll represent me?"

James allowed his lips to curve. If Nicholas thought he was that foolish, he was about to be disappointed. "As I said, I'll consider it. We don't make it a habit to represent rival vampires—or any vampires not within our own kiss."

Nicholas frowned, his chiseled features dark and menacing. "You are the one always talking about blending with human society to ensure our longevity. I assumed you would be more open to working together than some of the others."

James stood, signaling an end to their interview. "Nicholas, as I said, I'll consider it and be in touch."

After a pregnant pause, Nicholas stood as well. "Thank you for your time, James. I look forward to you making the right decision for all of us." Nicholas turned toward the door to go.

"Oh, and Nicholas?" James waited until he turned to face him. "Consider yourself un-invited until we decide if we will be working together." James' words revoked Nicholas' ability to enter the building or any lair of James' without his direct permission.

Nicholas' eyes flashed fire, but he quickly reined in his temper. It amused James to see the struggle on his face. Maybe that was the entire reason he'd come here today. After all, he had to know James would refuse to represent him.

After a long moment of tense silence, Nicholas nodded. "Understood. Again, I look forward to hearing from you."

James sighed. Now he had to go to Ariel, kiss her without being castrated, and then figure out what Gabriel had meant when he said something had already happened to Logan. Just another routine day.

CHAPTER NINE

Ariel pulled the comforter tighter around her and tried again for sleep. Thoughts of Logan in bed with Charity kept running through her brain and each time she saw the imagined scene, another slice furrowed deep into her aching heart.

She heard a soft whoosh of air and in the next instant, she stood holding a dagger to a man's jugular. She tightened her hold so if he struggled, he'd slice himself on the knife. Nothing like nine-hundred years of instincts to get you up in the morning.

"Ariel," James croaked.

She took a minute to register the scent of musk and man, which always clung to James before she loosened her grip and let him go. "Don't sneak up on me, James," she said as she deposited the knife back under her pillow. "I could have killed you."

She held up a hand as she realized what she said. "Okay, I could have made a big mess on the carpets, which Logan wouldn't appreciate."

Ariel turned back to face him and her breath caught in her throat. She and James hadn't spoken any more than necessary since he walked in on her and Logan, and this was the first time they'd been alone. Yet, the bastard had the gall to come into her room looking extremely good while she was still vulnerable from the hurt with Logan. No, actually he looked spectacular, which only served to irritate Ariel further. *Too bad vampires don't have to get permission to enter individual rooms rather than just the entire building.*

He wore a suit—Armani if she wasn't mistaken—and looked every inch the sexy GQ businessman. His dark hair, ebony eyes and bad-boy good looks were a killer combination, one she decided she was finally immune to. Especially the sexy scar over his right eye—the one she'd inflicted when they'd rolled out of a hayloft during a particularly rowdy round of sex. She'd changed to stone before they'd hit bottom, but he'd cracked his head against her stone one. Why hadn't he ever healed it? He was a vampire, after all.

James stood confidently, oblivious to Ariel's inner dialogue. He unbuttoned his suit jacket and made himself comfortable, sitting in the chair next to the bed. His lips quirked up into a smug grin.

Smug, not cocky, she reminded herself. *I like cocky. Smug is just damned irritating.* "Why are you here?"

"I wanted to talk to you without everyone else around. And it seems the only times and places you're alone lately, aren't very healthy for a vampire." He smirked—another irritating habit, which caused her to fume.

"Fine, I'm here. What did you want to talk about?" She sat down on the bed and glared over at him.

"I've been trying to find out who is after Logan."

She figured as much. "And?"

"And, most of the vampire circles don't even know who Logan McAllister is."

She deliberately cocked her right eyebrow at him. "You've got to be kidding, he's a famous songwriter."

James leaned back and stretched out his long legs in front of him, crossing them at the ankle. "Ariel, the vampire nation isn't exactly the country music demographic."

"I'm not an idiot," Ariel said. "But most of you older vampires are now in governments around the world, or in other positions of power. And that means they have access to all kinds of media—including those about country music celebrities. But you said most of them haven't heard of him. What about the rest?"

He sighed indulgently, sparking her temper again. "As a person in a powerful position, I wouldn't think a songwriter would be much of a threat or an asset to me, and neither do they."

"Fine," Ariel said when she couldn't think of a suitable response. "So why are *you* so interested in Logan?" She fixed him with a steely stare, daring him not to answer. "What do you get out of all of this?"

A faraway look came into his eyes, but before she could do more than wonder about it, it disappeared. "I spent my time getting into the music business—legitimately," he added when she narrowed her eyes. "And one night I went into a little hole in the wall bar in Dallas, and there he was." James smiled at the memory. "I knew I needed to help him so the world could hear his songs."

She didn't believe for a minute that he had altruistic motives in mind—there had to be something in it for him. "How noble of you," she said as sarcasm dripped from her voice. She leaned back against the chair, crossing her arms over her chest.

James' gaze turned deadly and he stood to loom over her. "Whatever you think of me, Logan is one of the good things I've done with my life. And after Jaclyn, I…" He snapped his mouth closed and glared down at her. "Never mind."

"Who is…?" she began.

The sharp look of utter desolation on his face stopped her question mid-sentence.

"Don't. I can't talk about her right now."

She nodded, but curiosity burned through her. Would Gabriel answer her questions about Jaclyn if she asked? Ariel looked up and her heart lodged in her throat—never had she seen James look so devastated. Granted, after she found out he was a vampire, she hadn't seen him again until last week. But somewhere deep inside where she still boxed up the feelings she had for James, she hurt. His pain was because of some other woman, which meant he loved her enough to allow her to cause it.

He continued to stare down at her, no doubt waiting

to see if any emotions would play over her face. She refused to give him the satisfaction and glared back at him, keeping her face a mask of stone.

After a long war of wills, James dropped his gaze and the tension level in the room slowly seeped away.

She noticed James still stared, just not at her face. She grabbed her robe off the chair next to the bed, and pulled it on over the silk teddy she slept in. It was a damned shame vampires had perfect night vision. "If you announced yourself, I could've aimed for your heart," she snapped.

"Good morning to you too." His lips curved in a smile, letting her know his humor had returned.

"I don't consider the crack of dawn morning anymore, James."

His eyes bored through her thin robe, and memories of being in his arms flashed into her mind. Memories so vivid and real, they took her breath away. She staggered to the bed and sat down hard.

When her mind cleared, she glared up at him. "I'm not one of your human bimbos. I know your vampire mind tricks for what they are."

Shock crossed his face. "I...I'm sorry, I always thought gargoyles were immune, so I didn't bother shielding my thoughts." He suddenly found his shoes to be of great interest. "My apologies."

She searched his face, but she could find no trace of deceit. Maybe he hadn't meant it. She sighed. It was hard to stay mad at him when he was like this. "Before I found out who you really were, you asked me for permission. I think that's why I'm *not* immune."

James locked eyes with her, his dark brows knitted together. "I don't remember asking you."

She tossed the hair out of her face and looked up at him. "The first time we made love, you asked me to open my mind to you. I remember feeling like we were inside each other's heads, but at the time I didn't understand the significance."

And now, she wished she could erase the memory, because no other being besides a vampire could give her that same experience. Although being with Logan had been incredible without it. She shook her head to dislodge the unwelcome thought.

Logan is Charity's now. Get over it.

"You mean, you thought it was a normal part of sex between two people." James had the grace to look sheepish.

She blushed and nodded. Feelings for James she'd kept buried for two centuries bubbled to the surface and threatened to spill over.

"Ariel." He sat down on the chair next to the bed and took her hand in his. "I'm sorry about walking in on you and Logan."

She dropped her gaze, deciding it was her turn to study James' shoes. Anything but meet his inquisitive eyes while they discussed this.

"I wasn't prepared for all the feelings I still have for you, or for my reaction to seeing you in Logan's bed." He used his index finger to tip her chin up and then locked his gaze with hers. "I know you're not a whore. I'm sorry I implied otherwise. I was jealous…and hurt. Can you forgive me?"

She fell into the deep chocolate of his eyes, and knew it had nothing to do with vampire powers and everything to do with him. Her heart sped up and she had the sudden sensation that time had suddenly rewound two-hundred years.

She remembered a time when she was deliriously happy and in love. A time when being in James' arms made life worth living.

He stood and closed the distance between them, crushing his mouth to hers. She found herself pulled to her feet, the full length of a very masculine vampire pressed against her.

She waited for the familiar fireworks, the slow burn she remembered so well...but it wasn't there. She only ached for Logan to hold her like this.

"I guess you were right, James. Although I seem to have interrupted before you could get her into bed."

Ariel jumped and pushed James away at the sound of Logan's angry voice from the doorway. She turned and saw barely contained fury simmering in Logan's eyes. Guilt stabbed at her, but she'd be damned if she'd apologize. After all, didn't he have a pregnant girlfriend he conveniently forgot to mention before he pulled her into his bed?

She squared her shoulders and faced him. "At least you already knew James and I had a relationship. I don't think you can really be throwing stones in your present situation, do you?" It took everything she had to hold back the tears and maintain her aloof expression, but she refused to let him see her cry.

Logan glared at her for a long moment, and then turned and walked away.

She let out a breath she hadn't realized she'd been holding.

"Terrific, doesn't anyone ever knock?" she demanded.

"You have a bad habit of leaving the door open," James said and then flinched away at Ariel's pointed gaze. He held his hands up palm out. "Sorry."

She sat down on the bed and buried her face in her hands. "James...." she said from between her fingers.

She heard him sigh and the bed shifted as he sat down beside her. "You don't have to say it. I figured we could go back to the way things were, but..."

Her head whipped up until he could meet his gaze.

"You mean, you didn't feel anything either?"

He bristled a little at her comment, no doubt his male ego was smarting. "I wouldn't say 'nothing'. Kissing a beautiful woman is always pleasant."

She raised her eyebrows at him until he looked away.

"Okay, I thought we could go back to what we had. I'm still not sure why we couldn't."

He sounded so forlorn, she almost felt sorry for him. "We are very different people from who we were then." She took a deep breath and was about to ask who Jaclyn was when he finally nodded.

"I'm sorry." He turned and searched her face with his piercing gaze. "I'm truly sorry about Logan seeing us. It was never my intent to hurt you even more."

She knew James' expressions well enough, even after all these years, to know he meant it.

But that didn't change the last few days of her life. Who was going to walk in on her next? She was fresh out of men.

*****

Logan slammed the door to his office and went directly to the liquor cabinet. Pouring himself two fingers of Jack Daniels and taking the bottle with him, he crossed to his desk chair and setting aside the liquor, buried his face in his hands. Maybe if he got stinking drunk, he'd get the picture of Ariel in James' arms out of his head.

He downed the Jack and poured himself more. *How did I get myself in this situation? And can I still get out?*

The morals his aunt and uncle beat into him growing up niggled at the back of his brain. He knew he would have to marry Charity—make an honest woman of her. But why did this feel so wrong? Something deep inside his gut held him back from saying those words out loud and hearing the cell door slam shut on the rest of his life. He'd told Ariel he believed the baby was his, and for some reason, he did. But the idea of a lifetime with Charity stretched in front of him like a never-ending dark tunnel.

But, a baby—he was going to be a father? He never imagined himself having children, but the thought of a child—his child—thrilled him.

Damn, why couldn't Ariel be the one pregnant? We didn't use any protection.

Logan shook his head. Maybe that was for the best as well, now that Ariel had turned her affections back to James. This left him open to do his duty to Charity. He scrubbed his hands over his face. He'd done the deed, he'd pay the price—and that would be spending his life with a woman he didn't love and who had no love for him. Ominously, the key turned in the lock—dread for the direction his life was taking.

Just to make sure he still could, he took a few breaths and then reached for more Jack Daniels.

He heard the door open and he looked up to see James' large frame filling the doorway.

Logan scowled and sloshed liquor into his glass. "What do you want? I figured you'd still be busy with Ariel." He gritted his teeth against the bitter pain his words caused. He tossed back the whiskey waiting for the burning to take away the pain gnawing inside him.

James sat down in the same chair Ariel first sat in when she'd interviewed with him. "I think you and I both owe Ariel an apology. Things between she and I are over."

"That's not what it looked like a few minutes ago."

James laughed. "Nothing involving Ariel is ever simple, is it? Let's just say Ariel and I were proving to ourselves that there's nothing left between us."

"So, she's finally over you. That figures." A bitter laughed welled up and he let it loose as he poured more whiskey into his glass. "Just when she gets past her hang-ups with you, I find out my destiny lies elsewhere." He downed his whiskey and cradled his head in his hands. "When all I want is her...," he whispered to himself.

"Interesting choice of words." He heard James shift in his seat and the desk moved as he leaned against it. "What the hell did I miss, Logan? What's happened?"

The sense of hopelessness, which had threatened to engulf him since Charity's announcement, swallowed him. He raised his head to look at James. "Charity is pregnant."

James' eyes rounded and his lips parted in shock. "Surely you don't think it's yours? Charity has warmed more beds than an entire brothel."

Logan shook his head. "I thought the same thing. But I believe her. I checked out her story and she convinced me. My destiny is with Charity." He thought about the prophesy. Things always happened for a reason, as his mother used to say. This time he could see pieces of the prophesy fall into place like the chains of a shackle around his neck.

"What proof do you have that this baby is yours? How far along is she?"

Logan placed the glass down carefully on the desktop and leaned back in his chair. "Two and a half months. The timing works out." He sighed. "As I said, I can't explain it, but I *know* it's mine. The child of my blood."

James narrowed his eyes and studied Logan. "That sounds rather formal. You haven't had any visits from a fairy lately, have you? Or maybe some dreams?"

Logan remembered Alonna's warning. Even though it would be the first time he'd ever lied to James, he couldn't take a chance with the prophesy. He looked down and began to study the glass, turning it slowly between his fingers and shook his head. "Weren't zombies, a crotch-eating vampire and a succubus enough without adding fairies into the mix?"

he asked quietly.

James' gaze bored through him, but he continued to turn the glass carefully avoiding meeting his friend's eyes.

After what seemed like hours, but was probably only minutes, James said, "I suppose you're right. There's no need to borrow even more trouble."

Logan looked up and searched James' face. He knew James wasn't fooled from the way he watched him so closely but he must have decided to let it pass. Grateful, Logan let out a breath he hadn't realized he'd been holding.

"What are you going to do about Charity?" James asked quietly.

Logan gripped the glass so tightly he was surprised it didn't shatter. "I'm going to marry her and raise our son." He realized too late that there was no way at two and a half months he would know the sex of the baby and prayed silently James wouldn't notice his slip.

"And what about Ariel? I know you're in love with her."

Logan ran his right hand through his hair in what he recognized as a nervous gesture. "Before a few minutes ago, I thought she'd find happiness with you." He leaned forward placing his palms on the desk on either side of the glass. "Are you sure there's nothing between you anymore? I want her to be happy." He looked down at the glass. "I want both of you to be happy."

James shook his head. "You spoke of destiny a few moments ago, Logan. Ariel isn't my destiny. I still think she's yours."

He took a deep breath and let it out slowly. "I wish it was true. But it seems like life has something else in store for me."

James made a noncommittal sound in the back of his throat. "I consider you my family. I'll stand behind you no matter what your decisions. But that doesn't mean I won't be watching Charity Taylor like a hawk."

CHAPTER TEN

James stepped out into the hallway and ran straight into Charity. *Well, well, just the person I wanted to see.* He reached out to steady her, and watched as her mouth rounded in surprise. The smell of her fear scented the hallway like a heady perfume. James battled his own inner beast to keep from basking in it. He'd never been particularly fond of Charity, and it was admittedly petty, but still immensely satisfying to know he scared her now.

James drew himself up to his full height and did his best to tower over her. But when he spoke, he kept his voice soft and charming. "Good evening, Charity. I just heard you were here."

She pulled her arm out of his steadying grasp and took a quick step back. Then, as if she realized what she'd done, she squared her shoulders and straightened her robe, her chin thrust up at a defiant angle. "Not just here, but here to stay." Her tone was defensive. "So you'd better get used to it." She crossed her arms over her chest and glared at him.

His earlier conversation with Gabriel ran through his head. *Something has already happened to Logan, but it's not life threatening. At least not yet.* So this was what Gabriel meant. James looked down at Charity and tried not to throttle her for ruining Logan's life. He just wished he understood how all the pieces of this puzzle fit together, and more importantly, how they affected Logan.

He expanded his senses and reached out toward the child. He tentatively touched the small life force thriving inside her, which proved she was actually pregnant. But no spark of recognition flowed between them. James battled between relief that this wasn't Logan's baby and anger at Charity for this charade. He wanted to find out what she hoped to gain beyond the obvious before he exposed her. But he couldn't expose her without exposing Logan too.

As a rule, vampires couldn't tell the paternity of a child, unborn or otherwise. But if this were truly Logan's baby, it would have James' blood running through its veins as well. James was very glad the secret of Logan's paternity had been so closely kept. Jaclyn had objected, of course, she wanted Logan to know the truth. But James knew Logan would always be in danger simply because there were those who would want to destroy anything James held dear.

Jaclyn had paid that price already. James couldn't bear to lose Logan too.

James' fangs snapped forward inside his mouth in response to his anger at the past and the present. But he made sure they were firmly tucked away before he spoke. It wouldn't do to have Charity suspicious of his vampire nature. "I suppose congratulations are in order as well." He carefully watched for her reaction to his next words. "That is, as long as this is truly Logan's baby."

The smell of Charity's fear flooded the hallway, her heartbeat sped up until it was a loud bass drum inside James' ears, and her eyes dilated so that only the black pupil was visible. Finally, she puffed out a breath which ruffled her perfectly coiffed blonde bangs. "I've already had this discussion with Logan, and it's none of your business." She glared up at James. "And since Logan and I will most likely be getting married, you'd better watch yourself or I'll fire your ass the first chance I get."

For the first time in the conversation, laughter bubbled up inside James and he let it flow free, making sure it trickled down her spine. He saw her shiver and laughed even harder. "Don't overestimate your power, Charity." He stepped forward and smiled in satisfaction when she stepped back again. "And don't ever threaten me." He reached out a hand and laid it against her flat stomach. "And if this is Logan's baby, we'll find out soon enough. But if not, you'll regret trying to use him. That I swear upon my very existence."

He stepped away and walked past her before she recovered enough to move.

James shook his head as he headed down the stairs. He'd bet his soul—if he still had one—that this had something to do with a prophesy. How he could find out without the gargoyles blocking his progress? Maybe he could charm Alonna into talking to him. She was still angry at him about when he walked in on Ariel and Logan, but she was one of the few who probably knew the entire truth from all sides. Not that she would share it with him. Alonna was a mysterious creature in her own right.

He continued down the hallway and took the stairs to the first floor. Charity's frantic footsteps finally sounded when he reached the bottom steps and he allowed a smile to spread across his face. It wasn't very becoming to enjoy his power of fear over people. But in this case, he'd definitely make an exception.

Stepping into the library, he pulled the door shut behind him. The smell of rich leather and old books hit him like a blow, and reminded him instantly of Jaclyn. He closed his eyes and took a moment to savor his memories. Logan knew this had been his mother's old house when he'd bought it. Did the memories of Jaclyn constantly call to Logan as they did to him?

He sighed and breathed deep. Jaclyn had spent countless hours in this room. He could still picture her reclining on the brown overstuffed leather sofa with a book in her hand, a serene smile on her lips and her ever-present glass of iced tea on the table by her side. James stepped forward to run a hand over the supple leather on the back of the sofa and tears stung the back of his eyes.

God had Her reasons, of that James had no doubt. But Jaclyn and Ariel—he'd lost them both, all because of who and what he was. He bit back a sigh.

Life isn't fair for anyone, Dark Redeemer, but I think The Creator has gone out of Her way to be generous to you in the past, you should trust Her with your future. Gabriel's words played through his mind again.

"I know, and I do," he muttered.

"Hello, James. Feeling nostalgic?"

James started and turned to see Dara sitting Indian style on an overstuffed leather love seat at the opposite end of the library, a pile of books beside her on the floor and one open on her lap. Her blonde hair fell in a wavy mass around her face that made James want to run his fingers through it just to see if it felt as silky as it looked. Green eyes, the color of a cat's watched him with curiosity and her slow smile highlighted a dimple in her right cheek which he'd always found fascinating.

Pulling himself away from his perusal, he took himself to task. He needed to pay more attention to the here and now and quit dwelling on the past, or someone dangerous to Logan was going to get past his guard. "I didn't mean to intrude. Just looking for somewhere quiet to think."

Dara studied him as she always did, with eyes that pierced right through to his soul—or could if he had one. He saw indecision for a split second and then, she patted the cushion next to her. "You look like you need someone to talk to, James. I'm a good listener as well as a healer, maybe I can help." He thought he saw hope in her eyes, but shrugged it away—probably just reading things into the situation.

Dara had always been the quiet one of the gargoyles, and he'd always been comfortable and at home around her. He shrugged. Why not? Dara had sworn to protect Logan, maybe it was time to trust someone. "Thank you, Dara. I'd like that." He crossed to the loveseat and sat down next to her. Not knowing what else to do, he smiled at her and enjoyed the way a pink blush crept up her porcelain neck to stain her cheeks.

She was so beautiful, it astounded him. Why had he never noticed that before? She wasn't striking like Ariel or lovely like Jaclyn, but she possessed the type of classic beauty one would see on a cameo brooch.

Dara cleared her throat and he realized he'd been staring.

"My apologies, Dara. You're so beautiful you captured my thoughts and drove them right out of my head."

Her lips curved and the enticing dimple was back. "Well, that was as nice a compliment as I've ever had." She laughed. "I suppose I've done my job then. The sadness is gone from your eyes."

Her comment startled him, but he realized it was probably true. She drove all of the sad memories away, even if only for a moment. "And I'm grateful for the reprieve. When I get in those moods, they are sometimes hard to break." He glanced down at the book on Dara's lap and felt like a schoolboy trying to talk to a girl he was enamored with. "So what are you reading?"

"Dante. He was one of our assignments back around 1300. He was being persecuted by the pope for his writings and we protected him for a few months." She flipped the book closed and studied the cover. "Quite the chauvinist, but I've had a soft spot for his works ever since."

A twinge of envy stabbed him when her eyes lit with pleasure as she spoke about this long dead man. "Did you and he…"

Dara blushed furiously and shook her head. "No, of course not. I never got involved with any of our assignments."

James thought there was more behind the simple statement than she'd said, but he left it alone to explore another time. "My apologies, I didn't mean to pry. I'm distracted, but that's no reason for my manners to slip."

She waved the comment away with a gesture. "No need to apologize." She looked up under impossibly long lashes and met his gaze, her green eyes boring through him. "Have you decided if you trust me enough to talk about whatever is on your mind?"

James sighed. "I always feel like you can see right through me, Dara. Why is that?"

She laughed again, the sound trickled over his skin like soap bubbles popping. Probably because I can. You're so incredibly easy to read—you wear your heart in your eyes."

Shock flowed through James. No one had ever told him that before. The general consensus he'd heard from people was that he was unreadable, inscrutable. It had always made him feel apart from everyone, even beyond what his choices and his existence forced him to be.

Dara's dimple still twinkled in her cheek and he realized she still grinned at him. "Don't worry, James. Your secret is safe. I've always had a knack for reading people that others don't have. I think it's one of my gargoyle gifts. So, what may be easy for me to read, isn't necessarily visible to others."

James wasn't sure if that made it better or worse. Dara being able to read him so easily should have left him feeling uncomfortable and exposed, but it didn't. He was almost relieved another being could understand him.

He took a deep breath, let it out slowly and decided to trust his instincts. "Dara, is there a prophesy going on that I don't know about?" At her shocked look, he held up his hand to forestall any objections and continued. "I was just speaking to Logan and he used words like destiny and child of his blood when referring to Charity's baby. Those sound distinctly like prophesy to me."

Dara studied him in silence until finally she spoke.

"You know as well as I do, prophesies are better left alone or we can unwittingly change their course."

He nodded. "I would normally and emphatically agree, but I may have some important information about this one which could alter its course."

Dara tilted her head to the side as if mulling over a difficult decision. "If you have such information, then I would share it with Logan and Ariel. As far as I know, they are the only two who know the details."

James sat shocked into silence. He had a suspicion that there was indeed a prophesy, but for Dara to tell him so easily shocked him. "Why..."

Dara interrupted him. "Why did I admit to you there is a prophesy in play?"

James could only nod.

"As I said, I'm good at reading people. I can see into their hearts." She shifted one foot out from under her and placed it on the floor, settling into a comfortable position with one leg tucked under her. "I used to berate myself for letting you get so close to Ariel and not realizing what you were. But after meeting you again, I know why I didn't."

Air backed up in his lungs. Did he want to hear this? "Why?" he whispered.

"Because I can see into your heart and soul just as I did then, and you're a good man. Whatever your station and purpose in life, you use it for good. I can't fault you for that—especially since you're doing it in a difficult position. It can't be easy to do good as a vampire, of all things."

He wanted to remind her he had no soul, but he was too shocked that she understood him so well. He wasn't used to having people *get* him.

"And before you disagree with my use of the word soul, let me explain. I believe someone's soul is their inner most being, the inner conscience, if you will. So, when you were turned, you may have given a "lien" against your soul to the dark one, but you've been negating that balance by being a good man ever since. I think it's only a matter of time before that lien is paid off."

"I'm not sure everyone would agree with your definition of soul, but I like it very much." He also realized he was beginning to like *her* very much. James had never seen the true Dara before, but now that he had, she intrigued him. "You're very insightful, Dara."

"Does that mean you'll talk to Logan and Ariel?"

James sighed, wishing it were that easy. "No, I can't. What I know would open up knowledge that could hurt Logan. The risk isn't worth letting him know right now."

To his surprise Dara didn't protest, she just nodded and looked thoughtful. "In that case, maybe you'd better choose someone you trust to talk to, so that two of you are aware of the situation. I don't think either Gabriel or Alonna will be very forthcoming. If there was something to tell, they would have already done so, or will do so at the time of their choosing."

He knew she was right and that even if he did talk to Alonna, she would only tell him what she was ready to. Again, James decided to go with his instincts and trust Dara with the ability to destroy him. "I trust you," he said softly. But even then, he knew he could only trust her with part of the truth. Not only for himself, but for Logan.

A crease formed between Dara's lovely brows, her full lips curved down into a concerned frown. "But I don't know what the prophesy is. How can I possibly help?"

James heard her unspoken question loud and clear. *Why would you trust me?* He'd come this far, he might as well trust his intuition the rest of the way. James reached out and took Dara's hand in his. Her face betrayed her shock at his actions, but she didn't pull her hand away. He began to trace small circles on the back of her hand with his thumb.

She was so incredibly soft. "I've never had anyone understand me, Dara. I think I like it."

"I...I have the advantage of being able to see the big picture in respect to you and Ariel. Please don't condemn her just because she didn't understand at the time. Hindsight..."

"Don't get me wrong, Dara. I don't condemn Ariel for anything. This isn't about Ariel, it's about you. You understand me like no one ever has and every instinct I have says to trust you with my very existence." He traced a few more lazy circles on the back of her hand and wallowed in the sensation of being able to touch her warm skin. "I need this to stay between us until you think this knowledge will help Logan. This is all about keeping Logan safe."

Dara nodded, but she kept glancing between their clasped hands and James' eyes. Yet she made no move to extricate her hand.

"After Ariel, there has been only one woman who captured my heart." He looked up to see her brow furrow with curiosity. "Her name was Jaclyn. And between us, we made something very special." James continued to gaze into Dara's eyes, willing her to understand what he couldn't bring himself to say.

Dara gasped and pulled her hand from his grip. Her eyes widened in surprise, her mouth in an adorable little 'o' that just begged to be kissed. Here he was about to find out if he'd just consigned himself to doom and all he could think about was kissing Dara.

"Why didn't I see it before? Logan, he's...your son." She shook her head and seemed to be struggling with this new realization.

Again, the adorable crease between Dara's brows was back. Logan's fingers itched to trace it, to smooth it away, but he held himself in check. He didn't want to ruin what he already had by being slapped by an extremely strong and ancient gargoyle. Although he didn't think Dara would go for his bollocks, his other body parts would hurt just as much when being ripped off.

He watched in fascination as she rebuilt her composure layer by layer until she was the cool calm woman he first sat down with. "Well, that actually makes sense."

James couldn't help but laugh at her reaction. "What do you mean by that?"

"I told you I can see into people's hearts. Well, both yours and Logan's feel similar. I wrote it off to you working together for so long, but I should learn not to doubt my own impressions." She reached out, squeezed his hand, and surprised him by continuing to hold it. "Don't worry, James. I won't abuse your trust, and I'll only use this information to protect Logan. I can see how if this came to light it would put him in even more danger. I hope I can trust you with the same depth?"

"Absolutely." He took a breath to say something further, but before he could think to form the words, Dara had closed the distance between them and lightly brushed her lips over his. Every nerve ending he had exploded and all coherent thought scattered to the winds. By the time he could even muster energy for awareness beyond Dara, she'd pulled back and stood.

"Good night, James."

He looked up at her in wonder. Her wonderful dimple twinkled at him before she turned to go and he could only nod at her retreating back.

*****

Logan straightened his jacket for the hundredth time and tried not to fidget as the limo pulled to a stop in front of the red carpet. He hadn't seen Ariel since a few nights ago in his office when they'd both agreed she wasn't his destiny. But he couldn't stop thinking about her. He sighed loudly and glanced over at Dara, who sat next to Charity doing an admirable job of not strangling her.

"Are you nervous?" Dara asked softly, ignoring Charity's continued primping.

Logan shook his head. "Not about the emcee gig, anyway."

Charity shot Logan an annoyed look. "Are we going to get out and walk the red carpet or sit here all day chatting with your bodyguard?"

Logan ignored Charity's outburst, much like he had every other tantrum and mood swing over the last few days. He knew some of this was just Charity's real personality showing through, but he was hoping to attribute a lot of it to the pregnancy, even if he knew better.

James, who sat next to Logan, broke in smoothly. "So much the better if we don't seem rushed. It will make your fans even more eager to see you."

Logan knew James must have been working hard not to bite his tongue off after that one. He shot James a grateful look. "Shall we?"

The driver stepped out his door and a few seconds later, opened the back door to the limousine. Charity stepped out first and began waving and smiling. Logan took a deep breath and stepped out behind her. The crowd was large and it seemed like half of country music was in attendance. He could see Toby Keith, Reba and Gretchen Wilson already on their way up the red carpet and a line of limos behind theirs that stretched around the block and out of sight.

He took Charity's arm and began to make what he had always called the walk of doom. Logan loved to write and even to perform in a non-pressured environment, but he'd rather face a succubus again than shake hands and do the fake smile thing for the next four hours.

Continuing to smile and waving now and then with his free hand, he tried to move Charity along. "Come on,

Charity. My face is going to freeze this way if I have to smile for one more minute."

Charity turned to Logan and beamed up at him like the most devoted woman in the world. Logan tried to keep a pleasant look on his face as he fought the urge to roll his eyes.

He heard Dara giggle behind them and his first genuine smile of the night curved his lips.

They'd taken no more than five steps when they reached the first camera point. A bleached blonde who had too many face-lifts thrust a mic into his face. "Logan, it's so good to see you here tonight, and with Charity Taylor."

Charity dived for the microphone like a bass angling for bait and Logan finally did roll his eyes skyward.

"Logan and I are just so happy to be here tonight. Between the two of us, we have so many fans, we just couldn't bear to disappoint them."

Logan noticed Charity's virginal mask was in full force for the cameras. He just wished she could wear it 24X7, then maybe it wouldn't feel like marrying her was signing away his soul to the devil.

Charity made a grand gesture pretending to brush the hair out of her face—as if the lacquered creation could even move after the stylist finished with it. And then a loud gasp from the overly happy blonde. "Is that an *engagement* ring, Charity?"

Logan glanced down and too late, noticed Charity wore a rock the size of the Alamo. He wasn't sure where she'd gotten it—he sure as hell hadn't bought it for her. *Damn it, Charity.* They had agreed to wait to announce anything to the press, partly because he was still coming to grips with it, but also because the gargoyles didn't want to put Charity in more danger by confirming her relationship with Logan. Charity hadn't been happy about the decision, but had reluctantly agreed—or so he thought.

Logan grabbed Charity's left hand and pulled it down away from the camera's view. "No," he cut in before Charity could draw breath. "It is *not* an engagement ring." He squeezed Charity's hand hard so she would keep her mouth shut. "In fact, this is the ring Charity is donating to be auctioned off for the Texas Children's hospital fund after the awards ceremony tonight. We're hoping that some of the other entertainers will donate items as well, so please pass the word." With a parting wink, he dragged Charity away from the camera and further down the red carpet.

"What the hell are you doing, Logan?" Charity asked between gritted teeth, but still through her fake smile.

Logan glanced down at her using every ounce of charm he possessed. "If you don't care about your own safety, or mine, then at least be woman enough to care about the safety of our baby. My bodyguards told us not to announce our engagement and that's that. So get ready to auction that ring."

She pulled her hand out of his grasp and for the first time let her mask slip. "I'll do no such thing," she hissed.

"What?" he feigned surprise. "You're going to disappoint all those children at the Texas Children's hospital?" He raised his voice until she shushed him. "What will your adoring fans think?" he whispered and took Charity's arm again just as the next set of cameras came into view. Under his breath, he added. "Don't ever try to manipulate me like that again, I'm not a doormat like your other boyfriends." She stiffened as they approached the cameras.

Ten minutes later, they finally approached the last set of cameras on the walk of doom. Logan bit back a sigh as yet another perky blonde stepped forward, this one with too much lip liner. She looked like she'd kissed a pink and black zebra and the color had stuck. He bit back a laugh and then stopped in his tracks.

Ariel. He sensed her nearby. He turned his head and saw her standing in the doorway of the auditorium where the red carpet would lead them next. Their eyes locked and held and the contact jolted through his entire body like a bolt of electricity.

She was stunning—even more beautiful than he remembered. Her dress was some sort of shimmery blue affair that melded to every curve, dipped amazingly low in the front giving him a tantalizing view of her cleavage, and made his mouth go suddenly dry. Her hair was pulled back away from her face, but left free in the back to cascade over her shoulders in a soft waterfall.

Suddenly, an elbow in his ribs brought him back to reality. He turned around and reluctantly answered some questions before dragging Charity away from the cameras and toward Ariel.

*****

Ariel took a deep breath as Logan turned his attention away from her and back toward the cameras. When he looked at her like that, she could never get enough air. But she secretly admitted she'd be willing to suffocate for the rest of her life, if only she could have Logan.

"*Be strong, Ariel,*" came Dara's voice inside her head. She glanced up to see her sister studying her intently. Thankfully, Logan and Charity were still interviewing with the camera crew, so she had a few minutes to regain her composure. "*Just think, maybe she'll trip and fall on her face during her performance later.*"

Ariel couldn't help but laugh, and at that moment, Logan turned around and locked eyes with her again. Then, before she knew it, he was standing in front of her, while Charity's evil glare pierced her skin like daggers.

"Logan." She nodded to him in greeting thankful her voice sounded strong and even. "If you'll follow me, I've already cleared your dressing rooms."

Logan seemed about to say something, but then he nodded.

Charity huffed an impatient breath. "I think we're backing up the red carpet line." Her breath held the same saccharine sweetness that always gave Ariel a toothache.

"No problem, right this way," Ariel said and then turned on her heel to lead them back toward their dressing rooms.

Finally, with Charity comfortably settled inside her dressing room, Dara closed the door, leaned back against it, and let out a long weary breath.

Ariel laid a gentle hand on her sister's shoulder. "You should get a sainthood for this."

"I should get a lot more than that for this. Talk about combat duty."

Ariel couldn't help but agree. "I'd better go check on Logan. I think I've put it off long enough." With a quick prayer for strength of character, she knocked on Logan's door and when he called out, she turned the knob and stepped inside.

His dressing room was a ten-foot square room, which held a couch, a chair, a makeup table and a small bathroom complete with a shower. The entire room glared red velvet including the wallpaper, which had small little dots on it. Her fingers itched to feel the texture of the walls.

Logan sat on the chair in front of the makeup table with his guitar in his lap. He looked up and she noticed dark circles under his eyes and wariness in his expression. "Hi, Ariel. I was hoping you'd come by." He looked down at his guitar again and stroked a hand over the polished wood as if it gave him comfort. "I missed you."

Ariel pulled her gaze away from Logan and slowly lowered herself onto the red velvet couch, careful not to muss her dress. "I missed you too, Logan." Her voice came out in a whisper and she blinked rapidly to keep the tears at bay, which suddenly threatened. "I was thinking." She cleared her throat and looked up to see Logan watching her. "There's nothing that says we can't be good friends. That we can't still see each other, even after all of this is over. You'll always be important to me."

Logan's eyes took on a watery sheen. Was his heart breaking as much as hers? "I'd like that."

Silence fell between them until there a discreet knock sounded on the dressing room door and a voice called out, "Mr. McAllister, you're on in ten minutes."

Ariel stood and turned back toward Logan. "You'll do great. I'll be just off to the side of the stage and I promise, no succubus interruptions tonight."

Logan smiled and took Ariel's hand in his. "Thank you," he whispered and then placed a kiss on the back of her hand before releasing her.

Ariel opened the door. "Oh, by the way, if you need me, or something doesn't feel right, just turn and look at me and wink."

Logan laughed. "You want me to wink?" he asked, incredulous.

"Well, we figured that would only enhance your reputation and it's something you can do on camera without having to explain it."

He started past her and out the door, but then stopped and placed his palm against her cheek. "For you, anything."

Time stopped as they looked into each other's eyes and Ariel's chest tightened with emotion. She placed her hand over his. "Go on, and try to stay out of trouble."

Logan walked past her and turned to throw her a charming wink over his shoulder. "Just practicing," he called as he walked toward the stage.

CHAPTER ELEVEN

Ariel scanned the crowd looking for anything out of place, or any vibes of evil emanating through the room. So far, everything seemed fine. Except the damn dress Kefira had chosen for her. Ariel knew this charity gala was A-list and she had to dress the part, but breathing would be a good thing here. And besides, if she needed to do a high kick in this thing, she'd rip some serious slits up the sides.

But when Logan had seen her in it, she'd seen the raw desire in his gaze. So she'd gritted her teeth and silently thanked Kefira for the plunging neckline and form fitting material. At least until she had to wear it for more than five minutes.

Her mood took a sudden and admittedly petty turn when she'd seen Charity. She showed enough that her normal form-fitting dress was out of the question tonight. Instead, she wore a loose-fitting floor-length that would no doubt start pregnancy rumors flying. But for the safety of all concerned, everyone had agreed to keep it under wraps for as long as possible. Despite Charity's attempts to get national coverage for her engagement.

The audience began to laugh and Ariel realized Logan's monologue was well under way and apparently very successful. She glanced toward him long enough that if he needed to signal her, she could catch his eye, but he continued his banter with the audience as if each were a personal friend he was having a beer with on a Saturday night.

Ariel turned her attention back to the crowd and suddenly felt clammy. Sweat broke out on her brow. She reached up to touch her forehead and her hand came away wet. She took a deep breath as she began to feel light-headed and her stomach began to roil. Leaning against the wall, she concentrated and contacted her sisters.

"Something's wrong—I think I'm going to be sick..."

Kefira appeared out of nowhere and slipped flawlessly into Ariel's post as Ariel made an end run for the ladies room. She made it into a stall before what resembled her stomach contents for the entire last year came up.

"Ariel, are you all right?" Dara stepped inside the stall and pressed some wet papers towels against Ariel's forehead.

After an eternity, the spasms in her stomach eased, and she reached over to pull a wad of toilet paper off the roll and blow her nose.

She tossed the paper in the toilet, reached up to flush the contents, and then leaned her forehead against the side of the stall. The cool metal calmed her and she sighed and closed her eyes. "I never thought a bathroom stall would feel so good." Her voice sounded hoarse in her ears.

She'd only been sick one other time in her entire existence. About eight hundred years ago in Greece, someone tried to poison her. According to Dara, in order to make Ariel sick, it had to be enough poison to take out the entire Greek population. But who the hell would want to poison her now?

"*Logan's fine*," Kefira said inside her head, answering her unasked next question. It would have been the next logical step to assume whoever poisoned her would try to kill Logan.

Ariel breathed a sigh of relief and glanced over at Dara. "What the hell is wrong with me? And why aren't you out with Charity?"

Dara gently reached down and brushed Ariel's hair away from her face. "Don't worry, Odeda is out with Charity. And when I left, she was having a terrific time needling her about her 'baggy' dress." Dara made quote marks in the air with the first two fingers of each hand. "As for you, I doubt it's poison, you ate what everyone else ate. But let's get you back to the hotel and I'll look you over."

Ariel's stomach made urgent gurgling sounds. "I don't know if I'm going to make it back, and I can't leave Logan here with minimal protection."

Dara put a comforting hand on her sister's shoulder. "I hardly think James, Kefira and Odeda are minimal protection. But if you're going to be stubborn, you can sit back in Logan's dressing room and be sick."

"I don't want to be sick in front of Charity." She knew it was petty and very vain, but she'd rather sit out back at the dumpster and be sick than do it in front of the blonde queen of the saccharine smile.

"She's up next, so you probably won't even have to see her."

Ariel took a deep breath and let it out, willing her stomach to stop rumbling. "Do you think God will forgive me for hoping she gets some disfiguring disease—after the baby is born, of course?" she bit out as she leaned over the toilet for round two.

Dara pressed damp paper towels to Ariel's forehead. "If it's one thing I know about God, it's that She understands the phrase 'only human', even when it applies to us."

*****

Logan read the teleprompter and kept the smile firmly pasted on his face. He'd noticed when Kefira took over for Ariel almost two hours ago. He also noticed, she'd never come back. Worry gnawed inside him, and he sighed gratefully when he introduced the next act and was able to finally exit the stage and grill Kefira about Ariel.

"She's not feeling well," Kefira answered his terse question.

The concern knotting his insides twisted tighter. "Is she okay?"

Kefira's blue eyes flashed. "Ariel will be fine. Your...girlfriend," she said with distaste, "has requested you visit her in her dressing room. You won't be needed again for about thirty minutes."

Logan knew when he was being dismissed. He also knew he deserved it. Ariel's sisters treated him professionally and courteously, but they would never forgive him for hurting her. "I never meant to hurt her."

Kefira's gaze searched his until she nodded. "Good intentions don't excuse it."

"I wasn't asking to be excused. I just hope she understands I'll love her for the rest of my life." He turned and walked toward Charity's dressing room, forcing himself not to look back into Kefira's accusing gaze.

When he reached the door of the dressing room, he took a deep breath before turning the knob. How could he spend the next sixty years dreading seeing his wife and the mother of his child? Sighing, he pushed open the door. Charity sat draped on the single couch in her bathrobe. Odeda stood in the corner, her arms crossed over her chest, a mischievous grin quirking her lips.

Logan nodded toward Odeda as Charity sat up and glared at him. "What took you so long? "I've been in here stuck with...*her*." She gestured dramatically toward Odeda.

Logan bit his tongue against the acid retort that came to mind. He may have to marry her, but she had another thing coming if she thought he would allow her to treat him like her lackey. "I was on stage, Charity. As you already know. What's the problem?" He purposely ignored her patting the couch next to her.

"I just needed to see you, Logan." Her eyes welled up with tears as if on cue, and Logan ignored the artifice. "And your bodyguard is being mean to me!" The classic Charity pout was back and she looked at him through lowered lashes.

He wished they didn't have to hide the gargoyle's nature from Charity. He understood the necessity, but it would get rid of a lot of Charity's whining if she knew

Odeda could lift small cars without breaking a sweat. He turned toward Odeda. "I thought Dara was protecting Charity. Is everything all right? I heard Ariel was sick."

Odeda narrowed her eyes and then nodded. "Dara is with her, she'll be back in a minute. Probably just something in the food that made her sick."

"Wait a minute," Charity interrupted. "We all ate that food." She put a hand on her stomach and struck a pose as if about to faint—her other hand on her forehead. "Shouldn't we have it checked or something?"

Logan looked over in time to see Odeda hide a smirk. He stifled a sigh of relief. If Odeda still needled Charity, then Ariel wasn't in any danger. He turned his attention back to Charity. "I'm sure the food is fine. Now if you no longer need me, I have to get changed for my next cue."

"But, Logan. What are you going to do about this?" Charity pointed at Odeda.

Logan sighed, but turned back to face her. "Charity, you've never once asked me why I suddenly have security guards. I can only infer from that you don't care. You got what you wanted, I acknowledge the baby as mine and when things die down, we'll start planning a wedding." He sighed as the strait jacket that had become his life tightened around him. "But if you think I'm going to be at your beck and call, you're wrong. You're getting a husband and a father for our child out of this, not a butler."

Her outraged gasp followed him as he turned on his heel and left, closing the door behind him. Guilt assailed him, but he squelched it quickly. If Ariel were the one he'd gotten pregnant, they would both be happy right now instead of miserable. He sighed and turned toward his dressing room. "If wishes were fishes..." He chuckled as he repeated what his mother had said to him so many times before she died.

He opened the door to his dressing room and stopped short. Ariel was lying on the sofa with a bucket sitting next to her on the floor. She held a damp washcloth over her eyes. Her skin held a pallor and glistened with sweat like she had a fever. He rushed toward the couch, dropping down on his knees in front of her and gently stroking her arm. "Ariel? Can I get you anything?"

She pulled the washcloth down to look at him. "Sorry, I thought I'd be gone before you got back. Must've just caught a bug or something."

Logan laid a gentle hand against her forehead. Her skin was clammy, her eye makeup smudged from the wet washcloth spreading dark makeup circles under her eyes. And even now, Logan thought her the most beautiful woman in the world.

Ariel started to sit up, but then moaned and collapsed back onto the couch. "You weren't supposed to need your dressing room until the last hour of the show," she said through gritted teeth. Then she leaned over and heaved into the bucket.

Logan held her forehead in his right hand and rubbed her back with his left. Then when she finished, he wiped her mouth and helped her to lay back. "The finale starts in half hour. I'll get you another washcloth. Don't move, I just need to change, then I'll get out of here and let you rest." He changed quickly, trying to keep the noise to a minimum. He knew when he was sick, noise of any kind just made it worse.

He stopped short at his last thought. With a shock, he realized he'd never taken care of anyone before when they were sick. Not only did the thought of someone being sick usually make him squeamish, but he studiously avoided others when they were sick. It made him feel helpless and weak. Things that reminded him of the night he found his mother.

A vivid picture sprang into his mind of her broken body lying on the floor, her throat a bloody mess that looked like so much hamburger, and a dark red pool of blood growing underneath her. In his mind's eye, he stepped closer and realized she still clutched a large silver cross in her right hand, and smoke rose in lazy wisps from the metal, although he could see no burns on his mother's hand.

His legs buckled and he reached out a hand to the wall to steady himself against the impact of the vision. He'd never seen this much of it before. It usually stopped where his dreams did, with her screams he heard from the top of the stairs after he snuck out of the linen closet. *Will I ever remember what happened in its entirety?* He sighed as his mother's staring eyes still burned inside his mind, her fear a tangible taste on the back of his tongue.

"Logan?" Ariel asked, placing a tentative touch against his shoulder. "Are you all right?"

Worry for Ariel pushed away the vivid memories and he turned to gently take her arm and lead her back to the couch. "What are you doing?" he chided without heat. "You should be laying down, you're sick."

She swayed and he caught her, lowering her to the couch before replacing the washcloth on her forehead. He let his fingers linger against her cascade of silky hair until a brisk knock sounded on the door.

"Twenty minutes, Mr. McAllister." Logan jumped as if he'd been caught doing something he shouldn't. Then, when he realized what he'd done, he chuckled at himself.

"Thanks," he called back as quietly as he could and still be sure he was heard.

"Go, Logan," Ariel said from under the washcloth. "I'll be fine."

He stood and looked down at her still, pale form. Logan closed his eyes and said a quick prayer. *Lord, you'd better have a damned good plan, if you expect me to trust you like this.*

Then he quickly left the dressing room, closing the door softly behind him. When he turned back around, he was face to face with the loveliest woman he'd ever seen. This was saying quite a bit since he'd met the gargoyles.

She had a straight lustrous fall of auburn hair, which extended nearly down to her calves and her eyes were the most luminous gray he'd ever seen. Hip huggers and an extremely tight tank top encased a sculpture perfect female body. Was she one of the presenters? Maybe a super model or actress? "Excuse me," he said and took a step back away from her. "I didn't see you there."

A flash of irritation sparked in the depths of her eyes, but then she smiled and the dark hallway seemed to brighten. "I would be happy to see you anywhere you'd like," she said, in a Marilyn Monroe voice, leaning forward to allow him a free view of enticing cleavage.

How quickly life changes you, he thought to himself and stifled a sigh. Not long ago, he would've jumped at the obvious offer.

But then he met Ariel.

"I'm flattered, but I need to be on stage soon."

Storm clouds gathered inside the woman's eyes and her perfectly shaped auburn brows furrowed. "Don't rush away on my account," she said and reached out a slender hand to rest it lightly against his chest. And then, to his surprise, she began to hum under her breath.

The warmth of her hand permeated his suit jacket, he started to remove it, but then the melody she hummed caught his attention. The woman stared into his eyes and began to sway back and forth a tiny bit, in time to the haunting music. It was lovely and enticing, filled with haunting dissonances and a wonderful minor key, which gave it a mysterious air.

Logan began to picture the notes written down in his mind's eye when he realized he'd heard dissonances. In order for there to be dissonances, more than one note had to be hummed at the same time. He shook his head, that wasn't possible with the human voice. Which meant this woman was another supernatural beastie come to prey on him.

Terrific, another day, another being who wants to castrate me.

Suddenly, his dressing room door flew open behind him and Ariel appeared in the doorway.

Logan instinctively started forward to protect Ariel, but faster than his human reflexes could act, the woman before him hissed and struck out, raking her fingernails over Ariel's chest, shredding the front of her dress and exposing her breasts. Several deep furrows oozed blood, but Ariel looked more irritated than injured.

Ariel's hand snaked out and grabbed the woman's wrist much as she had Jeb's the first day he'd met her. The next thing Logan knew, the woman knelt in front of Ariel with both arms twisted behind her back at a painful angle. Logan opened his mouth to ask the woman's identity when he heard footsteps and looked up in time to see James jogging down the hallway toward them.

The woman gasped, her eyes rounded with fear when she saw James and she tried to bow her head down to touch the floor, but was caught short by Ariel's grip.

"Ariel." James' deep voice echoed down the dark hallway. "Are you all right?" he asked, his gaze obviously assessing the damage to her chest.

Several doors down, another dressing room opened and a new boy band Logan couldn't remember the name of filed out. Logan held his breath, but the men merely snickered as they passed by and kept walking. He shook his head. Nothing fazed these people. That's why he was content to remain a songwriter and not a performer.

Ariel spoke, bringing his attention back. "I'll be fine. Can you handle our *guest*?" She said the last word with obvious distaste. "I'm still not feeling well from earlier, and Logan needs to be on stage."

"Forgive me, sire," the woman simpered, her voice sultry, but no longer the breathy Marilyn Monroe. "I did not know this one was under your protection." She gestured toward Logan with her head. "Please…" she begged, "have mercy upon me. *I* meant him no permanent harm."

Shock at the exchange caused Logan's mouth to fall open and he quickly closed it. "Sire?" demanded Logan. "Is she one of yours?"

James shot Logan an irritated look. "Of course not. She would call any ancient, sire."

"What the hell is she?" Logan asked, wondering what kind of horrible creature he'd stumbled onto this time.

"She's a klatch witch," Ariel answered. "They are a form of fairy whose sole purpose in life is to pursue earthly pleasures. They aren't harmful creatures, but they are protective of their *company*."

Ariel started to sway on her feet and Logan reached out to steady her. "James, can you take her so Ariel can go back and lie down?" James motioned for Ariel to release her hold on the klatch witch, which she did. The witch immediately prostrated herself before James, touching her forehead to the floor before rising up on her knees in front of James in a very suggestive position.

Charity chose that moment to open her dressing room door. All heads including the witch turned to face her.

Charity took in the scene and then crossed her arms over her chest and stared at James with obvious distain. "Isn't a public performance even a little kinky for you, James?"

Logan sighed. "Charity, let's go, we're due on stage." To James he said, "We'll discuss your groupie there later." Grabbing Charity's arm, he led her forcefully toward the stage.

CHAPTER TWELVE

Everyone disappeared leaving James alone with the klatch witch. He sighed. At least this one would probably talk. Klatch's were extremely respectful of any ancient being and wouldn't purposefully cross James. "Rise and tell me your name, sister." He used the ancient form of address for her.

The woman rose and faced James, her curiosity evident even through her fear. "I am Delwyn of the First Order of Klatch."

First order meant she was almost as old as himself. The klatch were created in ancient Ireland as one of the first races of fairies. So what was such a powerful klatch doing attending to Logan herself? He knew most of the ancients treated the klatch like the lower class of the ancient beings. James decided to try a tact he knew none of the other ancients had done with her. "Delwyn," he said and gave a short formal bow before her and took her hand in his, raising it to his lips and placing a soft kiss on the back. "Perhaps we can discuss this situation over some refreshments?" He stood straight and smiled his most charming smile.

The look of utter shock on her face confirmed his strategy. Then, her face blossomed with happiness, her lips curved, and she took a deep breath, which enhanced the display of her impressive cleavage. "If it pleases you, Sire, then I am happy to accompany you."

Soon, they were both sitting comfortably in one of the dressing rooms, Delwyn enjoying her second glass of champagne.

"Are you quite comfortable?" James asked. At her emphatic nod, he continued. "There's no reason for our discussion to be uncivilized. I do understand that you hurting Logan's gargoyle protector was purely out of instinct. She understands too, or you would be dead right now." Of that, Logan had no doubt. Especially since Ariel looked more inconvenienced than injured.

Delwyn's eyes clouded for a moment before she smiled brightly once again. "Yes, Sire. I would never deliberately hurt a gargoyle. In fact I did not realize there were any of their ilk left until I smelled her blood on my fingers."

James leaned forward, keeping his face pleasant. "Now, Delwyn," he said again, using her name deliberately. Those who knew your name within the realm of fairy had power over you and he knew she would not withhold it from him or any other ancient out of both fear and respect. "Let's discuss why you are here tonight. Did someone send you to seek out Logan?"

Delwyn emptied her glass of champagne and James smoothly refilled it even as she began to speak. "Yes, Sire. I was approached by another ancient, like yourself." She gestured toward James and then took another sip of champagne. "I know not his name, but only that he wished for me to castrate the human." She scowled and set down her glass on the mahogany table beside her.

James knew that for a being such as this, who lived for all pleasures including sexual, such a request would resemble sacrilege. "Of course, I respectfully refused. For a moment, I thought he would kill me for my insolence and be done with it."

When she didn't speak right away, James prompted her gently. "What happened, Delwyn? What did the ancient do then?"

"After his face cleared of the storm clouds, he smiled. Bright as the sun, it was. Then he said he admired a woman of convictions—whatever those may be." She waved away the word as if it were of no consequence.

James gestured to a tray of crab puffs and waited while she sampled one before he continued. "So, after he admired your convictions, then what did he say?"

Delwyn slipped another crab puff between her lips and chewed thoughtfully. "Then he said he would offer me a trade. If I brought him Logan, he would allow me a night with his entire kiss."

James wasn't shocked by the knowledge an ancient vampire was the one who approached her. Or that he'd offered her his kiss in return. Delwyn would prosper from the powerful energy gained through sex with an entire kiss of vampires, and since klatches were much more indestructible than any human and didn't have issues with pain or the taking of blood, as long as it was done during sex, she was the perfect vampire playmate.

"Delwyn," he began. "You said you didn't know the name of this ancient, did you hear anyone refer to him as anything but Master?"

She shook her head, her auburn hair swinging lightly with the movement. "No, Sire. The only name I heard was for the one who brought me to the ancient. His name was Astor."

James' temper bubbled higher. It had been the right decision to leave Astor in place until he figured out what he was up to. But that decision could have cost Logan his life.

Oblivious to James' internal anger, Delwyn said, "Sire, may I be so bold as to ask a question of you?"

James nodded toward her. "What do you wish to know, Delwyn?"

"The boy, Logan. He was immune to my powers. He was interested in my music, but not enthralled. It was almost as if he filed away my music for later use, analyzing it." She looked distinctly irritated at the prospect. "He didn't even look at my body. Does he have ancient blood running through his veins?"

A smile curved James' lips. He may not be able to acknowledge Logan, but he was glad that some good had come out of the bloodline for Logan, at least. Apparently,

Logan had some powers no one was aware of, not even his own father.

James leaned forward. "Just between you and I, Delwyn?" When she nodded, he continued. "He has very ancient blood and is protected by the Angel Gabriel and the Almighty, Herself."

Delwyn's face looked stricken, and her half-full glass slipped from her hand to land on the carpet at her feet. "I did not know, Sire. Please, have mercy." She slid out of her chair and onto her knees on the floor in front of James. "Please, Sire."

James shook his head and pulled her back up into her chair. "Delwyn. I'm not angry. Logan is fine, and you've helped me very much." In the manner of fairies, her sunny smile came back in an instant.

"Anything I can do to help one such as this, Sire, I'm more than willing to do."

"Let's discuss where you were supposed to deliver him and then I'm going to make sure Gabriel protects you from harm until this other ancient is no longer a threat to Logan."

*****

Ariel pushed inside her hotel room and gratefully sank down on the plush king-sized bed. Her lovely dress had been a total loss after the klatch witch's tantrum, so she borrowed a shirt from one of the young men who had walked by them while they were holding the witch. Ariel may not have looked glamorous with a black t-shirt complete with a smiley face with a bullet hole in its head, covering the shredded top of her dress, but at least she wasn't topless for her walk out to the car.

The limousine ride had been torture, and they had to stop twice so she could throw up on the side of the road. All the while, she heard Charity's snide comments from the back seat. It made her wish gargoyles didn't have such good hearing. Or alternately, that Charity would end up with lots of badly placed stretch marks.

She kicked off her shoes and heard them thunk softly on the carpet before she closed her eyes, wishing she could just fall asleep and wake up feeling like herself again. Placing a hand gingerly over her chest, she winced as pain shot through her from the deep furrows. There hadn't been time or privacy to turn to stone and heal them earlier. She needed to do it now before she lost all of her energy. But her body stubbornly remained still, her eyes closed, her stomach roiling.

The soft slide of the hotel key in the door slot sounded just before the loud click of the lock releasing. *"It's just me,"* Dara said inside her mind.

Ariel was grateful, as the soft voice inside her mind was much less invasive than spoken words on her throbbing head. The bed dipped as Dara sat down next to her and touched a hand to Ariel's forehead. *"I've also called Gabriel."*

Ariel forced open her eyes as shock traveled through her foggy brain. If Dara had summoned the angel, it meant it was beyond Dara's power to heal her. Not a good sign, especially since this was the first time since their creation Dara couldn't heal anything that plagued her.

Before she had time to worry about it, the scent of cinnamon filled the room making Ariel gag. Dara held up the trash can and Ariel leaned over just in time for her empty stomach to stubbornly try to turn her inside out again.

At the cool touch of Gabriel's hand against the back of her neck, the nausea and headache receded instantly. Placing a hand to her chest, she discovered the furrows were also gone as if they'd never been. She took a deep breath and let it out slowly, sagging with relief against her sister for a moment, grateful her body was back to normal. "Thanks, Gabriel. I don't think I could've handled much more of that."

"Don't worry, I've taken care of it for tonight, and it will only last a few more months."

Liquid ice spread through Ariel's veins as the words penetrated her brain. She sat up and snapped her head around to stare at Gabriel. "What?" She tried to form a cohesive sentence inside her mind and finally had to settle for, "What the hell is wrong with me?"

Gabriel sat down next to her on the bed and Dara took Ariel's hand in her own. Ariel squeezed it in thanks for the much-needed support.

"What are you trying *not* to tell me, Gabriel." Ariel stared at the angel hard, as a slow smile bloomed across his face.

"Congratulations, Ariel. You're pregnant."

Time slowed as a vortex of conflicting emotions rushed through her body at lightening speed, in great rolling waves.

Pregnant?

There was no way she could be pregnant after everything that happened. Gabriel must be joking. He often liked to tease those in his charge. Hell, he'd teased her for centuries. She shook her head, trying to find her balance. Finally, logic intruded and her head cleared enough to perform some quick calculations.

In the last two hundred years, she'd had sex exactly twice, and both of those times were with Logan. But after nine centuries of periods, Ariel was extremely sure of her own cycle. Feeling more confident, she stood and faced Gabriel defiantly with her arms crossed over her chest, her chin thrust upward. "Gabriel, the timing doesn't work out. I wasn't even close to ovulating."

Gabriel smile positively glowed and he gestured toward the heavens. "Her will be done."

The back of Ariel's neck prickled, her mouth fell

open and a bowling ball lodged in her stomach. The realization of what Gabriel implied spread through her like wildfire, the conflicting pool of emotions washed over her again, threatening to drown her.

She was pregnant…with Logan's baby.

Ariel's legs buckled under her and she sat down hard on the floor, afraid she would fall if she tried to take the few extra steps to the bed. "Oh, dear Lord, I'd been about to turn to stone to heal," she whispered under her breath in horror. The gargoyles had learned the hard way with Kefira that turning to stone while you were pregnant would abort the baby.

Gabriel made an upward motion with his hand and Ariel floated up to a sitting position in mid air. "You need to take better care of yourself than that, Lioness of God. After all, there are two of you now. And besides, you *didn't* turn to stone and all is well with the baby."

Dara turned to Gabriel. "Do you mean to say God altered her cycle so she could become pregnant? Does this have anything to do with the prophesy?"

Ariel gasped. She'd forgotten all about that. Tears burned at the back of her eyes. "Oh no…the prophesy." She looked between Dara and Gabriel in growing horror. "If Charity is carrying the child of Logan's blood, then I must be carrying the daughter of his destiny."

Gabriel remained quiet and looked at Ariel with sympathy obvious in his eyes.

Dara pierced him with a stern glare. "Maybe it's time you told us about the prophesy, Gabriel. I think protecting Ariel and the baby are worth the risk of everyone knowing."

Gabriel shook his head slowly. "I cannot. Prophesies are not mine to reveal to anyone. Only Alonna or a human with free will can divulge the details. Alonna has her own orders from the Almighty."

A shimmer appeared in the air and quickly coalesced into Alonna. "You summoned me, Gabriel?"

"I did *not* summon you," Gabriel chided. "And you very well know it. You just wanted to have an excuse to be here."

Alonna ignored him and fluttered over to land on Ariel's shoulder. "Giant cousin, don't fret so. I'm very happy for you." She clapped her tiny hands together. "Just think, a baby." Her voice took on a dreamy quality.

Ariel took a breath to respond to Alonna, but Dara cut her off. "Alonna. We think it's time we discussed the prophesy. We can't keep Ariel safe if we don't know what's going on."

Alonna cocked her head as if assessing her options. "Some people are not meant to hear all pieces of the prophesy. Some are meant only to hear one. But for my giant cousins, I can share another piece yet."

Dara turned to Ariel. "Let me get everyone in here and then Alonna can fill us in as much as she can. Hopefully between what you, James and Logan know, we'll have the whole thing."

Ariel wrapped her arms around her stomach and began to rock gently back and forth. "Not Logan. I don't want Logan to know," she said, not meeting Dara's eyes. "And not James—he would definitely want to tell Logan."

Dara stood and crossed to her sister laying a gentle hand on her shoulder. "But, Logan's the father. He has every right to know."

Ariel forced herself to meet Dara's troubled gaze. "He can't. The fate of the world rests on this, Dara. Please promise me, Logan must never know."

Dara opened her mouth to argue, but Alonna fluttered up into her line of sight, forestalling her objection. "James can know this new piece, but not the man-thing. As much as I like him, I have shared all I dare with him."

Alonna landed back on Ariel's shoulder. "Mayhap, we should start with your sisters and you can best decide how to proceed from there."

Dara nodded toward Alonna. "All right. We've always trusted you, Alonna, we aren't going to stop now." And then to Ariel, she said, "But I still think you should tell Logan about the baby."

Ariel squeezed her eyes tight against the tears and rocked back and forth more urgently. "Please, just get Odeda and Kefira."

Within minutes, Ariel's sisters gathered around her. They all sat on the king-sized bed, Ariel leaned against the headboard, a pillow cradled in her lap like a shield against the inevitable. Gabriel sat in the corner, hovering above the TV, his brow furrowed, his blue eyes dark with concern. Alonna perched on the headboard beside Ariel, her tiny feet swinging lightly over the side.

Odeda kicked off her shoes and leaned back more comfortably on the bed. "I had to tell a whopper of a lie to get James to stay with Charity and Logan. I told him gargoyles have a special ritual at 'that time of the month' and then he shut his mouth, practically shoving us out the door."

A small smile curved Ariel's lips at the thought of James' discomfort with feminine hygiene, but soon the seriousness of the moment weighed on her once again as she realized what she'd have to tell her sisters. She closed her eyes and said a quick prayer for strength.

"Granted," Gabriel murmured from the corner.

Ariel glared over at him. "If you're not willing to help fill everyone in about the prophesy, then you're welcome to go."

When Gabriel only continued to sit and look at her with concern clear on his face, she returned her attention to her sisters.

Alonna cleared her throat, which sounded like bells clacking together. "I can not repeat the part of the prophesy I shared with the man-thing. It was his choice to share it with the one who holds his heart, and hers to share it with you now. Once she's done, I can add one more piece."

"How long is this freaking prophesy, anyway?" asked Odeda with obvious frustration.

"Prophesies as a rule, are quite large. But since this one affects the war between good and evil, it's the largest I know of."

Odeda sighed. "Great. I thought it was a rhetorical question, but I think I liked *not* knowing better."

Kefira reached out and laid a comforting hand on Ariel's ankle. "Tell us, Ariel. We can tackle anything together."

Ariel looked into her sister's face and swallowed hard against a sob, which threatened to bubble out of her throat. Until now, she hadn't realized how hard this would be. But remembering Kefira's own lost child, Ariel realized she might be slicing old wounds open at the same time she shared her news. She buried her face in her hands, prolonging the inevitable, then looked up into Kefira's face as she spoke. "Well, before we get to the prophesy, Gabriel just told me I'm pregnant."

All color drained from Kefira's face until her freckles looked like specks of brown floating on a sea of milk. She ran a hand through her already tousled red hair and then when she looked up at Kefira again, a large smile blossomed on her lips. "Pregnant? Truly?"

Ariel released a breath she hadn't realized she'd been holding. She was shocked at Kefira's reaction, but then chided herself. She should have known that even though Kefira had lost her own child, she would be happy for Ariel.

"Well at least we know why you've been puking all over the place," Odeda chimed in, her eyes dancing with pleasure and her smile as bright as the sunrise.

Ariel turned to Dara, met her worried stare, and then remembered that the celebration of her sisters would be short lived.

"There's more."

"If this is about Charity, then don't you worry." Kefira sat up straighter like a mother bear protecting her cub. "Logan would never turn his back on his child. He'll want to be a part of this child's life. And if he knows this one is his too, he may choose to follow his heart rather than his sense of duty like he is now." Her scowl showed clearly what she thought of Logan's decision.

Tears began to steam down Ariel's face. "That's exactly why Logan can't know. Ever."

"He's the father, he has every right to know." Odeda scooted forward on the bed so she could grab Ariel's hand under the pillow.

Ariel leaned back against the headboard, the weight of the world pressing down upon her. "This involves the prophesy. I think it's time you know as much of it as I do."

Odeda held up a hand to stop Ariel. "Wait, are we sure we *should* know? I mean, if we all know it, we could misinterpret it, we could twist it toward evil and not even know it." She made large agitated gestures with her hands as she spoke. "It's too dangerous."

Dara spoke up for the first time since the meeting began. "I think at this point, it's too dangerous not to know. We have to protect Ariel and the baby, not to mention Logan, Charity and the other baby. Any information we have could help."

Odeda puffed out a breath. "I still think it's dangerous, but when you put it that way... If Ariel's baby is involved, then I'd gladly risk my life to protect it and her."

The three sisters nodded to each other, then turned expectantly to Ariel.

Ariel swiped at her tears with the back of her hand. She should have known her sisters would stand behind her no matter what. "Logan didn't remember it word for word, but it had to do with the son of his blood and the daughter of his destiny. He said he got the impression that if he raised the son, it was a good thing, but if he raised the daughter, evil would prevail." She glanced at each of her sisters in turn before continuing. "And there was also something about if Logan ceases to exist before his fated time, the son of his blood would avenge him with rivers of dark blood and the heavens will shine on him."

A heavy silence descended on the room as everyone digested what Ariel told them.

Kefira's next words were so soft, Ariel had to strain to hear them. "And since prophesies are usually linear, that would mean if Charity's baby was created first, it must be the son of Logan's blood."

Ariel's heart constricted in her chest as her sisters now fully understood why Logan could never know that the child she carried was his.

"Wait," Odeda said startling everyone out of the tense silence. "Alonna, does this actually mean that Ariel's baby is the child of destiny?"

Alonna shook her head sadly. "I can not offer explanations or options within the prophesy. I can only deliver it and hope it is interpreted correctly or incorrectly as it is meant to be."

Ariel started at the strange wording. "You mean sometimes they can be meant to be interpreted incorrectly?"

"Of course." Alonna's wings began to flutter as they always did when she was thinking and she began to rise slowly above the headboard. "God allows free will, but by Her very nature, She is omnipotent. She allows the free will and yet She knows all outcomes. How can She not?"

A pounding started behind Ariel's eyes as she tried

to work through the endless logic loops that line of thought could cause. She closed her eyes and sighed. When she opened them again, everyone was looking at her. "So, in other words, you can't tell us anything more about the part of the prophesy we already know."

"True." Alonna slowed her wings until her feet touched the headboard and she stood. "The part I can share is this, 'should the secret seed be revealed before the appointed time, the destruction will be twofold.'"

Dara gasped and Ariel noticed the blood drained from her sister's face. "Dara?"

Dara's head snapped up as she realized everyone in the room was watching her. "Then I think we have a dilemma."

"You mean besides the fact that this confirms I can't tell Logan?" Ariel asked.

Dara gazed at each of the sisters in turn and then looked back at Ariel. "I have another piece of information that could possibly pertain to the 'secret seed'. But unfortunately, I don't know if it really *is* the secret seed referred to in the prophesy, or if it's Ariel's baby or even Charity's. I think it's best for all involved to keep all of them as secret as we can for now. Alonna said James could know this new piece, but beyond that, everyone who doesn't already know, should stay in the dark."

A small flame of hope sparked, but she damped it down. Just because there were other possibilities she hadn't considered, didn't mean she could ever tell Logan about their child. But what would he think of her for keeping this from him, even if he knew it was for the best of all concerned? She wasn't sure she was prepared to find out.

Dara took charge once again, breaking Ariel out of her thoughts. "Alonna, you said James could know this new piece. Is it all right if I tell him, or do you need to?"

Alonna smiled. "I will stay with Ariel while you are

gone, cousin. I know of several herbal remedies for morning sickness."

CHAPTER THIRTEEN

James watched as Logan stood and began to pace across the suite they shared with Charity. Charity had tried to get Logan to share her bed, but so far he'd resisted, saying he was worried about the baby. James, perfectly happy with the arrangement, liked the fact he was close enough to keep an eye on Charity and Logan. Not to mention proud that Logan could use his gift of genetic intuition.

Logan probably didn't understand why he was so resistant to Charity, other than her horrific personality, but he followed his gut nonetheless. James resisted the urge to smile with parental pride at the obvious display of Logan's abilities.

Charity sat down in the armchair Logan had just vacated and began brushing out her long blonde hair. "Why don't you sit down, Logan." She dropped her voice to almost a whisper. "Or come to bed."

James couldn't miss the sultry undertone in her voice, or her pointed glare at him to leave them alone, which he studiously ignored. He snapped the open paper he was reading between his two hands and continued to scan the headlines.

Logan turned and began to pace to the other side of the room. "Something is wrong with Ariel and they aren't telling me what it is. Why would they keep me in the dark on this?" When he reached the far side of the room, he turned and began to pace back again.

James lowered the paper in time to see temper flash across Charity's face, her jaw set, her eyes narrowed.

James cut in smoothly before Charity's tantrum hit boiling point. "I'm sure Ariel is fine. She's always been healthy and strong. Everyone gets a bug now and then."

"Why do you even care that one of your hired help has caught some cold?" Charity demanded of Logan. "You should be worried about taking care of me and the baby, not pining after some fat, unattractive, blue collar worker!" She yelled the last three words and stood, clenching her fists at her sides.

James watched as Logan's head whipped around, his anger a palpable force in the room.

Dara's quiet voice laced with steel interrupted before anyone could speak. "I may have sworn to protect you, Charity, but as soon as you give birth, I owe you a fist right in your expensive nose job."

All eyes turned to see Dara standing in the doorway, her normally serene expression suffused with rage. Her eyes narrowed to angry slits, her fists curled at her sides. James noticed the way wisps of her blonde hair had fallen out of her clip to curl around her face. He longed to tuck the hair back into place, just for an excuse to touch her.

"Dara, I'm sorry you had to hear that." Logan stepped close to Charity. "I'm sure Charity is sorry and is just tired from a busy day." When Charity opened her mouth to protest, Logan grabbed her arm and steered her toward her bedroom. After pushing Charity inside, he turned back to them before closing the door. "She and I need to have a talk. Will you two excuse us?"

"I can't believe Logan ever slept with that woman! I'd like to wring her scrawny neck."

James gestured for Dara to sit in the chair Charity had vacated. "I believe there would be a line for that particular honor."

Dara sat and then chuckled despite her anger. "Don't make me laugh when I'm still trying to be angry."

"I've never seen you lose your temper. It's quite an interesting display." He leaned forward to take her hand in his, but she snatched it away.

Realizing what she'd done, color crept over her milky skin and her cheeks burned bright red. She cleared her throat. "I've come to tell you of the prophesy, as well as a new piece Alonna just told us."

James' brow furrowed. "Why now? A while ago, it was all secrets and silence. Is Ariel seriously ill?" His gut clenched at the thought of anything bad happening to her. He may be over his romantic feelings for her, but he would always care for her.

Dara hesitated before answering. James immediately studied her closer. He'd never known any of the gargoyles to lie, but he saw all the physical signs of one about to start right now.

Finally, she said, "Ariel's condition isn't serious, it will just take a few months to clear it up. But she will be fine."

From all of Dara's physical reactions, she'd told the technical truth, but James knew she'd told a lie of omission by the way her blood pressure spiked and her pupils dilated. Interesting. He'd bet his fangs this also had something to do with the prophesy. There was no other reason for her to omit information from him. "I'm glad to hear it's nothing to be concerned about. You will let me know if there's anything I can do to help? I will always care for Ariel."

Dara breathed a small sigh of what looked like relief at not being questioned further about her statement. "Of course, James."

James leaned forward and studied the long line of her neck. He could sense the life pulsing through her veins and wondered what she would taste like. When he realized what he was doing, he shook his head to clear the thought and sat back. He'd fed earlier tonight. There was no reason for these thoughts and sexual attraction wasn't enough to make him think of taking a bite out of Dara. *What the hell is going on here?*

"James?" Dara's soft voice interrupted. "Are you all right? You look a bit pale. Have you fed?"

"Forgive me, Dara. I think the stress of the last few

months has been taking its toll." He gestured his weakness away. "Please, tell me about the prophesy."

Dara studied him critically for a moment. Once she seemed satisfied he was all right, she settled back more comfortably in the chair and told him about the prophesy. He asked a few questions, but finally, exhausted, he sat stunned, rolling over the implications in his mind.

Should the secret seed be revealed before the appointed time, the destruction will be twofold.

That could mean one of two things. He wasn't supposed to reveal the truth about Charity's baby or he wasn't supposed to reveal that Logan was his son. And he couldn't afford to guess at which the prophesy meant.

Dara tapped her unpolished fingernail nervously against the arm of the chair. The little 'click, click' sounded loud in the tense silence which hung between them. "So you understand now why I didn't choose to tell anyone about you and Logan." Again, her physical reaction showed she hadn't told him everything.

"Dara, you wouldn't be hiding something from me, would you?"

She huffed out a breath and met his direct gaze. "Because of the newest part of the prophesy, we all decided to keep the information exchange to a minimum. The only reason I filled you in this far was that Alonna insisted you could know these parts."

James laughed out loud. This woman was a delight. "I've never met a woman who admitted she lied to me so eloquently. And without actually lying," he added.

Dara smiled innocently. "I didn't lie. I just told you I'm not telling you everything, and I gave you a perfectly rational explanation of why."

"I know. That's what I find delightful about you." He leaned forward. "You're a puzzle a man could spend centuries unlocking.

Dara shot to her feet. "I'm not a puzzle to be unlocked, James. And I'll thank you to keep all of your puzzle keys to yourself." With that parting shot, she quickly left, closing the door behind her.

"Well, well. I do seem to have the ability to fluster her. I think I like it."

*****

Nicholas motioned for Astor to enter his office and went back to scanning the morning paper. Finally, after letting Astor stand shifting from foot to foot for several long minutes, he spoke. "I'm scanning the entertainment page and I don't see anything about Charity's engagement to Logan. Only a small article about Charity donating the rather expensive engagement ring we gave her for a charity auction." He carefully folded the paper and set it aside before turning his deadly gaze toward Astor.

"I don't know what happened. They were quite an item just a month ago, and Charity can manipulate any man. She's a natural." He seemed ready to babble on indefinitely.

Nicholas cut him off with a wave of his hand. "Apparently not natural enough. You said Logan was weak. You told me if she pressured him on the red carpet, to save face, he would go along." He let his voice rise to a menacing level. "Logan is *obviously* resisting her." He took a deep calming breath and let his anger flow away.

When he spoke again, he made sure his tone was cool and cultured. "But I did see something extremely *interesting* on the news this morning." Nicholas picked up a remote control from his desk and clicked on the TV inset in the far wall. It flared to life showing a scene from last night's charity event.

Charity chatted happily for the camera, while Logan turned away as something else caught his attention. When he didn't turn immediately back, the camera followed his line of sight and showed a shapely brunette gargoyle

Nicholas knew James had been involved with in London once upon a time.

Nicholas hit the pause button and the woman's intimate moment with Logan froze on the screen. "I think *this* is the reason Charity is having problems controlling Logan. He's fallen in love with someone else while we were all busy fucking Charity senseless and implanting her with the child of Destiny."

Astor's pale face turned even whiter as he ripped his gaze away from the screen and turned toward Nicholas. "But that's only Ariel Knight. She's the bodyguard James hired to protect Logan. There's nothing to worry about, I'll…"

"You fool." Nicholas let power flow through his fingertips and watched in satisfaction as Astor flew across the room like a rag doll. "Ariel Knight is a gargoyle. A warrior for God." Nicholas stood and walked around his desk to lean back against it so he could watch Astor struggle to sit up. "She works directly for the angel Gabriel. So, if she's involved, it only confirms that Logan is the one the prophesy refers to. When there is a gargoyle involved, you always worry about it or you'll find yourself a pile of ashes."

Astor wiped blood away from his bottom lip with the back of his hand and pulled himself up to stand unsteadily in front of Nicholas. "But if she's supernatural, then she can't be carrying the child of blood. Gargoyles have been around for centuries and none of them have ever become pregnant, according to James."

Nicholas snorted at the ignorance of this young one. "You are so weak, I don't know how James puts up with you. If you didn't still have some further use, I'd kill you here and raise the collective vampire IQ." Nicholas toyed with the idea of killing him anyway. His main plan for infiltrating James' lair had backfired when James revoked all of his access, even after Astor had invited him. But waste not, want not. Astor could still be of some limited use before Nicholas had the pleasure of killing him.

He brushed a piece of lint from his slacks and glanced back at Astor. "God created the gargoyles personally, and in the nine hundred years since their creation I've never heard of one of them giving birth either. If they were capable of reproduction, someone would have knocked them up long before now. They are quite attractive."

Astor seemed relieved that Nicholas agreed with him. Nicholas ended his comfort with a single sharp look. "But," he held up his hand stop sign fashion. "Since God released them from service, their status could have changed in that area. They can now glamour their wings and walk in the daylight. It would be just like God to allow them to carry the child of blood, thinking the infant would be safe with a pack of gargoyles protecting it."

Astor looked as if he were weighing his options. Speak and risk Nicholas' wrath or remain silent and get it anyway. Finally, his timid voice sounded, barely reaching even Nicholas' supernatural hearing. "So, we should kill her so Charity has a chance with Logan?"

Nicholas sighed and tried not to snap the younger man's neck in two. It would be immediately satisfying, but in the end would negate all his hard work at infiltrating James' organization. "It would be best if we can eliminate all three at the same time. The gargoyle and her spawn as well as Logan. That way we avoid the revenge of the child of blood and Logan is unable to make another child of blood."

"But, then how will Logan raise the child of destiny?" Astor asked in a quiet whisper.

"Once he's dead, Charity can go public with their engagement and the fact that she carries Logan's baby. The world will raise this child as Logan's. There's no risk of revenge in the prophesy if the child of blood dies with him."

Astor started for the door.

"Astor?" Nicholas waited until he turned back. "Try not to screw this up. My patience with you is at an end. Enlist some of the human servants to help so we have round the clock pressure on them to die."

Astor nodded and left.

Nicholas sighed. That was the interesting thing about the prophesy. It had a way of twisting around to happen the way it was meant to anyway. He would have to follow all of the nuances that would allow the Dark One to win. God always played fair, so there had to be a way for evil to reign. Nicholas just had to ferret it out, or his Master would be extremely displeased.

Everything seemed to be in place. Now if he could just figure out how to use the latest piece of prophesy he'd come across. *Convert the secret seed of darkness before the child of blood is birthed and evil shall reign.* He had tortured a priest for four days before he'd gotten that piece of the prophesy. He was determined it not go to waste.

*****

Logan closed the door behind him, muting out James and Dara's words. He took a cleansing breath and turned to face Charity. He wasn't sure what to say to her, but this wasn't going to work. His entire being screamed at him that he was going down the wrong path. And with the prophesy at stake, not to mention the well-being of his child, he had to go with his gut.

When he turned to face Charity, evil emanated off her in visible waves and fire sparked in the depths of her eyes. But when he blinked and looked again, he saw only Charity's lovely face, reddened with anger. *I've been having lots of strange visions lately. Maybe that succubus bite affected me more than I thought. Then again, maybe the universe is trying to tell me something.*

"You have no right to embarrass me in front of the

hired help. Let her threaten me and then drag me in here before I've had a chance to defend myself."

Charity's tantrum continued long after Logan stopped hearing her. Her words became a buzz inside his ears and a sense of foreboding and dread told him everything he needed to know. Logan stood in front of her for what seemed like hours until finally she wound down and stood staring at him with her arms crossed over her chest.

"What the hell are you staring at?" she demanded.

"Now that you've gotten that out of your system, why don't we sit down and discuss this like two civilized human beings." Logan gestured for Charity to precede him.

She watched him for a moment, but then turned and walked over to sit down on the king-sized bed. Logan followed, taking the armchair facing the bed.

"Charity," he began, his mind racing for what to say next. "I think it's time we put all our cards on the table."

"Finally," Charity harrumphed. "Let's discuss this and maybe you can get your priorities in order." She leaned back on the bed regally and eyed him with disdain and triumph.

Logan shook his head. She wasn't going to make this easy. A sense of profound peace flowed through Logan's body and he knew what he was about to do was the right path. He couldn't explain it logically, but he *knew*. "I'm sorry this has been so difficult for both of us. You and I never had any kind of a serious relationship. It was all about the sex for me. For you, the hope of propelling your career forward."

She looked stunned at the unexpected turn of the conversation. "Logan, how can you think I don't care for you?"

Logan cut Charity off with a gesture and stood. "Don't. The time for the bullshit has passed. You know every word of what I just said is true." He ran a hand through his hair and then straightened to face his future.

"I'm ashamed to say this, Charity, because I'm no longer the same person you knew. But I never meant to have you be anything to me other than a passing diversion. And if you weren't pregnant, we wouldn't even be having this discussion. We have absolutely nothing in common other than that we work in the same industry. I was a shallow and extremely selfish person. But then all of the attacks started—attacks that you know nothing about, because you aren't even interested enough in my well being to find out."

Charity opened her mouth to retort, but Logan mowed over her.

"That's how I met Ariel. And she changed my life. I finally found out what it was to truly care about someone else more than myself." Logan stepped forward to tower over Charity. "I will give our child my last name, my time, my money and my love. But I belong with Ariel, and I can't do *this* anymore." Using his index finger, he pointed back and forth between the two of them. "But I'd like for us to be friends and I want to very involved in my child's life."

He watched as Charity's eyes flashed fire and her whole body vibrated in anger. "You can't do this to me." She shot to her feet and stood toe to toe with Logan. "No man has ever turned me down. You have to rethink your priorities, or I'll go public with the fact that you got me pregnant and then won't even acknowledge your own child!"

Logan shook his head. Even pregnant, Charity only thought about herself. What had he ever seen in her? He dropped his eyes to her heaving chest and a small internal voice reminded him exactly what he had seen in her, as well as what he hadn't. *You got yourself into this mess because you lusted after an extremely fine set of tits and a nice tight ass.* He shook his head as once again he wished hindsight revealed itself beforehand.

"Charity, you can threaten me all you want, but even

a scandal like that would only improve my career. And besides, as soon as you try to bluff it through and take me to court, I'll be agreeing to support my child, asking for visitation and wanting to be a part of its life." He put a hand on each of her shoulders and met her angry gaze. "This is better for both of us. You aren't any happier with me than I am with you. You wanted what my career and songwriting could offer you."

Logan saw the calculation in Charity's eyes as she started to protest and then switched tactics. In the next instant, tears filled her eyes and her chin trembled. He resisted the impulse to applaud.

"But, Logan," she said and blinked just enough to allow a fat tear to roll down her cheek. "How can I live without you? You're my whole world. Please, just give me another chance. I can change." She pressed herself against him, tried sobbing convincingly as an excuse to rub her breasts against his chest.

This was the mother of his child and he'd willingly gone to her bed. They needed to make peace between them if this was going to work. He hugged her and she melted against him. Glancing down, he saw the feral smile flash across her face before she replaced it with more weeping. "Charity," he said, continuing to hold her and resting his chin on her head. "I think we can do this together if you'll drop the drama, be yourself and allow us to be friends."

She stiffened in his arms and then pulled away. "You bastard!" she shouted and then grabbed a vase off the nightstand and lobbed it at him.

Logan ducked as the vase narrowly missed his head and shattered against the wall behind him, sending crystal shards of glass flying around the room. "Charity," he began, but then had to duck again when a lamp followed the path of the vase. He ducked again, but when the crashing sound of the vase never came, he looked back to find Dara holding the vase unbroken and James holding Charity's wrist to keep her from throwing anything else.

She glowered at James for a long moment and then in a flash, the cool calculation was back. "I'll have my lawyer call you to discuss the details. You *will* be providing well for this child and if you want to see it, you'll make sure to keep me happy." She turned to face James. "Let go of my hand." When he finally complied, she said, "I no longer want to be cooped up with your white trash hired help and your pet manager. If you have no desire to be anything but *friends*, then I'm done here. I'll see you in court."

She turned to walk away, but Logan stepped into her path, blocking her. "You're in danger if it gets out that you're carrying my child right now. There have been several attempts on my life and I don't want anything to happen to you or the baby."

She glared up at him, all pretenses dropped for once. "I gave you a chance to play the humble father and husband. You've told me you prefer the help. I'll hire my own protection and send you the bill." She stepped around him and continued out the door.

Dara put her hand on Logan's arm to keep him from following her. "Odeda will shadow her until she finds someone to keep her safe."

"I think I'll call one of the members of my kiss to come and take her home. He can protect her as well as keep her entertained."

Logan sat on the bed long after James and Dara left him alone with his thoughts. He knew Charity was just using him and he knew he'd done the right thing. So why did he feel so miserable? At times like this, he missed his old self. The self who could walk away from a woman without regrets or conscience. But he also knew he couldn't raise a child while he was living a lie.

He dropped his head into his hands and did

something he hadn't done since his mother died.
   He prayed.

CHAPTER FOURTEEN

Logan stepped into the cockpit of the private plane and slipped into the co-pilot's seat. He buckled himself in and then glanced over at Ariel, who expertly operated the controls. After searching for something to say to break the silence, he said, "Can all gargoyles fly planes?" All that had come out of his mouth since they'd boarded the plane had been one-liners and lame icebreakers.

Ariel laughed, the sound of it bubbled over his skin in the enclosed space. "No. But a few years back a foreign diplomat we were protecting took flying lessons. So, I got to learn along with him."

Another heavy silence fell between them and Logan grimaced. After her sisters told her about the discussion he'd had with Charity, he'd hoped for a more intimate feeling between them. It was as if Ariel held him at arm's length for some reason, but he could tell it was with reluctance. He shifted in his seat to face her and tried again. "I'm surprised the others didn't want to wait an extra day and go back on the private plane – there's enough room for ten or twenty people back there." He nodded his head toward the back of the plane. When Ariel didn't respond, he tried again. "And thanks for staying with me. It's easier for me to be available now than to wait for a space in Tim's schedule."

Ariel glanced over at him, her face lit with excitement. "Are you kidding? It's not every day a girl gets to meet Tim McGraw. It was really sweet of him to sign those autographs for me to take to my sisters." She returned her gaze to the equipment panel and flipped a large toggle switch in front of her, which Logan suspected had something to do with altitude. "Besides, it's probably best if you and Charity aren't on the same plane until she cools down." The cool tone in her voice was obvious.

"So you did hear about that. I wondered since you

didn't say anything." When silence descended in the cockpit again, he sighed. *Should've stayed away from that subject.* He turned toward the window to see fluffy white clouds sail by. They looked like soft swirls of cotton candy and they were so close, he thought he could reach out and grab one.

Finally, Ariel cleared her throat. "Are you going to write that song for Tim?"

Grateful to have another chance at a conversation, Logan answered. "Probably. But I told him it wouldn't be ready for his next album. I have a few other songs already in my head I need to get down on paper before they are gone." *Mostly songs inspired by you...*

When he glanced over at her, it worried him to see her face devoid of color. He touched her arm and confirmed his suspicions. Her skin was clammy and cool to the touch. "Ariel? Are you okay?"

She didn't turn her head to look at him, only nodded and swallowed deliberately before answering. "Would you mind grabbing some of that tea in the black tin out of the galley and bringing me some hot water? I think I'm still getting over my...cold."

He detected the slight hesitation before the word "cold," which only assured Logan she kept something from him. But confronting her now when things were still fragile between them didn't seem like a good way to get her to open up. When she was ready to trust him again, Logan was confident she'd confide in him. And now that he'd straightened things out with Charity, they had all the time in the world.

Logan returned with the tea a few minutes later and handed her the steaming cup.

Ariel flipped another toggle switch on the console he assumed was the autopilot since the controls began to move on their own. She held the mug between her cupped hands as if basking in the warmth emanating through the ceramic.

After blowing away the steam, she sipped tentatively and then sighed.

Almost immediately, her color began to return and the knot that had formed inside his stomach began to loosen. "Wow, that's fast-working tea."

She nodded and took another sip. "Alonna's recipe for supernatural health."

Logan absently rubbed the spot on his inner thigh where Alonna's permanent purple lip prints remained. "I'm glad she gave you something that helped." *And yours isn't even permanent.*

He relaxed against his seat and began to study the cockpit. There were hundreds of gauges, knobs and levers, some of which he could decipher with common sense or from various movies he'd seen. But others reminded him of being inside an alien spaceship and they looked foreign and ominous.

The gentle sounds of Ariel's sips were the only punctuation to the drone of the engines, and for the first time since he'd boarded, the silence settled between them comfortable and warm.

The mountains in the distance grew larger and he returned his attention to inside the cockpit. Maybe she'd be willing to teach him to fly. It looked like just as much fun as driving his cars.

Suddenly a loud popping sound startled him, reminding Logan of the pop gun he had as a boy. The plane shuttered and a wrenching sound shimmied through the metal beneath his feet. Then without warning, the plane lurched to the left, smoke and the sound of rushing wind filling the air around them. Pain seared along his arm as hot tea spilled across Logan's bare skin. He looked over in time to see Ariel's head bang into the side of the cockpit with a resounding crack. A trickle of blood blossomed on her temple, but she wiped it away with the back of her hand and began checking the plane's gauges.

"We've lost the left engine," Ariel yelled over the noise. "We'll have to jump."

"Can't we restart it?" His voice sounded far away as if he was on the outside watching this happen instead of here in the thick of it.

"Lost as in it is no longer attached to the plane," she yelled over the din. "Someone must have planted a remote detonator."

"Shouldn't we start calling mayday on the radio?" he asked, swallowing his panic.

Ariel only shook her head. "No time." She unbuckled her belt and he followed her toward the back of the plane as quickly as he could. Logan couldn't understand why they couldn't still fly on one engine, but then another wrenching sound convinced him Ariel's course was the only way.

The scene in the back of the plane filled him with horror. There was a small hole in the side of the plane, the edges charred and black. Wind rushed past them whipping his hair and clothes against him in painful slaps. The plane lurched again and he realized they were in a steep dive. He stepped toward the compartment where the parachutes were kept, but Ariel shook her head and pulled him toward the hole.

"Hold on to me tight," she demanded.

Before he could let himself think about what he was doing, he threw his hands around Ariel's waist. Ariel threaded her hand through his back belt loop and jumped out through the hole taking him with her.

Icy air surged past them stinging Logan's face and arms, and then he made the mistake of glancing down. The ground sped toward him and he tasted bile and panic in the back of his throat. Then suddenly, he saw Ariel's wings materialize on her back. He breathed a sigh of relief, the impact of the resistance of the wings against the air jarred him so hard his teeth clacked together. But once he recovered, he realized that their descent had slowed.

"Are you hurt?" Ariel asked against his ear, her voice soft and tentative. He shivered at the feel of her warm breath caressing his skin.

Logan shook his head and reached up to check the cut on Ariel's temple. Blood coursed in a steady stream down the side of her face and he pressed his hand against the wound trying to staunch the flow. "You've lost a lot of blood. We need to land somewhere and get you medical attention." She nodded and he noticed her face looked pale and white. Blood continued to ooze through his fingers and he wished he could maneuver enough to pull off his shirt to press to the wound, but any movement he made seemed to require her to correct their course, so he tried to stay still.

An ear-splitting explosion made them both jump and he almost lost his grip on Ariel. He anchored his arms around her neck, careful not to limit the motion of her wings and craned his neck to try to see the source of the explosion.

In a valley between two large mountains, the remains of their plane still blazed. Logan swallowed hard as he realized that without Ariel he'd probably be down there with the wreckage. He breathed a sigh of relief as Ariel continued past the wreckage and finally set them down in a small clearing surrounded by pine trees.

"I never thought I'd be so happy to have my feet on firm ground again," he said.

Ariel smiled up at him weakly and then panic shot through him as her eyes fluttered closed and she sagged against him.

*****

Ariel woke to the smell of pines and a crisp breeze caressing her face. The tittering of birds and skittering sounds of small animals sounded softly all around her.

Hazy light filtered in through her closed eyelids, letting her know it was either dusk or dawn. She took mental stock of herself and realized she wasn't in any pain, other than a headache, and was lying on a soft, cushiony bed of—pine needles by the feel of them through her shirt.

She reached out instinctively to her sisters, but her head pounded and she winced, the connection never completing.

Where is Logan? And how did I get here? Wherever here is...

She slitted open her eyes and saw a cerulean blue sky through a maze of pine tree branches, which swayed gently in the wind. The sky to the west was brighter, telling Ariel the sun was setting not rising.

"Ariel."

She turned her head in the direction of Logan's voice and smiled as relief washed over her, even as her head protested the sudden movement. What kind of protector was she if she passed out and left her charge vulnerable? But at least she apparently got him to the ground safely and he didn't look any worse for the wear.

Logan knelt by her side and helped her sit up. "How's your head?" he asked, examining her temple.

She hissed as he touched a sore spot. "It was a dull roar before you touched it," she snapped and then instantly regretted her outburst. Apparently, plane crashes left her a tad cranky.

Regardless, Logan's face blossomed into a blinding smile. "If you're that feisty, it looks like you'll live. It could have been worse," he said gesturing to her temple. "I kept pressure on it until the bleeding stopped. But I was really worried." He handed her a silver beer can. "It's all I could find to put water in, drink it. You need to hydrate."

Ariel took the can and sipped so she didn't make herself sick. She looked past him and realized they were sitting on the edge of a small clearing. Her earlier deductions had been correct—they were in a forest. But where? Her memories of the explosion and their flight to the ground were hazy. A few snatches flashed through her mind of explosions, Logan's face, and the ground hurtling toward her. But she had a hard time putting them in order or making much sense out of them. She recalled nothing about actually landing safely. "I don't remember a lot from the crash. How long have I been out?"

Logan leaned back against a tree trunk. "Almost twenty-six hours. I was concerned about a concussion when I couldn't wake you up." He leaned over and took her chin between his long fingers. "You don't know how happy I am to see you open your eyes." Logan leaned slowly closer.

Panic skittered up Ariel's spine and she wrenched her chin from his grasp. If she let him get too close, she'd be tempted to tell him about the baby. But she couldn't, especially not with the newest piece of prophesy Alonna told them. Too much was at stake.

Placing a hand against her stomach, she instantly connected to the new life within her for the first time since she'd found out. She would do whatever it took to protect this child, even if it meant keeping its existence from Logan. And even if that fact alone would tear at her heart.

Ariel looked up to see a hurt expression raw on Logan's face.

Firming her resolve for her unborn child, she changed the subject. "Any idea where we are? I can't remember any landmarks from yesterday."

Logan was silent for so long she thought he wouldn't answer. "Well, as far as I can tell, we are somewhere in Northern Arizona."

"How do you know?" Ariel rubbed at her sore temple and then leaned back against a tree, facing Logan.

He stretched out his long legs and crossed them at

the ankle. "I saw the Grand Canyon as we flew over yesterday."

"We didn't fly over the Grand Canyon, our flight plan was a bit south of that."

Logan grinned. "I didn't say the *plane* flew over the canyon—I said *we* did. Or at least close to it."

Ariel concentrated and tried to remember anything from their escape from the plane, but her mind remained a blank void. Frustration running rampant, she stood, handed him the can and stepped toward the clearing. Logan seemed content to watch her in silence, and she wasn't sure if she was disappointed or grateful. On one hand, a comforting touch from Logan could take her mind off her frustrations, but on the other hand, it would crumble her already shaky resolve.

She stood and clearing her mind, she visualized her wings. As they materialized on her back, the solid weight of them forced her to adjust her stance so she didn't topple over. Flapping them experimentally, she winced.

"My wings are a little sore," she said more to herself than Logan. He continued to watch her, taking in every movement and she turned away from his intense scrutiny. Flexing her wings gingerly, she extended them open as far as they would go. But even in the small clearing, they kept snagging on the trees, so she had to keep angling between the branches to open them to their full ten-foot extension. After one last stretch, she returned them to their tattoo form and rolled her shoulders. "I guess that will have to do until I can find a gargoyle-friendly Jacuzzi."

Ariel's stomach rumbled. Logan stood and stepped toward her, nodding toward her stomach. "I was just getting ready to build a fire and then find us some breakfast when I saw you were awake."

Food sounded terrific, but Ariel had more important issues on her mind. She grabbed Logan's arm as a wave of nausea roiled through her. He steadied her, but then the strong taste of bile rose in her throat and her mouth watered, so she pulled away and made it to a nearby tree before her stomach emptied itself. When the spasms finally eased, she turned to find Logan there to support her and help her back to the side of the clearing to sit.

He squatted in front of her and captured her gaze in his steady one. His blue grey eyes were soft and concerned and she resisted falling into them.

"What are you keeping from me, Ariel?" His gaze never wavered and gave her no room to look away. "I know there's something wrong." His voice was mesmerizing and she could almost feel it caressing her skin.

Not able to meet his concerned gaze and lie, she looked down at the blanket of pine needles on the forest floor. "I've just got a supernatural form of the flu, and now I've lost Alonna's herbs, so I'll have to deal with the symptoms. Or maybe I just sipped the water too fast."

He made no move to stand and his gaze settled over her like a heavy weight. After holding out as long as she could, she looked up, not at all surprised to see him still studying her. "I'll be fine. Really," she insisted, when he remained silent and motionless. "I just need to heal so I can contact my sisters."

Logan's brow furrowed, his dark expression a striking contrast to his sandy blonde hair. "You can't contact them?"

"Don't worry, I'll figure out how to get us out of here." Her thoughts turned to formulating a plan to get them back home.

She was shocked when suddenly, Logan loomed so close his breath feathered against her face and his hands gripped her upper arms. His eyes had gone dark and hard and she could tell he resisted the impulse to shake her. "You arrogant female," he said, his voice low and dangerous. "I can find my own way out of the wilderness. I'm not some helpless child you found orphaned on the side of the road. I'm concerned because if you can't contact your sisters, it means you're hurt badly and I have no way of getting you proper care. And I don't even know what care you need because you're too damned pig-headed to trust me enough to tell me what's wrong with you." He huffed out a frustrated breath and stood.

She watched, stunned, as he stalked off toward the center of the clearing, where a charred ring of rocks already stood. He began gathering twigs and wood for the fire. The truth of his words pierced her like angry daggers. She treated him as if he was helpless and she had definitely withheld information. She pushed away her guilt at the latter, but she admitted fault on the former.

A picture of Logan fighting the zombies popped into her mind and she smiled. She could still visualize perfectly how calm and competent he looked holding the shotgun, even when the vampire attacked. No one seeing him then would ever think of him as helpless.

"Logan..." she began. "I'm sorry. I didn't mean to treat you like you were helpless."

Logan continued to arrange the wood inside the rock circle and then turned to her expectantly. "And?"

Ariel smiled at him reluctantly. This frustrating man held her heart, and all the prophesies in the world couldn't change that. Even if it prevented her from being totally honest with him. "And I'll even admit I'm pig-headed...at times."

He returned her smile. "And?" he asked, his voice a sultry invitation.

And we made a baby I'll cherish forever. Aloud she said, "And I'm fine...really. Gabriel said this would take a few months to get out of my system, but then I'll be good as new." At least she hadn't lied. Gabriel *had* told her exactly that.

Logan searched her face and when his smile widened, she let out a breath of relief. He stood and closed the distance between them until he knelt in front of her once again. "I'm glad you're all right." His eyes bored into hers with an intensity that made her skin tingle and her breath catch.

He cleared his throat, and reached out to trail a calloused finger lightly along her jaw line. "I should've found the courage to say this on the plane—at least before it crashed." He grinned, mischief dancing in his eyes. "I'm sure you've heard it from Dara, but I want you to hear it from me."

Ariel's swallowed against a lump inside her throat. She *had* heard about Charity and Logan's fight from Dara. But the words she'd been dying to hear since Charity came into their lives now threatened the balance between good and evil. It almost sounded like a cosmic soap opera. But unfortunately, it was very real and had become her life.

She couldn't be with Logan because he couldn't raise their child. And both her heart and her hormones needed to remember that.

Oblivious to Ariel's inner turmoil, Logan continued and shifted closer. So close, she could smell the musky scent that was uniquely Logan. "I love you, Ariel. Charity was never anything but a diversion to me and I'm a different man since you've come into my life."

The sun sank lower and the dusk raised the feeling of intimacy around them. A band squeezed around her heart so hard she thought it would explode. The skin on the back of her neck ruffled, breaking the spell of the moment. Her head snapped up in an automatic gesture to better scent the unseen enemy.

"What is that?" Logan whispered. The smell of pure evil so strong that even Logan seemed to sense it.

Ariel stood, keeping Logan behind her and whatever she sensed in front of her. "Vampires. Several from the smell of them."

"Smell, hell. All the skin on the back of my neck is about to crawl off." Logan stepped even with Ariel and pulled a hunting knife with a wicked looking blade from his boot. "I know, aim for the heart."

Ariel stared and then chuckled. "You're just full of surprises, aren't you?"

"Flying on private planes definitely has perks." Logan grinned over at her, and her heart melted.

"Do you always carry that?"

"I'm a country boy. We never go anywhere unprepared. We're like boy scouts, only better." He grinned at her, his lopsided grin creeping past her defenses.

Once again, she'd underestimated him. Ariel swore it would be the last time. But she also swore she'd keep him as far out of harm's way as possible. "Let's go see what's hunting us. Because I'll bet they're the same ones who put the detonator on our engine."

Logan adjusted his grip on his knife. "Vampire for dinner, it is."

*****

Odeda ran into Logan's living room and found Dara and Kefira sitting on the sofa discussing the awards ceremony, a cozy fire blazing in the fireplace beside them. At her arrival, they both fell silent and stared up at her, concern clear on both lovely faces.

"Charity is gone. Have either of you seen her?" Odeda demanded, her breath coming in short gasps since she'd done a running search of Logan's entire property already.

Kefira bolted to her feet and shook her head. "I saw her in her room a few hours ago, she said she was going to read and then go to bed. How did she get past all three of us without being noticed?"

Odeda ground her teeth in frustration. "I could care less if that spoiled bit of plastic fell off the planet, but Logan's baby—the child of blood—needs to be protected."

Dara, always the voice of reason, spoke up. "Let's contact Ariel and let her know to keep an eye out for Charity." She turned toward Kefira. "When are Ariel and Logan supposed to be back?"

"Charity told me Logan's message said they'd get in late tomorrow."

Odeda nodded. "I'll contact her." She closed her eyes and concentrated since it was harder to pinpoint Ariel at this much of a distance. Her sister's presence hovered just out of reach. Odeda could tell she was alive, but she couldn't connect to communicate. Opening her eyes, Odeda glanced up and met her sister's worried expressions. "I can't reach her. Something's wrong."

Odeda waited impatiently while both Kefira and Dara tried to reach Ariel. But she knew she would've done the same thing in their place.

Kefira growled low in her throat. "Charity. That bitch lied to us about Logan and Ariel."

All three sisters exchanged a practiced nod and then stepped forward to join hands to form a circle. Power sparked through Odeda and flowed out to both Kefira and Dara. Their power doubled back to fill her body. Of their own accord, her wings materialized on her back and her skin slowly began its transformation back to stone.

Humans came from dust and returned to dust, but the gargoyles—they came from stone and only became dust upon their deaths. But all of their power stemmed from the stone.

As the last of her body flowed from flesh into cold, white granite, Odeda opened her senses and allowed herself to merge with her sisters. Their joint stream of power snaked out, seeking the last part of themselves—seeking Ariel.

"Be careful not to touch Ariel with the power or she'll turn to stone and kill the baby," Dara warned.

Odeda sent her wordless consent through the stream of power and received Kefira's in return. Their bodies left behind, their joint consciousness flowed up through the roof and out into the early Texas morning.

In this form, they couldn't feel the wind against their bodies or the dwindling rays of the sun as it sank beyond the horizon, only the utter cold that permeated them in their stone forms. But their destination pulled at them like a magnet. They raced through the sun kissed sky faster and faster until only a blur of color and sensation was visible.

After what seemed like only seconds, they hovered over a large forest of pine trees. Their energy moved slower now as all three of them sensed danger.

"She's close by," Kefira said inside Odeda's head.

"And so are several vampires," added Dara.

Odeda glanced down through a space in the canopy of pine branches and saw both Ariel and Logan look up to search the sky. Both seemed unharmed and the joined consciousness of the sisters breathed a sigh of relief.

"Ariel?" they tried together.

Ariel nodded but tapped her temple. Odeda received a flash of pain and frustration at Ariel not being able to contact her sisters.

"Is the baby all right?" Dara asked.

Ariel placed her hand over her stomach and nodded. Unable to hear the exchange, but sensing something, Logan whispered something to Ariel. When she nodded, he waved toward the invisible trio.

"He senses our connection extremely well for a human. There's got to be something supernatural in his family tree somewhere."

Odeda, joined with Dara, gleaned the knowledge of Logan's connection with James and would have smiled if she were in her solid form. *"Of course. I should have seen it earlier. With ancient vampire blood, he'll definitely be sensitive to all things supernatural."*

Odeda sent reassurance through their connection to both Ariel and Logan. Then they relaxed and let the pull of their bodies drag them back without conscious thought.

Odeda's consciousness snapped back into her body like a rubber band and her skin stung as she adjusted to the confinement of the stone. Taking a moment to savor the healing quality of the stone, Odeda allowed the stone to flow away leaving behind her human form.

"Where are they?" James asked startling Odeda, and by the way Kefira and Dara jumped, both of them as well.

Odeda turned to James. "A few miles south of the Grand Canyon."

"They're all right," Kefira added. "But there are several vampires close by and Charity lied to us about when Ariel and Logan's plane was supposed to get in."

"God help me…," murmured James.

Odeda saw only a blur and then nothing where James had stood a second before. "I'm going to stake his feet to the floor. I hate it when they do that."

Dara stepped forward, her wings fluttering in an unconscious gesture. "Stake him later. Right now, we'll have to fly hard just to catch up."

CHAPTER FIFTEEN

Logan adjusted his grip on his hunting knife and stepped toward the stench of evil.

"Wait." Ariel grabbed his arm to stop his progress. She seemed to search for the correct words before she began. "I'm not underestimating you. I've learned my lesson with that. But I'm better equipped to fight vampires than you are."

"We don't have time for this discussion," Logan said and began to push by her.

Ariel refused to release her grip and as much as it galled Logan to admit it, he was no match for her supernatural strength.

"Actually we do. The sun hasn't fully set, we have about ten minutes. I'll know when they get close."

He concentrated and was surprised he was able to sense the distance inside his head. "Wow, I see what you mean."

He hadn't said it with sarcasm, but Ariel narrowed her eyes as if she didn't believe him. "Anyway, about the vampires…"

Logan glanced over at his knife and wished for his shotgun. Sighing, he admitted, "You're right. But just because you are better equipped to fight them, doesn't mean the vamps will let me sit on the sidelines quietly—not even if I was willing to. Which I'm not."

Ariel turned to face him, her brows knit with concern, her full lips curved down into a frown. "How about a compromise?"

"Fair enough. What did you have in mind?" Compromise would be better than her asking him to let her fight them alone.

"My wings are pretty indestructible. Not impervious, but almost. If we fight back to back, they won't be able to surround you, and you'll get some protection from my wings." After a slight pause, she added, "And it will help keep me from being surrounded as well."

Logan knew she'd added the last comment for the benefit of his ego. He'd seen her when she fought the zombies. Being surrounded didn't necessarily hinder her. He sighed. She made an effort to sooth his pride, the least he could do was let her. "Bring your wings out and let's test it. I still need to be able to maneuver, or the knife is useless."

Ariel turned her back on him. Her fairy wings tattoo glinted softly in the waning daylight and he couldn't resist stepping close and tracing the edges gently with his fingers. Ariel shivered and then spun away from him, her face flushed, her breathing labored.

"Now isn't the time for that," she snapped at him.

He let her see his satisfied smile. "Maybe not. But it proved you're not immune to me. So, let's see those wings."

She stood glaring at him for a full minute and then suddenly her wings just *were*. It still amazed Logan to watch them materialize out of nothing. Extending his index finger, he twirled it slowly in the air until she turned her back on him again. He faced away from her and stepped back so her wings protected his sides and his back.

"Try swinging the knife. And don't worry. My wings are tough enough to withstand that blade. It takes something heavily supernatural to even nick them."

Logan stabbed at an invisible partner a few times, trying to ensure a full range of motion. Then he swung his hand back over his shoulder to start a larger swing. His hand connected with Ariel's wing and bounced off returning the knife in a downward arc toward his stomach. He stopped the motion of the knife just in time to keep from impaling himself.

Ariel coughed, a bad cover for her laugh. "Yeah, I'd watch that. They're pretty rubbery."

Logan saw Ariel's smirk as she looked back over her shoulder and through her wings. He ignored her. Curious, he reached out and touched her wing. It was warm and smooth, almost soft. But when he squeezed, it had the consistency of a car tire. Hard and rubbery.

"So, what do you think?" she asked.

"Cool," he said chuckling and squeezing the wing again between his fingers like a brand new stress ball.

Ariel snorted and shook her head. "I meant about the fighting back to back."

The reek of evil filled Logan's nostrils and he coughed as panic skittered up his spine. "It will have to do. They're here." Darkness descended quickly, but the moon shone full, so they could still see. Stars began to dot the black velvet of the sky.

"They're close," she corrected. "If they are projecting fear, there's an ancient with them. Be very careful."

"Let's go."

They made their way down the side of a hill and into a small clearing next to a stream.

"Let's make a stand here," Logan whispered. "Enough room to fight without getting caught from someone hiding. And it's the best use of the moonlight so we can see to fight."

"You mean, some-*thing*," Ariel said. "But I agree."

"Can't we just fly out of here if they get too close?" Logan asked.

"Unfortunately, vamps can fly too."

"Damn, it's always something."

Logan's skin began to crawl as if hundreds of bugs crept just under the surface trying to escape. He shuddered. *Get a grip or they'll beat you.* Taking his own advice, he closed his eyes, took a calming breath and let it out slowly. When he opened them again, the creepy sensation was gone along with his fear. Only his concern for Ariel remained.

The sound of clapping hands broke the stillness of the forest and a man in an expensive suit stepped out of the trees and into the clearing. Logan couldn't tell if the material was grey or blue, but he looked out of place among the conifer and pine needles. But even beyond that, Logan had the nagging feeling he'd met him before. The man's presence reeked evil and ancient. This must have been the vampire Ariel meant.

"Bravo, Logan. I'm impressed," said the man, interrupting Logan's thoughts.

The deep voice reverberated through the clearing and tickled at the edges of Logan's memory. He'd heard this voice before, but he couldn't remember where.

"And forgive me for being rude. Greetings to your gargoyle whore as well." The man sketched a mock bow toward Ariel, a sardonic smile plain on his face.

Logan took a step forward and then realized he was being goaded as Ariel grabbed his arm and the vampire burst out laughing. The cultured laugh irritated Logan and ripped across his skin like talons. "Who the hell are you?"

"You may call me Nicholas. After all, we're almost related."

Ariel tightened her grip on Logan's arm, no doubt to keep him from doing something stupid, like getting into a pissing contest with an ancient vampire. He laid his hand over hers and squeezed it in reassurance. He had no intention of dying today or of letting anything happen to Ariel. Although it would be satisfying to break a few of the blinding white vampire teeth grinning at them that were visible even in the moonlight.

Turning his attention back to Nicholas, he said, "I don't see how that's possible."

"You and I both shared your mother." His cultured laugh rang out again and Logan saw a flash of his mother's face, her eyes cold and staring, her mouth still open in a silent scream. "You may have had her first, but I definitely had her last. And she was delicious, I might add."

Logan saw himself as a young boy running down the stairs in his pajamas, following his mother's screams. When he reached the bottom of the stairs, he saw Nicholas bent over his mother, drinking from the gaping wound in her neck. He opened his mouth to scream, but no sound came out.

"Logan!"

His legs still rubbery and weak, Ariel's voice brought him back to reality. After years of his subconscious bubbling scraps of memories into his nightmares and even his waking hours, he finally had all of the puzzle pieces. He glared at Nicholas with all of the hatred and pain of losing his mother.

"Interesting," said Nicholas and took another small step forward, half his face erased in shadows. "I erased your memory all those years ago. No one has ever broken through my mind block. Care to tell me who your father is? Your mother refused, that's why she's dead." Emphasis on the last word made it feel like a knife thrust straight into Logan's gut.

Logan wouldn't tell this man who is father was even if he knew. There was only his mother. And his aunt and uncle said they never knew who'd fathered him. But now he knew who'd taken his mother from him. "Go to hell, you bastard." Ariel placed a comforting hand against his back and a measure of calm stole over him from the touch. Letting Nicholas stir his emotions would get them both killed. He'd have time to grieve for his mother after he'd taken his revenge.

"Let's all go, shall we?" Nicholas laughed and it echoed around them in a macabre whirlwind. "Once I kill you and the child of blood, the world will belong to the Dark

One."

The sky suddenly darkened further with angry wisps of clouds that floated in front of the moon. Streaks of lightning punctuated the tension with angry barks of thunder.

Logan sensed more vampires behind them and stepped behind Ariel to assume their back-to-back fighting stance. Immediately, several vampires stepped out into the clearing, all of them dressed for a boardroom instead of the forest. In another circumstance, he'd think it funny, but the situation was too dire to see the irony now.

Ariel assumed a fighting stance behind him, but she kept her wings slightly extended to offer him maximum protection. He appreciated the gesture. She'd been right about him not being equipped to fight these creatures. He still remembered when the vampire at his ranch had thrown him against the wall like he was a rag doll. And that was just one, not the dozen or so that surrounded them now.

Alonna's words sounded inside his head with unnerving clarity.

"Your prophesy—and mind it well—is this. If you raise the son of your blood, he will become a champion for good. If you raise the daughter of destiny, she will swallow the world in darkness. If you cease to exist before your fated time, the son of your blood will avenge you with great rivers of dark blood and the heavens will shine on him."

Keeping an eye on all of the new vampires, he said, "If I cease to exist before my fated time, Nicholas, the son of my blood will avenge me and the heavens will shine on him. Meaning you'll lose." He said a silent prayer that Charity was still safe at the ranch with Dara and Odeda.

"That's only if he's still alive to avenge you." His eerie laugh rang out again, bristling along Logan's skin. "Take them," Nicholas barked to his vamp army.

Ariel's movement behind him told him she already fought behind him. The vampire directly in front of Logan winked at him, although he wasn't sure how he knew that in the dark. Then the vamp became a streak of light tracking directly toward him, but he traveled in slow motion. Logan tracked the vamp's progress and as soon as he materialized, Logan plunged the knife into his heart. There was a loud popping sound as the vamp's body disintegrated and Logan screwed his eyes shut against the foul ashes.

"Fools," Nicholas called. "I told you he has something ancient and supernatural in his bloodline. Your vampire tricks won't work on him."

Shock traveled through Logan at the statement. Could his unknown father have been an ancient being? *I wonder if James knows who it is?* After all, he was the only ancient being Logan knew besides the gargoyles. Then his body froze as another thought percolated through his brain. James had always been extremely protective of him. Had even treated him like a brother. Or had Logan just taken it for brotherly concern because he thought of James as a peer?

"Logan," Ariel called, breaking him out of his thoughts. "Watch your right side."

Logan slashed his knife to the right in time to slice a long hole in a very expensive looking suit jacket. It didn't injure the vampire, but it did make him angry. The vampire lunged for him, talons extended, lips curled back to expose his fangs, but Ariel's wing tip extended as she executed a front kick and it knocked the vamp back to land on his rear. As Ariel had to lunge to avoid a hit from another enemy, Logan almost lost his balance and fell outside of the protective area between her wings. But just as he began to fall, her left wing righted him. "Damn, you're dexterous with those things!"

"I've had nine-hundred years of practice," she called over her shoulder.

They fought for what seemed like hours and Ariel kept extending her wingspan to keep the vamps from getting too near Logan. And while his pride smarted at not being more involved in the fight, he knew she was right. He was no match for these beings.

"Enough!" Nicholas' deep voice reverberated through the clearing.

The remaining vampires retreated to a loose perimeter surrounding Ariel and Logan.

Nicholas stepped forward. "We've wasted enough time here today." He held his arm out to the side and a new vamp emerged from the trees dragging Charity by one arm. Charity cried and whimpered, her makeup smeared down her face, her blouse torn.

"Damn!" muttered Ariel under her breath.

A band around Logan's heart squeezed painfully. *The baby. God, please. Protect my baby. Take me instead, or use me how you wish, just please keep him safe.*

A peal of thunder rang out quieting the world around it in awe. One small crack in the cloud cover opened, allowing a larger stream of moonlight to peek through. Logan smiled to himself grimly. *I'll take that as a yes.*

"Let her go, unharmed, Nicholas, and you can have me."

Ariel clamped her hand around Logan's wrist. "Don't, Logan. He'll just kill you both."

Logan placed his hand over hers. "I have to do this. I can't let my child die. Just remember I'll always love you, Ariel." He leaned in to kiss her tenderly and saw the sadness and the desperation in her eyes. But she reluctantly removed her hand from his wrist.

"I find that an acceptable deal, Logan." Nicholas pulled Charity away from the lesser vampire and pressed her in front of him. His hand rested on her softly rounded stomach. "Step away from your gargoyle whore and we'll do a trade."

Logan gave Ariel's hand a final squeeze, took

several steps forward, and stopped. Nicholas pushed Charity and she stumbled forward toward Logan. "Charity, are you all right?"

She lurched against him, and he brought his arms around her to steady her. When she tipped her face up to look at him, the cruel smile that crawled across her face, made him stop short. So did the gun she pulled from behind her back.

She held the gun against his stomach and took a small step back. When she spoke, her voice was dangerous and low. "I'm perfectly all right, Logan. Especially since Nicholas has given *me* permission to kill you." She pushed her hair back over her shoulder, all the while keeping the gun trained steadily on Logan's stomach.

Fear washed through him as he tried to understand this new turn of events. "What are you doing? Put the gun down." He held his hands out to the side, palms open. "There's no reason to kill me. I need to be around to raise our child, remember?"

"Oh, you will. The child of Logan McAllister will be raised in the spotlight and will be the next prodigy of the music world. Especially after the tragic way her father died."

"Charity," he began, his eyes widening as he saw her squeeze the trigger, a smug smile curving her lips.

The deafening boom of the gunshot rang in his ears and the world slowed to molasses speed. He watched in petrified fascination as the bullet left the gun and crept toward him. He closed his eyes as he waited for the pain. But a whoosh of movement and a feminine grunt of pain caused him to open them again.

Ariel lay on the ground beside him, a large hole blossoming blood from her chest. She'd jumped in front of him to shield him from the bullet. "No!" He knocked the gun from Charity's hand and then retrieved it and rushed to

Ariel's side. He breathed a sigh of relief when she opened her eyes to look at him. The blue depths swam with pain, but she gripped the hand he offered. He pulled off his shirt and pressed it to the wound, but the hot thick fluid that was Ariel's life kept pouring forth. "Turn to stone," he whispered to her through his tears. "I'll protect you while you heal yourself."

"I can't," she said back. She reached up to cradle his face in her hand. "It will kill our baby."

"Bitch!" Charity screamed. "I *knew* you were carrying the child of blood. I'll kill both of you!" She started forward, but one of the vampires grabbed her around the waist and pulled her back.

"We need the child of destiny safe, hellcat," he told her.

Logan felt numb. Ariel carried the child of his blood. That was what she hadn't wanted to tell him, because she thought she carried the child of his destiny. So she'd kept it from him to try to protect him from raising the child, which would allow evil to rein. Everything finally clicked into place. A dangerous calm flowed through his veins and all his fear and doubt receded.

Logan stood over Ariel and faced Nicholas. Words flowed through his mind and knew he had to say them aloud. "I claim Ariel as the mother of my son—the child of blood. The child, who is blessed by God Herself. And I'll protect them both with my life and my eternal soul."

Nicholas growled low in his throat. "So be it." He gestured and the remaining circle of vampires began to tighten around them.

*****

James flew across the sky faster than he ever had in his long existence. The last rays of sunlight stung against his skin, but he ignored the irritating discomfort. He knew in the back of his mind, the only part still rational, that it would drain his power and he would be vulnerable to being noticed on modern radar. But the front of his mind had decreed he get to Logan as fast as possible, everything else be damned—even if he was sighted or shot down as a UFO or spy plane.

He opened a mental link he'd never used before, his link with his son, with Logan. If Logan's life were in danger, taking the chance another vampire would sense and understand their connection was worth the risk. The link snapped into being as if they had been using this form of communication since Logan's birth. James sensed a vampire charging Logan and used his own abilities to allow Logan to track the vampire's movements.

He returned his attention to flying and gauged how far away he still had to travel. Probably another ten minutes or so, he guessed. But James' parental joy was short-lived as he received a flood of anguish and emotional pain through their link. Concentrating, he allowed himself to see through Logan's eyes and the sight made him falter and lose altitude. Ariel lay dying, a gaping wound marring her chest, her eyes filled with love and pain.

James jerked as he fell into someone's arms and was propelled forward. He opened his eyes to see Dara's worried frown. He took a breath to tell them about Ariel and then realized through their link with her, they already knew. Feeling he had to say something, he said, "Thanks, I can't remote view and fly." He glanced to either side to see Odeda and Kefira flying hard, intent on their goal.

Dara's leaned close to his ear so the wind wouldn't steal her words. "We can't remote view, but we can feel her dying. You view, we'll fly."

James nodded and closed his eyes to concentrate. The rushing sky fell away, replaced by Logan's view of Nicholas. "Bastard!" he shook with fury and Dara's arms clamped around him more firmly. He forced himself to keep his eyes tightly shut so as not to sever the remote viewing link. For the benefit of the gargoyles, he said, "Nicholas, another ancient, and six other vamps are facing Logan and he's only armed with a hunting knife. Ariel has a chest wound, but Logan packed it with his shirt, so I can't tell what kind. She must be pretty weak if she's not healing herself."

"She can't, James." Dara's voice was sad and low. "It would kill the baby."

James' head snapped around, his eyes flying open wide to stare at Dara. "Baby?"

Dara nodded and continued to stare past him toward their destination.

The weight of the world settled on James' shoulders as everything suddenly made perfect sense. Ariel, his ex-lover was pregnant with his grandson.

He was the grandfather of the child of blood.

His heart swelled with emotion until he remembered that three people he loved were in the hands of Nicholas. James squirmed out of Dara's grip and continued flying on his own, willing himself to fly even faster.

Finally, the clearing came into view and James was happy he had excellent night vision. Logan stood over Ariel with his knife brandished before him. Covered in blood, probably his own, from the almost pristine condition of the vampires.

James angled into a dive, with the gargoyles on either side of him, just as Astor stepped forward and raked extended claws across Logan's chest.

"No!" James heard the word echo in his ears and only then did he realize it had come from him. Astor stared up at James with a smirk. Logan took one last stab at Astor and managed to wedge the hunting knife deep into Astor's jugular before falling to his knees. Astor's hands flew to his spewing wound and he stumbled away as Logan fell face first across Ariel's legs.

Rage and grief burned through James until his vision tinted with a red hazy of fury. He landed just behind Astor, knowing Dara would go immediately to Ariel and Logan. If anything could be done for them, Dara would do it. Astor, his hands still pressed to his spraying neck, turned to face James. Never faltering in his step, James extended his talons, plunged his hand into Astor's chest and pulled out his still beating heart. Astor's face showed shock and surprise just before he disintegrated into ash and blew away on the evening breeze.

James heard fighting around him and dimly understood that the gargoyles were fighting the lesser vampires. He knew they could handle it. His gaze never wavered from Nicholas.

"*He killed her...*" James stopped dead in his tracks as he heard Logan's voice through their still active connection. A picture flashed through his mind. It was Jaclyn, lying on the floor in her own blood, Nicholas leaned over her, drinking from her ruined neck. The picture faded to be replaced by the present day Nicholas. James knew Logan had found his mother dead. He never knew he'd seen her killer, but then Nicholas had probably erased his memory. James spent years trying to find out who had killed Jaclyn, but he'd always run into a dead end until now.

"Good evening, James." Nicholas smiled at him as if they were meeting on a street corner during a Sunday stroll. "I've waited over thirty years to find out who Jaclyn was rutting with. She had the signs of the prophesy even back then."

No emotion reached him but deadly calm. "I claim the right of vengeance." The ancient words spilled from his lips. It was a direct challenge between two equal vampires, which meant the fight would be just between them, to the death. "You, my brother of the original men turned, have defiled and killed my mate."

"Your *mate* shouldn't have been involved in the prophesy and neither should you."

James continued unheeded. "You have also injured my son and my son's son—the child of blood."

Nicholas' lips quirked. "Not to mention your ex-lover, the pretty gargoyle, eh, James?"

Nicholas laughed at his own joke and James punched him square in the face. Nicholas did stop laughing, but his eyes turned deadly. "I acknowledge my grievances and would like to add one more—your death."

James didn't bother to retort, but raked his hand across Nicholas' chest, shredding the cloth of his suit and the top few layers of skin. Killing or even injuring an ancient vampire was much more difficult than the younger vamps. This would be a long fight. He poured all of his rage and grief into every blow and found himself saying something he'd heard Logan say in bar fights. "Bring it on."

CHAPTER SIXTEEN

Ariel's heart constricted as she saw Logan's chest ripped open in front of her. She tried to will her broken body to stand, to protect him, but she had lost too much blood and was past the point of being able to make a choice. She'd already decided in favor of their child and now had to live with that choice—if she even lived through this. Her sisters would come for her, she was sure. But for the first time, she was afraid they would be too late, for the baby, for Logan and definitely for herself. Having no energy left for tears, she saw Logan fall to his knees beside her and then topple over to land on her legs, face down.

"Logan," she whispered. With the last of her strength, she reached down and laid her hand on top of his head. His hair felt soft and warm against her fingers. Memories of the times she ran her fingers through his hair while they made love came back to assault her. Maybe this was how heaven would be, getting to cherish the good memories she'd experienced in her long life.

Dimly she heard the sound of wings and then Dara's cool touch feathered across her forehead. "I'm here. Hang on."

"Check the baby and Logan first," she croaked.

"Saving the baby means saving you, so be quiet and conserve your strength." The iron behind Dara's words brooked no argument and Ariel relaxed and put herself in her sister's hands. The wound in her chest burned as Dara removed Logan's shirt and began to clear away the blood so she could assess the damage. Logan's weight shifted off her legs and as the cool air stole the warmth from where he'd lain, she felt bereft. "Logan," she whispered. Then Logan lay beside her, his hand in hers. She smiled. Her sisters, bless them, must know they'd want to be together. She threaded her fingers through his and received a sluggish squeeze from Logan.

She tried to turn her head, but her muscles wouldn't cooperate. The ground was cool and the last of her warmth seeped into it. All except where her hand touched Logan's. He was her lifeline and she held on for the sake of their child. "I love you, Logan," she whispered and hoped God would allow him to hear it as the last of her strength ebbed away.

Lord, Your will be done in all things. I've served you faithfully for centuries. I would ask that if it is within Your plan, please save Logan and our son.

*****

James staggered back from Nicholas' latest blow and spit a mouthful of blood into the dirt before straightening and lunging for his opponent once again. Sweat and the metallic tang of blood permeated the wind. They'd fought for what seemed like hours, but the moon hadn't moved in the sky, so it was probably only minutes. Both were bloody and shredded, their stamina waning.

"Our Master will win, James. You fight in vain. Why don't you join us, kill the child and his sire and all your transgressions will be forgotten." Nicholas ducked under James' blow, then pivoted on his right foot and caught James in the mouth with a left front snap kick.

James' head snapped back hard and a loud buzzing began in his ears. He shook his head to try to clear it. "The Dark One has not been my master for a very long time. I turned to God long ago, and it's to Her I pledge my life and allegiance."

Nicholas bared his fangs. "So much for the last tidbit of the prophesy, since I can now see you're the secret seed of darkness. As soon as I learned you were Jaclyn's lover, I knew you were the traitor. There's a whole branch of the prophesy around the traitor to the Dark One." Nicholas leapt forward snapping his fangs where James' throat had been only seconds before.

James stumbled back, out of reach of the deadly fangs, and lost his footing. He landed hard on his back, his breath whooshing out in a painful rush. He rolled to the right just in time to avoid another attack from Nicholas and then twisted back around to pin Nicholas to the ground, his face pressed into the pine needles lining the forest floor.

James plunged his hand through Nicholas' back and wrapped his hand around the engorged heart. Full of the blood of humans he'd terrorized and killed for the last nine hundred years. He squeezed and Nicholas winced. James leaned down near Nicholas' ear, but not so close as to be in range of his sharp incisors. "This is for Jaclyn and if it ends up being for Logan as well, I'll follow you into hell itself to extract my revenge."

James crushed the heart and then ripped it free of Nicholas' body. He tossed the mangled heart to the forest floor and then stood to ground it under his heel. But Nicholas was an ancient and there would be no disintegrating to ashes for him. Complete darkness descended like a heavy cloak and the air stilled to leave an eerie feeling of something to come.

James stepped back quickly as the ground around Nicholas' body cracked open. Flames directly from hell licked up around the inert form and only when engulfed in fire did the screams begin. James had killed two other ancients in his lifetime and knew that the Dark One punished failure cruelly, bringing the unlucky soul back to awareness as he burned them alive and only then took them back to hell.

After the final screams died away and the crack in the ground closed as if it had never been, the heavy cloak receded and moonlight and starlight shone once again. James finally allowed his exhaustion to overwhelm him. He turned to see Ariel and Logan lying on the ground side by side, their hands linked. Stumbling closer before falling to his knees on the ground, he sought out Dara, his unasked question clear in his expression.

When Dara refused to meet his gaze, but only shook her head, his heart broke and tears welled up to stream down his face unchecked. This was the first time he'd cried since he'd been human, more than nine hundred years ago. A great emptiness welled up inside him and a desperation like he'd never known, not even during his years as an evil vampire, threatened to choke him.

James raised his open palms to the heavens and spoke directly to God. "I beg you, Lord. You spared my life centuries ago when I tried to walk into the sun. Since then, I've pledged my life to you and served you loyally." His voice echoed in his own ears across the still air around them. He pressed his fists to his eyes, hopelessness suffocating him. "I know my life isn't worth even one of theirs, but please, I beg you. Take me and let the three of them live."

When only silence greeted him, he collapsed forward in defeat.

A spare breeze played against his skin and he sat up and opened his eyes. The sky steadily lightened until a ray of soft light shone down over him, a beacon in the darkness. The rays warmed him and chased away his despair. The scent of cinnamon tickled his senses and he turned to look behind him and directly into the cerulean gaze of Gabriel.

Kefira, Dara and Odeda knelt and placed their right fists over their hearts.

Gabriel nodded at them and they rose before he turned his attention back to James. "Dark Redeemer, the Lord has granted your prayer." Gabriel's smile was kind, but laced with sadness.

Gabriel stepped away from the circle of light past Kefira and Dara and toward the still forms of Ariel and Logan. He knelt between them and placed a hand on each of their chests, a soft glow emanating from the contact. Then finally, Logan and Ariel stirred and slowly sat up. "Be well, your lives have been spared." Only then, did Gabriel stand and return to James.

Gabriel reached out a hand to rest it lightly against James' forehead. The hand warmed where it touched him and all of the energy left in James surged forward toward the contact and up into the angel. "Thank You," James whispered before his awareness disappeared.

*****

The burning in Logan's chest slowly receded until he knew his body had been totally restored. Ariel's hand gripped his tightly and he opened his eyes to see Gabriel looming over them. "Be well, your lives have been spared," he said in a kind voice before rising and returning to James.

Logan wanted to ask what happened while he'd been unconscious—he was afraid to ask if he'd been dead. He wasn't sure if he wanted the answer.

Gabriel stood and walked toward James, then reached out to lay a gentle hand on his head. James whispered something Logan couldn't hear and then collapsed at Gabriel's feet in a heap.

"James!" Logan lurched to his feet and rushed to James' side. Gently turning him over, Logan cradled James' head in his lap, then looked up into Gabriel's steady gaze. "Why?" he whispered, pain and betrayal flowing through him. He sensed more than heard Ariel step close behind him and lay a comforting hand on his shoulder.

Gabriel looked down at James, compassion clear in his gaze. "God granted James' last request. James offered to trade himself for the three of you." Gabriel gestured to encompass Logan, Ariel and the baby.

Conflicted emotions flowed through Logan. James, the father he hadn't know he had, willingly traded his life for all of them. Logan remembered all the times James had been there for him as a manager, a best friend and a confidant and emotions rose up to form a large lump in his throat. "Why didn't he ever tell me? About my mother, about him…about everything?"

Gabriel sighed and stepped forward to kneel next to Logan. "He and Jacqueline were involved for a few years and then his assignments took him elsewhere. Five years later, she sent him an urgent message that she thought her life was in danger. He rushed back to find her dead on the floor and a son he didn't even know he had."

"Why didn't he keep me with him? I could have grown up with a father." Logan studied James' face looking for similarities to himself. He obviously inherited his mother's coloring, but now that he looked for it, he saw he and James shared the same shape face, high cheekbones and even the cleft in their chins.

"James knew if he claimed you, your life would always be in danger, so he took you to your aunt and uncle and made sure to come back into your life when he could help you the most—as an aspiring songwriter and musician. That way he had a reason to keep you close without putting you in danger."

Ariel stroked a hand along the back of Logan's neck. "That sounds like James."

"God always has reasons for whatever She does. And not to sound callous, but now that the existence of the child of blood has been proclaimed, he will need an appointed protector." Gabriel met Logan's gaze and then glanced down at James.

Logan didn't understand what Gabriel was trying to tell him with the pointed gesture, but he knew it was something. But before he could ask what, Ariel broke in.

"Our child has protectors—me, Logan, my sisters—"

"Lioness of God," Gabriel chided. "You never did have much patience. You and Logan cannot be the child's protectors because as the parents of the child of blood, you have your own destinies and purposes. As do your sisters, although all of you will be very helpful in watching out for the child."

Logan broke in before the conversation could follow any more tangents. "What exactly are the requirements for a protector of the child of blood?"

Gabriel beamed at him as if he were a prize pupil. "The protector must be able to withstand attack by all supernatural beings and have great stamina. One of ancient blood would be preferred purely for experience and strength. And they must be able to care for the child 'round the clock."

Kefira started to say something, but Logan cut her off. "Someone like an ancient vampire, maybe?"

A collective silence fell over the group as everyone realized where this conversation was headed.

Ariel's hand tightened on Logan's shoulder as she addressed Gabriel. "An ancient vampire who no longer had restrictions of avoiding sunlight and drinking blood would be ideal."

Gabriel grinned over at Ariel like they shared a private joke. "True. But the appointment of the protector is purely up to the two parents of the child. God has given them leave to protect the child as they see fit."

Logan smiled over at Ariel and nodded for her to continue. "As the mother of the child of blood and with the consent of the child's father, we request James Wellington as the child's protector. But in order for him to carry out his duties effectively, he would need to be able to withstand sunlight and have his reliance on blood removed."

Gabriel looked at Logan for confirmation. "I concur."

"Then it is done." Gabriel stepped away from Logan and dropped to his knees, his eyes downcast.

The whitest light Logan had ever seen beamed into existence in front of him until it coalesced into the form of a beautiful woman with skin the color of creamy coffee. Her dark hair flowed around her and she seemed to be clothed only in shifting light that kept her appropriately covered no matter her movements.

She smiled and the world around them visibly brightened, flowers suddenly blooming at her feet. Only then did Logan realize everyone else in the clearing knelt with bowed heads.

He quickly averted his gaze and dropped to his knees beside Ariel.

Her voice sounded like birdsong carried on the wind when she spoke. "You've done well, Logan. Make sure to take good care of my gargoyles and your child."

The words caressed Logan's soul and he finally lifted his gaze to see her step toward James.

"Dark Redeemer, rise and fulfill your duties as protector of the child of blood. I don't make personal appearances for just anyone." She leaned down to brush a kiss across his forehead before vanishing.

James' eyes fluttered open, almost stopping Logan's heart. "James," he whispered.

"You bastard," James said to Gabriel with a smile.

"I'll second that," Kefira said as Logan helped James sit up.

Logan noticed all the gargoyles glaring at the angel. Odeda spoke first. "What the hell was with all the theatrics?" she demanded. "Why didn't you just tell us?"

Gabriel laughed and the inevitable placid calm descended on everyone as it always did when the angel laughed. Logan shook off the feeling and waited for the angel's answer.

"I can't get involved in the ins and outs of the prophesy that don't concern me. I have a specific part to play in Her plan as do all of you." He reached out a hand to James to help him stand. "But I'm glad you're back, James. You may feel a bit unsteady for a while, it's quite a task for a vampire's body to remake itself."

Thunder clapped, startling them.

"Nothing She can't handle, however," Gabriel conceded. And then under his breath, he said, "There's no reason to be testy." A ripple of wind sounding suspiciously like laughter played through the trees.

James stood unsteadily with Logan and Dara supporting him on either side. Kefira stood off to the side next to Odeda, her hands on her hips, her red hair shining black in the moonlight.

"What did you mean about my body remaking itself?" James asked.

All attention turned to Gabriel and he smiled so fully it caused the cinnamon smell to grow stronger. "The parents of the child requested you as his protector with a few modifications. You can now walk in sunlight as well as darkness and you no longer have to survive on blood, human or otherwise. But you retain all of your previous powers."

James looked stunned, but then threw his arms around Logan and dragged him closer to Ariel so he could throw an arm around her as well. When he pulled back, tears shone in his eyes. "The best of both worlds. Thank you. I'll protect the child with my life."

"You mean your grandchild," Logan said softly.

James dropped his arms and faced Logan. "I hope you'll forgive me, I did what I thought was best for you. Although I won't blame you if you don't see it that way. You grew up without a father and even without a mother because of who and what I am."

Logan studied James, the man he'd known and trusted for years and realized he had nothing but love and admiration for who and what he was. "Knowing now that

I'm going to be a father, I can understand your decision. All these years I've wished for a father of my own and now I have one. And as an added bonus, he's my best friend."

The men stood looking awkwardly at one another until finally, James pulled Logan into an emotional embrace. Logan gasped for breath inside the vice-like grip, but didn't want to break the mood of the moment. When Logan pulled back, his eyes were heavy with moisture and he blinked rapidly to keep the tears from falling. There was a tap on his shoulder and he turned to face Ariel.

"I think it's my turn."

A wide and probably silly-looking grin bloomed across Logan's face. "I thought you were reluctant to fall in love with me. Something about trust issues with this jerk behind me." He chucked his thumb over his shoulder in James' direction.

"Glad to see I'm so loved and appreciated now that I've come back from the dead to watch over your offspring," James said from behind him.

Ariel and Logan both ignored him and Ariel stepped forward to twine her arms around Logan's neck. "Ever since I found out I was pregnant, I've wanted nothing more than to tell you about *our* child. But I was afraid…"

"I know, you thought you were carrying the child of destiny. But now we know the truth."

Ariel pulled away from him and huffed out an impatient breath, crossing her arms over her chest. "Can I finish?" she asked imperiously, but then ruined the effect when she smiled at the end.

"By all means," Logan conceded.

"I don't want to waste any more time with misunderstandings." She drilled a finger into his chest. "Do you love me or not?"

Logan couldn't help but be amused at her highhanded tactics, especially if the outcome was what he'd wanted all along. "Yes—"

Ariel cut him off, "I love you too and we belong together—the three of us. So is there anything else to say?" Then she pressed her lips to his giving him no more chance to argue.

Logan had never been happier to be interrupted. He pulled Ariel against him until he could feel the heat of her skin through their clothes and let her lead the kiss.

"I wonder if she can kiss and fly, I'm hungry," complained Odeda.

Logan pulled away and looked down at Ariel. "Put a hold on your stomach, Odeda. I've got one more thing to say." Logan stepped back from Ariel and knelt down in front of her, still holding her hand in his. Blood still caked what was left of her lavender top and she was grimy and dirty from their ordeal, her hair in disarray—and she'd never looked more beautiful. "Ariel Knight, in the presence of God and all those you hold dear, will you marry me and be my wife…"

Ariel smiled down at him and opened her mouth to answer, but it was his turn to cut her off.

"Before someone else comes up with some obscure piece of the prophesy that will cause us more misunderstandings." Logan glared back at Gabriel who shrugged innocently. He noticed Alonna now perched on the angel's shoulder watching the proceedings with interest.

"What?" Alonna protested as all eyes turned to her. "I told you, I don't write those things! Just finish what you're doing, man-thing before you mess it up."

Logan turned back to Ariel expectantly.

"Yes," she whispered as she pulled Logan to his feet and into another mind-numbing kiss.

EPILOGUE

"My giant cousins look breathtaking," Alonna told Gabriel from her perch on his shoulder. "And Ariel looks so happy." She clapped her hands together in childish delight.

Gabriel smiled to himself and looked out over the crowd from their invisible perch in the rafters. The groomsmen already stood in their appointed places like sentinels next to Logan, all wearing black tuxedos with a lavender cummerbund. The music started and Ariel emerged through the double wooden doors dressed in a flowing white wedding gown, low in the back so the iridescent 'tattoo' of her wings remained bare. James, looking stoic and dark in his tuxedo, escorted her. Her sisters followed behind in gowns of smooth white silk, also low backed, their identical tattoos glinting in the light filtered through the stained glass windows of the old church.

"They're lovely," Gabriel heard himself whisper. The gargoyles had all insisted on the low backed dresses in case of emergency they needed to use their wings.

Alonna sighed with longing. "My kind never have joinings like these, I think we are missing out." She swung her legs, her small heels tapping lightly against Gabriel's shoulder. "Man thing looks handsome too, but the goofy smile isn't very becoming."

Logan stood in front of the pastor in a black tuxedo with white cummerbund and an admittedly silly grin. He'd been fidgeting as if he had hot coals inside his shoes until he saw Ariel. Now, his gaze riveted on her, tracking every movement, his mouth hanging open, no doubt at how radiant she looked.

"Alonna," Gabriel warned. "That just proves he's in love. Let the boy alone, everything worked out as it should." *Even if I had to nudge them along.*

She harrumphed. "It took them long enough. The prophesy left several clues and still they were confused."

Below, the guests, who consisted of friends, family, country music A-listers and press oohed and ahhed as Ariel and her sisters passed. Ariel reached the front of the congregation and James leaned down to kiss her cheek and place her hand in Logan's. Logan held her hand as if it were precious porcelain and guided her next to him so they could face the pastor together.

    The murmurs of the crowd quieted as the pastor's vibrant voice echoed through the church. Gabriel breathed deeply, enjoying the scent of gardenias and roses that emanated from all of the bouquets and arrangements adorning every available space. "There is still much to do. It will be many years before the child of blood can take his place among those fighting on the side of good."

    Alonna fluttered her wings absently and rose a few inches above Gabriel's shoulder. "That it will. And what of my other giant cousins?" She gestured down at them. "What role will they play in all this?"

    Gabriel paused to listen to Ariel's vows before answering.

    "I, Ariel, pledge before God this day to take you, Logan, to be my husband...to have and to hold from this day forward...for better or for worse...for richer or for poorer...in sickness and in health...to love and to cherish till death do us part."

    Gabriel spoke, his voice a mere whisper. "The other three have destinies that still await them. The prophesy is far from finished. It's been many thousands of years in the making." He nodded toward Ariel. "God is smiling down on her today. I remember the day she was christened, 'Lioness of God.'" Gabriel was surprised when a large lump formed in his throat and he swallowed hard to dislodge it. He turned to see Alonna watching him, sympathy clear in her lavender gaze.

    "She was the first created, and is the leader. It was

fitting for her to find her destiny before the others." She fluttered closer and laid a small hand against his cheek. "Besides, you're not losing her. And soon we will have a small one to play with."

Gabriel only nodded, afraid anything he said would give away the emotions coursing through him. Now he understood why fathers cried at their daughter's weddings. After all, the original five-hundred gargoyles were all like daughters to him. The four who stood before him were the last of their kind and more dear to him than he previously realized.

"I, Logan, pledge before God this day to take you, Ariel, to be my wife…to have and to hold from this day forward…for better or for worse…for richer or for poorer…in sickness and in health…to love and to cherish till death do us part."

Alonna sighed again and brushed a lavender teardrop from her cheek with the back of her tiny hand. "Oh, man-thing, that was lovely." She turned to Gabriel with unshed tears glistening in the liquid depths of her eyes. "But mark my words, if he hurts Ariel ever again, I'll give him horrible nightmares!"

Gabriel chuckled. He knew just how vindictive the little fairy could be when angered. A few hundred years ago, she'd haunted James' dreams for almost a year before Gabriel found out and put a stop to it. "Somehow I don't think that will ever be a problem again. They are totally besotted with each other."

"Shhh, I want to hear," she complained.

Ariel's clear voice rang out in the excellent acoustics. "With this ring, I thee wed." She slipped a silver wedding band on Logan's left ring finger. When she tried to drop her hand, Logan pulled it to his lips, to place a quick kiss on her open palm and then pressed the palm to his heart. The congregation including Alonna responded with appreciative murmurs and a flurry of camera clicks from the press.

Ariel blushed and dropped her right hand from his chest. She gave Logan her left hand while he retrieved a sparkling diamond solitaire and wedding band from James. Logan took her fingers in his and held the ring poised in front of her ring finger. He cleared his throat and his voice shook as he said, "With this ring, I thee wed."

"It is done then," Alonna said through a sheen of lavender tears. "Who is the next one to meet her destiny?"

A shaft of sunlight slanted down to glint off Kefira's fiery-red hair and Gabriel smiled. *Excellent, My Lord.* He turned his head to Alonna and said, "Kefira has been through much in her lifetime and has borne the most personal loss. Her destiny will find her next."

Alonna nodded emphatically, her blonde hair gyrating around her wildly from the movement. "You should have let me sick the succubus on Dagan for hurting her so. And the baby…"

"Dagan is off limits to your vindictiveness for now. We must focus on Kefira."

Alonna shrugged, clearly unconvinced. Gabriel chuckled and vowed to keep a close eye on the little fairy.

"I now pronounce you man and wife. Logan, you may kiss your bride…"